MW01532577

DAVE OLIVER was bor
Naval Academy. In the
and commanded a nucle
Airbus and as a political appointee in the Department of Defense.

Dave has consequently traveled six of the seven world continents as a naval officer, business leader and a political appointee. His novels use Dave's personal experiences to provide background to his stories.

Find out more about Dave and his work at www.daveoliverbooks.com

Gunlog J Millet
317 W Main St
Chester, CT 06412

INTENT
to
DECEIVE

DAVE OLIVER

SilverWood

Published in 2018 by the author

Copyright © Dave Oliver 2018
Images © Joan Covell 2018

ISBN 978-0-9994718-0-7 (paperback)
ISBN 978-0-9994718-1-4 (ebook)

British Library Cataloguing in Publication Data
A CIP catalogue record for this book is available from the British Library

Page design and typesetting by SilverWood Books
Printed on responsibly sourced paper

Dedicated to my Asya, Linda Bithell Oliver

KAZAKHSTAN:

where Europe and Asia grind against each other

CHAPTER ONE

The protective metal cover over the satellite's navigation receiver silently slid back. The crystal thus exposed had once been grown for 17 days in a pressurized chemical bath in a vibration-isolated room deep beneath the good Maryland loam three miles off Route 50 between Annapolis and Washington, DC. The crystal had then been carefully transported by an Otis elevator up one floor where it was laser-ground to nanometer perfection. On the same floor it had been fitted with a dozen millimeter fibers that conducted nearly as well as silver. It was then shipped, along with that day's milk, from the picturesque dairy farm built atop the top secret facility. Now the crystal was in space moving at 14,000 miles an hour gathering every lumen in the black environment.

The software at the end of the fibers discarded the moon and planet distractions and evaluated the star radiations. Millions of calculations and a tenth of a second later the satellite's exact position was established and the navigation cover began closing. Sixty feet away on the metal structure another aperture opened and a telescope began aligned itself with it's earth target.

Three hundred miles down the camera lens was Kazakhstan's Derzhainsk missile field. Most of the immense steppe was uninteresting, merely hundreds of kilometers of featureless prairie. However, in this case there were miles of concrete roads, doubled concertina-wire fences and dozens of guard towers. Under the turf here lay nearly 100 deadly missiles – snug in their steel and reinforced-concrete launching pads – carrying warheads powerful enough to take out an American city.

As planned, the satellite sweep was viewing the field in the midst of a planned missile upgrade. One of the new Satans was already lying undraped on its huge tractor-trailer, ready to be inserted; its four-story-long body gleaming from its protective oil. A few hundred yards along the paved road toward the next silo, a team of men in white and green snow garb, partially protected from the falling snow by a temporary tent, stood by to cut the old missile body to pieces – as required by the US/Soviet treaty provisions for these city-killing weapons – as soon as it was drawn out of its silo. The Americans would later note from their photos that some of the men had already begun testing their acetylene torches. The KGB embedded spy in the CIA had suggested that touch.

Five kilometers east of the work area was the 30-meter-deep trench the tunnel machine had dug one moonless night shortly after the work crew had completed their difficult task in the Urals. The trench had been immediately covered with camouflage until a different work team could install cement floors, walls, ramps at both ends and a reinforced latticed roof of the best Russian pine. Atop that was a foot of machine snow. Now, under a few more inches of the real stuff, a soldier sat smoking in an empty tractor-trailer truck in the bottom of the dark trench. He was waiting to enter stage left.

CHAPTER TWO

Half the world away, a winter storm threw snow crystals against the granite front of a building in Indianapolis, Indiana. Up on the fifth floor, in the oversized glass panes that looked north down Delaware Street, icy branches crept out from the four corners like drunken quilt stitches. No, Anastasia corrected herself, perhaps it was more like bony witch fingers. Whatever the best analogy, she knew she was chilled and uncomfortable.

"Do you like the chair, Ms Conner?" Asya obediently rocked slightly back, still looking beyond her handsome new boss's gelled hair and trim black mustache at the rapidly frosting windows. She could swear she heard the wind moan and saw a draft momentarily twitch the bottom edge of one of the corner window drapes.

Her chair and the drape's heavy fabric returned to rest. Unseen, below the edge of her desk, Anastasia's left hand slowly coiled and uncoiled a lock of her long hair. Maybe she should have cut it too. She refocused her eyes on her boss, her features arranged in a careful smile. She had practiced this very look. Attentive, but not encouraging. Outwardly dutiful, but deliberately dull. A young woman oblivious to anything inappropriate. The best approach, she had decided, during one of her many sessions with her mirror last week. She straightened herself to the full sitting height her 5ft 5in frame provided and, again, mentally and physically squared her shoulders. She could play this role.

"Just fine, Mr Snyder."

A year ago, Winsor had quipped, "Two careers and 26 years already in your rear-view mirror". He had been so right. And this was the first day of her critical third career. She needed to pay attention. Mr Snyder's lips were moving again.

She had probably been too anxious at the Farm. Maybe if she had only been willing to wait a few more weeks they would have found somewhere else, something more…someone less… Her new boss was now standing immediately in front of her desk, now quiet, but frowning, one hand smoothing his flat stomach, then unfolding a suit-coat pocket flap that had been partially tucked away, his other hand smoothing his red-and-blue striped tie, trying his best to avoid staring at the breasts she had carefully covered that morning with a professionally tailored suit. New clothes for a new job… Her inability to focus was certainly not getting her off to a flying start – and they had been very insistent on her remaining in her first position for at least 24 months…

"Did you need something, sir?"

A wry grin crossed his face as he took a half-step toward the door to his private office. "Nope. Take some time and meet the other executive assistants. Everyone important is on this floor. Coffee nook is two doors down. I like it black. Look at my calendar for this week, talk to Dorothy – she's the girl who's been my temp – about my routine. I have a meeting at nine, there are a series of calls I make every Monday at 11 and then I thought we might…"

His personal line rang. He made a quick glance at his watch, raised his hand to indicate he would answer it himself, and ducked into his office, closing the door behind him.

Anastasia reached out for the heavy brass letter opener that Dorothy, the 40-year-old 'girl' from down the hall, had left her, along with the hand-me-down ergonomic chair. She wiggled her butt to test the cushion, toed the plastic rug-protector and spun back and forth a quarter-turn. Surprisingly, the chair seemed fairly comfortable.

What else had she inherited? Two large monitors: one displaying Mr Snyder's daily, weekly and monthly schedule, the other apparently available to search the internet or serve as a word processor; one desk made from tight-grained rainforest wood; a top-of-the-line printer; a laptop; stapler; two-hole punch; six filing cabinets, the grain and sheen of which matched the desk. The letter opener she was unconsciously balancing in her palm.

She reflexively ran her thumb down the brass blade. The edge was so dull, it was hard to imagine it doing damage to any envelope that possessed even a wisp of rag content. Nevertheless, it was better than nothing. She rolled her chair back a foot, looked around to ensure no one was watching and flipped up the skirt she had asked the tailor at the Farm to cut a little fuller than he had first recommended. She slipped the letter opener into the empty leather sheath strapped to the inside of her left thigh.

When she rolled the chair back to her desk, she already felt calmer.

She booted up her computer and began deliberating on how to construct her new password. Suddenly the door to their office suite banged open and two men entered. The first held a bouquet of violets.

"Winsor!"

Anastasia pushed her chair back, took two quick steps across the room and threw herself into his arms. He had remembered! Winsor squeezed her waist once and then pushed her away, "I want you to meet my friend Alex, Alex Yates. I thought we would take you to lunch."

At the noise, her new boss immediately came out from his private office, looking for an introduction. As usual, Winsor took charge, crossing to him and extending his hand, "My name is Winsor Asher. I used to work with Asya and heard she was starting a new job here today. Alex and I work at one of those lettered agencies back in Washington. Since we happened to be in the vicinity, we stopped by to wish her well. I hope we're not a disruption."

Winsor was a sight for sore eyes. Asya hadn't seen him in months. He was still handsome. She had forgotten that he was so tall – a couple of inches over 6ft. She wondered if she had ever known how old he was. She guessed early thirties – a few years younger than her new boss. He certainly looked good. He was wearing the same expensive camel-hair overcoat he had worn in Kure, Japan, nearly a year ago, but rather than turned up against the rain, today, the beige collar protected against the Indianapolis sleet. The dark brown Australian bush hat that normally topped his longish blond mane was tucked under his left arm, along with the bunch of violets. He needed a haircut and she wanted to brush back the curly wave of hair threatening to fall over his forehead.

While Winsor charmed her new boss, Asya introduced herself to Winsor's friend. Alex was slightly shorter than Winsor, maybe a bit broader in the shoulders. She soon found out that they not only worked at the same agency, but had also been fraternity brothers. A couple of scars around his left eye probably marked him as a wrestler or boxer, since he mentioned that their Yale fraternity emphasized sports, but he didn't specifically say. He also steered the conversation away from his family, and, as Anastasia had her own back-story to protect, she was happy to keep the conversation on Washington politics. He seemed surprisingly liberal, but she had been out of the loop for a while. She did wonder if she might have detected one or two word choices symptomatic of someone who had begun life speaking a non-American syntax, but she was unsure; her own ears had been stuffed with Virginia accents lately. It had been difficult to completely focus on Alex, as she kept wondering what Mr Snyder and Winsor were discussing. They had apparently connected. Their relationship was backslappingly vigorous. She resigned herself to seeing her violets become a casualty of a male bonding process.

"Well, Asya," Mr Snyder helped her on with her coat. "I hope you found your first day interesting. Tomorrow you need to get a key made so you can lock up if I'm not here." He pulled the door shut while she pushed the button for the elevator.

"I thought your friends from Washington were really interesting. That was a great lunch, but I didn't have a chance to talk to you. We'll have to make time for a lunch with just the two of us tomorrow." The door opened, and she moved into the elevator and stood near the back wall.

No one else was in the elevator and it could have held eight to ten people, yet Mr Snyder stood closer than Anastasia preferred. She was immediately reminded of the uncomfortable way the day had begun. She crossed her arms over her breasts and stared straight ahead. Americans preferred a larger personal space than Europeans and Asians – his actions had to be deliberate. He didn't touch her, just stood uncomfortably close until the cing announced the ground floor, at which point he stepped aside. "After you. I have a company car. Is your apartment far? I'll give you a ride." She walked ahead of him as he paused at the lobby newsstand to buy a Wall Street Journal.

"No, but thank you anyway. It's just up on Ninth Street." She pulled a pair of pink running shoes out of her oversized bag, leaned up against the cold black lobby marble and exchanged the heels she had been wearing for Nikes. "I'll walk. It was a long day. The fresh air will clear my head."

Not waiting for a reply, Asya adjusted her scarf and pushed through the revolving door. She turned north and set off at a brisk pace into the wind. The cold air in her face felt great. It had been one of the longest days of her life. How awful. She would almost have rather spent the nine hours in interrogation. But finally her thoughts were her own. My frozen smile and I can't stand to be around you for even one more minute today, Mr Snyder. I am certainly not sure how I am going to last two years. Maybe you will be hit by a speeding gangster's car. If we are both lucky, you will be promoted to the New York office and be forced to leave me behind.

As an anonymous walking commuter, not having to worry about controlling her every reaction, some of the stress of the day began to be blown away by the same breeze that was trying to whip her long hair out of her scarf. One thing about Indianapolis, she thought, is that the wind felt familiar. Another thing that reminded her of home – she had only walked two blocks and already she was cold. It had seemed warmer when she left this morning. Six more blocks to the apartment. She first saw it yesterday. Would she even recognize it at night? It got dark so early here. Americans didn't control their time zones the way Moscow…

She was nearly past University Park, and that one ten-foot section on North Pennsylvania Street where Benjamin Harrison's statue casts such a deep afternoon shadow when a huge gloved hand with a dosed cloth wrapped nearly completely around her face. His other arm pulled her off the sidewalk.

A second man immediately appeared in front of her, grabbing her purse and driving his other hand into her stomach!

As her head was being jerked back and the man's fist closed the few inches, Asya mentally shifted into her old professional mode. Breathe chloroform like a baby? Succumb on a public street? Did these two amateurs not realize she was a professional? She tensed the sheath of stomach muscles that had prepared for an Olympic career and slightly twisted her torso while she waited for the blow to land. Unfortunately the man behind had caught us some of her hair. She was going to look like hell. Lucky he was pulling her further away from the other walkers, who all had their heads down against the snow. She stumbled a bit to help him move toward the alley she assumed was there. She brought her arms down, reached under her coat, and absorbed her assailant's blow while delivering her own.

She knew just how dull the letter opener was so she used both hands to drive it into his rib cage just to the left of this breastbone. Then she pushed past his amazingly bad breath. Did everyone in Indiana eat liver and onions for lunch? She twisted it as she looked in his eyes and waited for the blood to begin to dribble past his lips. He looked surprised.

The giant of a man behind her made some sort of noise and it was past time to sacrifice her hair. Asya pulled back her letter opener as she dropped. As soon as she got some movement, she executed a cross-step pivot and rose, her driving legs bringing clenched and linked fists, thumbs extended up, along with the brass hilt of the letter opener, under her assailant's coat and directly into his groin.

"Christ!"

He reached down to protect himself and as his head finally became reachable, Asya drove the blade into his right eye. As he fell back, she was already asking herself the key question.

Who betrayed me this time?

CHAPTER THREE

Pete O'Brien sipped his steaming coffee and leaned his 6ft 3in frame against the black onyx desk in the lobby of the Roxy Apartment building. He and Jane, the 70-year-old concierge for the Roxy Apartments, were both drinking vanilla lattes. Every 10 to 15 minutes, Jane nodded and spoke familiarly to someone who passed her desk. Pete's was the lone signature in the visitor log for today.

"You just beat the snow." Jane brushed back a pixie cut that did her hairdresser proud and took a small sip, immediately placing her Target charge card firmly of top of the hole of her cup to keep any steam from escaping. She had grudgingly accepted Pete waiting in the lobby, after a careful examination of his Navy identification card. After he had patiently and silently stood for two hours, and made a second Starbucks trip 20 minutes ago, her natural curiosity was winning out over any Midwest reticence.

"I hear the train is nearly as expensive as flying." She had a line of foam on her upper lip that she carefully blotted with the napkin Pete offered.

"Well, I have to be back in DC by Thursday to brief the Chairman of the Joint Chiefs of Staff. Snow shuts down the airports in DC pretty easily, so I bought tickets back on both the train and the plane. This trip is private business, so I used my own money."

He knew it sounded terribly wasteful and wanted to ensure she knew he wasn't throwing away taxpayer funds. He would have spent any money necessary after finally getting a clue to Asya's location.

And it had just been via a dropped comment!

On Sunday night, after their monthly outing to the Kennedy Center, when Bob and Sandi had put their two kids to bed and Pete had taken their babysitter home, the three had finally settled into their usual end-of-week discussion around the living-room fireplace. After the second glass of wine, and the usual chat about rising Russian influences, Sandi had unexpectedly broached an old subject, abruptly turning to her husband and saying, "Why don't you tell him she listed Pete as her only contact on the witness-protection form."

"Jesus, Sandi. Pillow talk is supposed to be exactly that!"

Luckily, the CIA routinely swept senior officer's private residences, because Pete was sure Bob wouldn't want to have the subsequent interchange recorded somewhere on tape. Bob Farrell, the Head of Operations of the CIA, the number-three officer in that premier organization, a man whose odd-shaped fingers on his left hand confirmed he had once survived 28 hours of torture in Lebanon, was a very tough man. Unfortunately, he had been called into work twice that week for all-nighters and, perhaps implausibly had been looking forward to catching up on his sleep over the weekend, hopefully accompanied by a little spousal comfort. And they all did need to keep their voices down so as not to wake the children. Whatever the rationale for his weakness, sometime between 2 and 3am, tempted on one side by the explicit promise of sex in the very near future, and bombarded by the threat of everlasting hell for ever more on the handball court, Bob had caved and filled Pete in.

Pete spent Sunday in his Pentagon office clearing his in-tray and calendar. After a discussion with the chairman early Monday morning, despite threatening weather reports, he caught the afternoon flight to Indianapolis and took a cab to the address Bob had given him. There he had met Jane, who was not about to let him past the apartment lobby.

"TV this morning said we're going to get 14 to 18 inches. Just like when I was a girl. The weather will be sweeping down from Canada through Chicago and moving east. People on the east coast, they don't know how to handle snow TV says they all stay home or just slide straight off the road." She laughed, "Course, some of those states back east are so itty bitty, you brake in one and come to a stop in another!"

"Do you have any idea when the woman in 406 will be home?"

"Nope. Haven't even met her. I work weekdays and she checked in this weekend. As the good book says, I wouldn't know her from Adam. I expect you to introduce us. You say you know her, right?"

Pete looked out into the snow that was now swirling beyond the lobby's revolving door. The streetlights had come on. The snowstorm brought an early dark. Yes, he knew her. He looked out into the stormy Indianapolis street and it was as if he were back on his submarine, looking out of *Grayfish*'s periscope – at the FSB gunship directly ahead lying doggo in the center of the Vladivostok channel.

Pete could feel the familiar give of the neoprene of the periscope eyepiece against his forehead. He had dipped the periscope as *Grayfish* passed abeam of the gunship. He considered running directly beneath the gunship and sliding back up to look when well on the up-channel side, but there might well be a second gunship drifting in tandem. Lying silent, a gunship was like a camouflaged hunter in a tree blind, waiting for a deer to venture into the kill zone.

Instead, Pete intended to cruise at a shallow depth, the periscope dipped just below the water. Each time the mast broke the water surface, the tiny countermeasures receiver located at its very tip would automatically sample the electronic environment and simultaneously copy any new alerts the National Security Agency might have slung their way. Checking frequently but quickly, he could better avoid surface-killers and still avoid showing themselves to the powerful radars on the surrounding mountains. He carefully threaded his long arms up into the maze of pipes in the overhead, so he could stand erect and stretch. He was too large to ever be comfortable aboard a submarine. This was especially true in the control room, where each overhead nook was crammed with a computer screen.

"Captain, everything aft is normal." The off-going Officer of the Deck quietly reported, "The number-two high-pressure air-compressor is down, Jones and Offerman are replacing the seals on the third stage. It should be back up in two hours. All air-bank pressures are good. We are also working the number-two carbon-dioxide scrubber, but have no estimated time of repair."

Pete ran his left hand reflectively over his bald scalp and then used his thumb and forefinger to press his growing headache back into his bushy black eyebrows – the only hair remaining from his morning shave. "Very well, Mr Ackerman." He caught himself before he reflexively reached down to massage the ache in his right knee. He knew it was only a phantom pain. When he was tense, his subconscious visualized the bullet he had forced himself to forget.

It was time for a look-see. Pete couldn't afford the luxury of multiple navigation bearings tonight. Two would have to suffice and he would accept the fix inaccuracy. "Up scope." As the periscope traveled the last few feet out of the well, he squatted to ride it up, pulling the handles down and rotating the barrel in the direction he anticipated finding his first navigation object, visualizing the image he expected to see. As the scope broke the surface of the water, he quickly swung it 360 degrees, announced "Nothing close", rotated his wrist to increase the magnification and centered the thin black crosshairs, calling out clearly as he did, "Smokestack, Mark."

The Quartermaster – a tall, thin youngster with a scraggy goatee he had been vainly trying to encourage since they last left Yokosuka – read the dial that mimicked where the periscope was pointed, reported, "034", and copied the bearing number alongside the object description into the ship's log.

Pete swung left and found the second landmark he had planned as a navigational aid: "End of jetty. Mark." He was mentally counting. he did not want to give any radars too good a look, three one thousand, four one thousand...

"292."

Pete suddenly stepped back, slapping the scope handles up as he did, his voice intense, his diction precise. "Down scope! Right full rudder! Back full!"

He deliberately squeezed the emotion from his voice as he announced to the control-room watchstanders, "I have a second FSB gunship dead in the water immediately ahead. Mark it on the chart, Navigator." Right now, the clouds were completely covering the stars and it was as black as the ace of spades out there. Remote cameras repeated the periscope scene for the other men in the control room, but none of the instruments was as sensitive at night as the human eye. As a result, every man aboard was tuned to the body language and voice inflection of the one man at the periscope. Luckily, Pete had spotted the gunboat's lookout watch before the periscope bent itself against the warship's gunnels.

Hell, they had been so close he had seen the tip of the man's cigarette suddenly brighten as the sailor inhaled.

With the periscope successfully down, there were now 20 feet between the *Grayfish's* sail and the surface. Hopefully, the gunship drew less than that and was drifting, not anchored, so there was no chain to avoid. The best clue as to whether they would miss was the rose of the compass. Come on, bow – turn now…swing! Pete swore silently to himself. It had been ten seconds. Only now was their bow beginning to rotate. According to his mental picture, they were passing down the starboard side of the gunboat. He let another ten seconds pass. "All stop." He could hear the Diving Officer's quiet "That's right, Macy. That's right" as the bow and stern-planes operators worked to remain on depth. They could use another ton of water aft to keep the stern down, Pete thought, but now…now…the bow was swinging smartly and they should be clear. "All ahead one-third. Left ten degrees rudder. Come back to 012."

Was there a third gunship?

"Up scope." Pete gave the command, and bent down to ride up, so his eye would break the surface simultaneously with the glass face of the periscope. As soon as the water drained from the glass, Pete again spun his body and the periscope in a complete circle.

Three seconds. Pete snapped the handles up. "Down scope."

"It's very black up there tonight, men, but it looks like our only surprise was the second gunship."

"Captain," the Executive Officer said, puzzled, "the last fix doesn't make any sense!"

Pete walked over and looked down at the chart. The two lines crossed at a point that indicated *Grayfish* was dangerously close to the shoal water on the north side of the Bay.

"Right, Exec." Pete kept his voice calm and conversational for the benefit of the men within earshot. "I'm sure I misidentified the jetty." He marked the upside of the situation with his inflection. "It's pretty dark up there, which is going to make our SEALs very, very pleased. We'll just motor on this course for a while and take another peek in a minute or two. I'll drop the jetty and pick up the right tangent of the Vladivostok Hotel."

Twenty minutes later, Pete finally located a landmark that was recognizable from the pictures he had studied back in Pearl Harbor. This bearing cut the line from the smokestack at a broad angle. He mentally breathed a sigh of relief when the Navigator reported they were only 50 yards left of the planned track and nowhere near the shoals. Three miles to go. They were now so close that every time the scope broke the water, the piercing racket of the harbor radars literally bounced around the control room. Pete had turned the volume control on the periscope electronic receiver counter-clockwise as far as the knob would go. Fortunately, none of the radars seemed focused on *Grayfish*'s sector.

Pete lived for times like these. It was why he had wanted to attend the Naval Academy. It was why he didn't sell soap, design bridges or argue cases in court.

Two hours to the rendezvous time. Two hours before he got to see for himself if the spy were as beautiful as the picture they had provided. Hell, she was supposed to be some famous gymnast. "Exec, inform the SEALs it's time to suit up. Ask Jim to come see me." As he gave the last command, Pete closed his eyes and slipped a black blindfold over his eyes. From now until the spy was on board, he would operate blind except when he actually had his eyes buried in the periscope's neoprene facepiece. Heightened senses and the best-possible night vision were essential for this next step.

When the SEAL Lieutenant cleared his throat, it was enough to recognize him by, and Pete spoke: "Change of plans, Jim. You don't need all eight guys on the pier. Why don't you have two of them take machine guns up on the bridge? This will give them the advantage of height as well as the protection of the steel cockpit if something happens."

There was silence while Jim thought. Then, laconically, he agreed. "Good idea, Captain. I think I'll make one of them Swede. He's my best gunner. You know him."

Jim was correct. Pete knew Swede. They had once been as close as brothers. Faded-blue tridents on the right biceps of each man attested to that bond as well as to a best-forgotten night in Pattaya Beach. He could still remember the feel of the cold dark water closing in around his body. It had truly been a kick. But one unlucky hunk of flying lead and the damage had been done. He definitely couldn't run ten miles anymore. Hell, the burn began after 20 yards. It was free weights for him for the rest of his life. On the other hand, he still had his leg, he could walk, and submarining had proven to be more interesting than he had expected.

Jim didn't immediately move away. "How long until we surface and the rest of my team and I can go over the side?"

Pete reached back for the leather captain's chair and, instead, bumped his elbow against a black onyx counter, as an unfamiliar woman's voice wrenched him back to the present.

"Mr O'Brien, the nighttime concierge is not as trusting as me. She might not appreciate your presence in our lobby. If you'll pay for a cab home, I'll skip my usual bus and have her come in a bit late."

"Jane, I would truly appreciate that. Would you like another coffee?"

"Maybe a sody water. I sometimes have trouble sleeping if I drink too much coffee. Be careful when crossing Delaware. It gets dark early this time of the year."

As he stepped out into the Indianapolis sleet, Pete's mind again drifted back to the South China Sea.

CHAPTER FOUR

Grayfish silently rose to the surface between two long Vladivostok piers, seawater streaming off her round black hull. The forward hatch swung silently up against the greased hinges and was locked open. Camouflaged figures flowed out onto the narrow path, where the non-skid paint provided some traction for their rubber-soled boots. Within 30 seconds, two inflated boats were being eased over the side and Jim's team of SEALs was waterborne. When they quietly ascended the nearest pier, a pair of seagulls, rousted from their night's rest, raucously bitched, took an awkward step or two, gathered themselves and reluctantly flapped away.

Pete keyed the special communication circuit to the bridge. "Swede, you set up?"

"Yeah, Captain. Like a pair of eagles in a tall nest."

He could picture the old warhorse settling his Mark 48 machine gun on the metal cowling and beginning surveillance around the deserted waterfront. It was nice to know Swede had his back.

"OK, Swede. I've also got both periscopes manned. Keep a weather eye on the freighter." The periscope gave Pete electronic monitoring and a 20ft height advantage over Swede, as well as night-vision capability. To the south, less than 50 meters distant, an old freighter, towering five or six rusted stories over the surfaced *Grayfish*, blocked his vision.

Pete had made a detailed observation of their next-door-neighbor-to-be before he had surfaced. The cargo-hauler was long overdue for a repainting. Orange rust streaks ran every few feet from her scuppers down to her normal waterline. Even lower, eight feet of peeling black bottom-paint was exposed, along with gray swatches of dying sea grass, both indications the ship was freshly unloaded. This was good news. In addition, the ship was carelessly moored. Pete had seen no tell tails or rat guards on any of the lines and the stern haul was loose. Every sixth or seventh swell, the freighter's stern rode a few feet away from the pier, only to be rudely shoved back against the pilings by the next sizeable wave. Those were all sure indications of a slovenly crew. Given their general demeanor, and with no cargo to guard, it was more than likely the freighter's topside watch was fast asleep.

The clock in the control room quietly tolled four bells: "Ding ding. Ding ding." The appointed rendezvous time. Pete swung his periscope back and forth. The piers were still as deserted as a Marseille waterfront church service. He had trained for times like these to force his heartbeat to slow. Beat. Hold. Breathe in. Breathe out. Again. It had helped him keep from making bad judgments in the past. He could drive his heart rate down into the low fifties under just this sort of pressure. He could also fire a weapon twice between heartbeats. He took another breath. Again.

After a repeated careful search of the entire waterfront, he motioned the Officer of the Deck to take the scope for a few minutes and stood back. From this position, Pete could see the clock over the diving stand. It was 20 minutes past the designated rendezvous time.

Two days ago, when Presidential permission had finally been received for the mission, it had included a provision that limited *Grayfish*'s risk by specifically stating the spy was allotted no more than half an hour to make her designated rescue pickup point. *Grayfish* was hard to see in the dark here between the piers, but all they needed was one drunken sailor to wander over to the wrong side of the freighter for a smoke and all hell would break loose.

"Ding ding. Ding ding. Ding" Five bells. Another half-hour of sand through life's hourglass.

His Executive Officer spoke from near the diving stand: "Captain, it's time." Pete could hear the anxiety in Bob's voice. "Want me to get the SEALs back aboard?"

"No, Exec. I think 30 minutes is probably only a standard time allotted for a spy pickup." He kept his voice light-hearted for anyone listening to their conversation. "For particularly good-looking ones, I believe there's an unwritten rule that I'm authorized to extend to forty-five or so."

Such were the prerogatives of command.

Forty minutes. Pete was back on the periscope. The two previously disturbed seagulls had shifted camp to the head of the freighter's pier. There they had discovered a discarded treat wrapped in paper near one of the cleats. From the flurry of wings and squawking, it was evident they had begun a discussion about finder's rights. Pete hoped the debate was providing entertainment for any night watchman awake aboard the freighter.

Fifty minutes. A wind was rearranging the thick overcast. A few stars were beginning to bathe the piers in soft light. Pete could now see each of the SEALs without the benefit of the periscope's infrared capability. One of the gulls wrestled something from the paper and flew back across the watery slip. The white-and-gray bird braked to a stop in the air and gracefully descended to *Grayfish*'s convenient stern, turned to make sure he hadn't been followed, and disgorged his treasure onto the afterdeck.

Several blocks to the north, Pete suddenly saw two lights turn a corner onto the waterfront road. The vehicle accelerated toward their pier. Pete spoke sharply to the men in the control room: "Action on the piers, Exec! Alert Swede and the SEALs!"

He rotated his wrist to increase the periscope's magnification and shifted back to infrared. He could see the white-hot blaze of muzzle flashes from both sides of the car. What was their target? Below decks as he was, he couldn't hear the booms, but he knew this Vladivostok district must be waking up fast.

Pete trained the periscope ahead of the car. A red blur cut across his screen. Another vehicle was running without lights and hurtling in their direction. It must be their spy – driving for her life!

Without looking away from the periscope, he reached over, picked up the bridge mic and spoke softly but clearly: "Swede, we got some bad guys chasing someone. The good guys don't have any lights, but will reach our pier first. As soon as the second car turns onto the pier, how about if you two give it a good hosing?"

"Right, Captain. Second car, not the first, Aye, sir."

"Attention in the control room," Pete announced. "As soon as the SEALs are back aboard, we are going to depart here as fast as we can. Inform Maneuvering that we are about to order flank speed."

Although the area near the piers was sufficiently deep for *Grayfish* to theoretically submerge, the sea room was so tiny, it would be a death trap if they stayed anywhere in the vicinity. Opening datum – in layman's terms, simply known as getting the hell out of Dodge – would add significantly to the Russians' problem in finding *Grayfish*.

He could now see the unlighted gray Volvo. "OK, Swede – our passenger is turning onto the pier now."

"I see her, Captain."

As Pete slowly trained his periscope, he could see the car with lights, a Russian GAZ, their military jeep, careen onto the long pier and accelerate toward the SEALs' position. The GAZ was now less than 50 yards behind the darkened Volvo.

Pete suddenly heard the solid staccato of machine guns from the bridge, and a few pieces of brass bounced down the escape trunk, He saw pieces of the GAZ begin leaping into the air. The GAZ veered sharply toward the edge of the pier until it plowed into a large metal cleat, bumped up for a moment as if caught in indecision, and then arced up and off it, grill first, like an Acapulco cliff-diver, into the water below.

"Swede, stay up on the bridge until everyone gets on deck and the forward hatch is closed. Keep a weather eye on the freighter. Don't worry about getting the guns down. Pitch them in the water and get your asses below!" Pete had more machine guns than he had time.

"Aye aye, Boss."

"Captain, all the SEALs and the woman are aboard. Forward hatch secured."

"All Ahead Flank. Steer 288. Swede, I want you off that bridge now!"

Swinging the periscope to look aft, Pete saw the still water suddenly churn white as the reactor's full power fed the huge screw and the resulting interaction with the shallow bottom began to drag the stern under water. Nonchalantly, the gull eyed the encroaching boiling water, calmly grabbed his prize, took one step and departed for a quieter dining spot. Behind him, Pete heard two boots hit the steel deck plates in the control room, followed by the thud of a second set and the metallic clang of the lower bridge hatch closing.

"Bridge hatch secured, Captain."

"Very well."

"Exec, go search the spy and ensure she doesn't have contraband or a weapon."

"Right, Captain."

Pete swung the periscope 180 degrees. Lights were springing up all around the harbor. Now it was going to get interesting. It should be at least five minutes before even the alert helicopters could get airborne. Pete looked south to check out the nest of K-class destroyers. No activity there yet, but those ships wouldn't stay moored for long.

He swung back to the waterfront. *Grayfish* was already a half-mile from the pier. She was accelerating every second, a wide path of white foam marking her wake. However, while he had been examining the harbor, half a dozen more GAZs and Kamaz troop trucks had pulled up to the pier, stopping alongside the spy's abandoned vehicle.

At least a dozen soldiers were firing at *Grayfish*, two of them dropping to a prone position to steady their aim. There were also some muzzle flashes from the vicinity of the freighter's bridge. Now that he was not so focused on getting *Grayfish* safely out from between the piers, Pete recognized he could hear the ping of bullets ricocheting off the sail above him. The Russians could put as many holes in the sail as they wanted, as long as a lucky shot didn't penetrate one of the periscopes. That would be a pain. "Lower number one." Better ensure he had a spare.

Now that he was clear of the pier, the electronic countermeasures receiver reported that nearly every radar in the hills above Vlad was exclusively focused on *Grayfish*. Probably the only person who didn't know where he was right now was his mother. That was good – she tended to worry.

Ignoring another volley of bullets clanging off the sail, Pete swung the periscope to look in the direction of the Vladivostok airfield.

"Navigator, how long before a helicopter can reach us from the nearest airfield?"

I need to get submerged ASAP. Definitely need to be down before a helo gets a visual. Pete decided not to wait on the Navigator's response.

"Quartermaster, when did I order the Flank bell?"

The Quartermaster quickly turned back a page as he looked up at the control-room clock. "Exactly fo–ur" – his young voice cracked and he flushed with embarrassment – "minutes ago, Captain."

Since the entire hull was more than a football field long, it would take at least 90 seconds to get *Grayfish* safely under water.

"Sounding?"

The Navigator grabbed the headphones and pressed a button. He listened to the return while watching the ping electrically burning a brown dash on the paper drum. "Thirty-five fathoms, Captain."

With 240 feet of water to play with, it was time to begin behaving like a submarine again.

"Sound the diving alarm. Ease your way down to 62 feet. All Ahead two-thirds."

"Miss Spy, I'm sorry – I don't speak Russian, so I'm afraid I can't properly introduce myself." She was sitting in his tiny stateroom, calmly drinking tea, while two sailors stood guard in the narrow passageway outside. Pete had left the control room to check on the object of his mission for himself. At the sound of his voice, she slowly turned and looked up at him.

He and the two guards squeezed to the side to permit two oncoming watchstanders to pass them. Pete half-stepped into his own room to get out of the way, stopping when he realized he was nearly bumping his hips up against the seated woman. After driving like mad and sprinting for her life, she looked amazingly calm. She wore a light-blue sweater that emphasized her curves and accentuated the gray in the tailored wool trousers. Her glossy black hair was caught in a ponytail over her left shoulder and still reached nearly to her waist. But it was the eyes above the sharp cheekbones that Pete found most arresting. He suspected they might have been the best weapons in her spy arsenal. He stared for a moment and shook his head. "By God, the pictures were right! You do have the damnedest blue eyes."

He caught himself. That was not the most professional greeting he had ever managed. But then, no harm done. Her face still contained the slightly quizzical look she had when he had walked up. It was obvious she didn't understand English.

He should have asked Jim or Swede to accompany him to translate, but too late now. A half-hearted gesture toward sign language only made him feel foolish. He immediately abandoned the effort. He had always done poorly at charades. It was either stand and stare or say something, so he shrugged and continued speaking: "I apologize for having the Exec search you, but we don't have women aboard and I'm not completely sure you're a good girl." Her eyes actually also held a tiny fleck of gray near their corners. "So, you're going to have to stay in this room until I can turn you over to someone who understands spies." Pete noticed he had forgotten to put his gold Naval Academy ring in his safe. It was perched in one of the desk cubbyholes.

"And if my ring is gone when you leave, I will search you myself. I suspect I have much more experience than my Exec in frisking women." The spy took a short sip of tea and slowly lowered her cup to the saucer, her large eyes not leaving his.

Pete was not sure why he was prattling like this to someone who didn't speak a word of English. He was probably still winding down from the adrenalin rush of the last couple of hours. How many skippers could say they had backed between two Russian piers? At night. To save a woman who didn't even speak English! "Good thing we stayed another 20 minutes while you did your nails or whatever. Someday a lucky man is going to be eternally in my debt."

Miss Spy inclined her head and stared at something in his room on the other side of the washbasin. Had he left something classified out of his safe? Was there an object she might be able to use as a weapon? Pete unobtrusively leaned his upper body a bit more into his stateroom, his hands holding onto either side of the doorway.

As he inclined forward, he became aware of a pressure in his groin. She was beautiful, but he was more professional than that! There was no way he was getting an erection just talking to a woman, was he? He focused on the bulkhead opposite him for a few seconds and willed the problem to go away. Nothing changed. If anything, the pressure in his trousers increased and he could feel a drop of sweat begin to run down the side of his nose. Several more relieving watchstanders excused themselves as they brushed by his back on their way to the control room. Pete casually wiped his face and looked down.

She was staring up at him, her wide eyes unblinking. After a moment, she deliberately swayed her upper torso slightly back. He caught a flicker of reflected light. Her right hand held a knife. The tip of the blade was tightly pressing against his khakis' zipper, the jeweled hilt firmly held by red-tipped fingers.

"You also have blue eyes, Captain, and anyone could search better than your Executive Officer. Now, before you try to break my arm, take my knife," she pulled her hand back a few inches, flipped the knife one-and-a-half rotations so the blade slapped into her palm and extended the dagger up to him, handle first.

"Since you were so kind to wait, you may call me Asya, which is my Russian diminutive. Now, I am curious: why is your ship stopping?"

CHAPTER FIVE

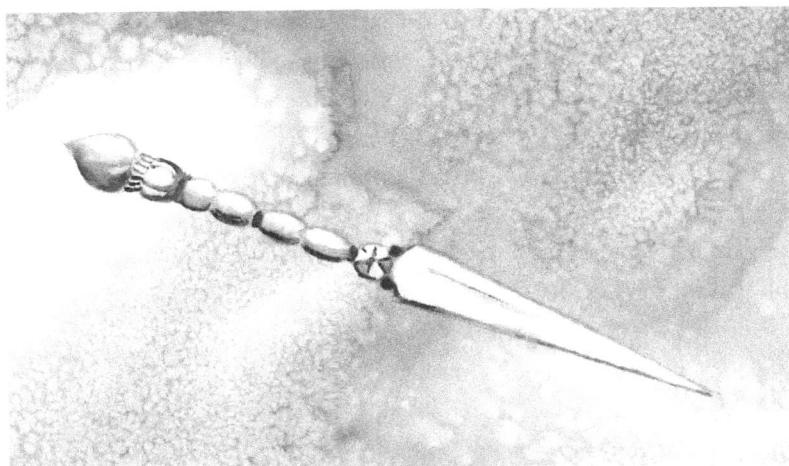

Anastasia hailed a crowded bus at Ohio and Meridian and worked herself to the back. She squeezed past an elderly man with a cane and a woman with several packages and slipped into a window seat. She turned her head to the frosty window and let the bus carry her away from the alley, silently damning the excruciatingly slow pace. The driver eased the bus to the curb to board or discharge passengers eight times in the 10 minutes it took him to get four blocks past her apartment. Still, there was no outcry. She couldn't stand to look at her watch, but it seemed forever before she could finally disembark and begin quickly walking back south. Her lodging would be a natural focus for any pursuers but at least she was now approaching from the opposite direction.

She should simply cut her losses and immediately leave town, but she had left for work that morning with only $50 in her purse. Her two assailants had contributed only a little over $1,000 to her new savings plan. Damn! She should have been better prepared. Two days back and already… Stupid! Stupid!

"Век живи́ – век учи́сь." She murmured one of her mother's favorite sayings under her breath. "Live for a century – learn forever," she had always said – a much more elegant phrasing than the Westerner's impatient 'live and learn.' A painstakingly constructed cover story was in imminent danger of dissolving around her ears.

If she could safely get into the apartment, there was a Glock behind the overhead heating vent in her bedroom – along with her passport and $10,000, the cash still in the bank's currency bands. Nothing else was important. Clothes could be bought. At least her attackers had gifted her a .38 along with the cash. Both men had been armed, but the professional in her had rejected the .45 the man with the bag had been carrying. That particular weapon was going to cost someone at least one finger someday. She had left it for some nice policeman who might need a new throw-down weapon.

Asya stopped at a news kiosk and bought a local baseball hat from the shivering vendor before stepping into the deep shadow of a doorway. There she looked into the window as she gathered her hair and shoved it through the plastic snap closure, and, testing the fit, cupped the sides of the baseball-cap bill down hard at the sides. She pulled the brim forward and checked her image again. If they only had her picture, the blue-and-white cap might provide a split-second advantage.

As she got within a block of the steps that led up to the Roxy, her heart was beating faster. She slowed her pace and began dialing down on her emotions. Time to add some ambience to her facade. An amble here, a little hip swivel there. Her head needed to be constantly scanning. She stepped momentarily against the apartment building and slipped her right hand down into her purse. Her fingers felt the reassuring sticky ridges of black tape someone had carefully wound around the butt of the .38. The American gangbanger weapon of choice. No cocking necessary No safety. Light trigger pull. Walking like this for the last few steps was awkward but necessary.

Thank goodness the wind is in my face so my hair stays back, she thought. Need to bring my pulse down one more notch. Want nothing to disrupt my aim. Not hard. This is my chosen profession. She hitched her purse strap a bit higher on her shoulder so her hand was deep in her purse.

She stepped back into the center of the sidewalk. Back to the hip roll and head bobbing. Another 50 meters – yards –still need to work on using American metrics.

Once she had exchanged pleasantries with old Ms Stroup – it would be up in the elevator to the sixth floor and back down the stairs to the fourth. She had been busy Saturday afternoon. It had taken but a few seconds to unpack her few things. The True Value hardware store had been three blocks over and was open until 8.

Her apartment was at the back of the building. On the fourth floor, a large window looked out onto the parking lot. A small pine table with a bowl of silk chrysanthemums was positioned in front of the window. A little puff of liquid nitrogen along with one blow from a chisel and the window lock had parted company from its frame. A spot of glue was now the only thing between Asya and an unalarmed exit to the outside. She had spent 15 tense minutes outside the window on Sunday night, driving a set of 16-penny nails in the brick mortar to form a bridge to the fire escape. The nails had held her weight then. Hopefully, today's cold hadn't embrittled them.

The closer she came to the entry to her hotel, the faster she was breathing. Damn. Six months at the CIA's Farm and you would think she had forgotten everything she had ever known. She forced herself to walk more slowly until she could see the door. It was opening. A couple was coming out. Good. They would partially shield her until she was completely in the lobby. A last look around, then up the four steps.

Ебать! It was a different concierge! And another big tough was leaning over the counter! Asya whirled and sprinted up the street.

*

Anastasia took a deep breath and another look around before inclining her leather chair backward. The train was finally sliding slowly out of Union Station. She was still slightly out of breath from running through the snowy streets, but no one could have possibly followed her, and she was certain she had been the last passenger to board. There was a Polish community in Chicago. She had enough money for at least two or three weeks. She would think of something.

She unbuttoned her coat and spread it over her lap, slipped off her wet tennis shoes and curled her legs up into her seat. Ever since the Grayfish trip, she had found the rolling motion of a train comforting — it felt just like a submerged submarine transiting under a storm. Goodness, she was tired. The 15 blocks from the Roxy to the Amtrak station had seemed more like 15 miles. She would probably have some Olympic-sized blisters tomorrow. She had nearly fallen on icy patches twice. She had even dropped her purse — fortunately it had not opened — and the .38 hadn't discharged!

The conductor stopped at her seat and she handed him her ticket. They were already on the outskirts of Indianapolis. The cars were swaying so much it would be difficult to walk in the aisles. She hadn't run that hard in years. She wondered why they didn't keep the lights on. Surely businessmen going to Chicago still read? She would never trust the witness-protection program again. Someone had betrayed her. She was going to have to buy moisturizer. This dry air was making her eyelids heavy. The steel wheels of the cars were beating ever faster against the rails.

As the crescendo of percussions rolled against the ship, and the metal behind his broad shoulder blades bent and reset, Pete was absent-mindedly flipping Asya's knife in graceful cartwheels, catching it each time by the handle. As the noise died away, he caught it left-handed in mid-air, two fingers clamping tightly on the sides of the razor-sharp blade. He reached in front of her and, holding one big hand up so she couldn't see the dials of his desk safe, spun it right, left and then back right again. He placed the knife and his class ring inside, then closed the door and spun the dial to relock the safe door before returning his attention to her. "If you hadn't insisted on bringing this noisy company along, we would already be on our way to safety. Your friends up there," he motioned toward the Bay's surface, "are going to delay our exit. We're going to have to remain here on the bottom until they believe we've already made our escape."

A frown wrinkled Asya's brow as she focused on what Pete was saying. "But won't they find you with their radars?"

The deafening explosion of another string of much closer depth charges punctuated her comments. The shock was sufficient to momentarily buck Pete's back away from the metal bulkhead. It also shattered the lens covering the passageway light immediately above his head.

He brushed the plastic shards onto the deck. A thin red line of blood began forming on his scalp. "Those aren't radars. Hear those sharp bangs and then the drawn-out whistles?"

Anastasia resisted the impulse to reach up and wipe away the drop of blood slowly forming near the Captain's right ear. The shrieking probes prying and pounding the water screamed for her attention. Grayfish's hull was reverberating like a snare drum at a rock concert. As the hull-pulsing increased, Pete moved closer to her.

She could feel his voice in her hair. "All this noise means those people up there on the surface are very unhappy because they haven't found us – yet." A particularly loud three-tone note whipped through the hull. Pete reached into his pocket, tore open a plastic bag containing a set of orange earplugs and offered them to Anastasia. She accepted and he ripped out another set for himself, visually demonstrating how to roll them until they were pliable, before screwing them deep into his own ear canals. She did the same and could feel the muscles in her neck immediately begin to relax.

She opened her eyes to his voice in her ear. "However, what depth charges do exceptionally well is stir up the water, the sand and the mud. This mixing produces underwater 'ghosts'. These are good spirits for us. They give the Russian sonars false underwater returns, which encourages them to drop even more depth charges on other swirling columns of sand."

Asya found his confidence comforting. "So, whenever the helicopters or surface skimmers think their sonars see something, they drop depth charges as fast as they can…"

"…that might kill us…"

Pete nodded and raised his voice. "But only if they are very, very lucky."

This man was very good-looking, and obviously smart, but he had absolutely no idea who she was. It had been a long time since she had met someone as kind as this submarine captain. Even Winsor, when he had recruited her in Los Angeles, had never really treated her like this. But here, on the bottom of a Russian harbor, danger all around, this handsome American was taking the time to ease her fears. She rewarded him with a smile. "But don't they also see our 'ghost'?"

"They do and they don't. Right now, we are part and parcel of one of your peoples' historical monuments to the Great War." He turned to the bulkhead and drew an imaginary bay with his finger. "Here in the middle is a sunken World War II ship. It is the grave of more than a thousand Russian sailors. The site is prominently marked with a large buoy and provides a sharp sonar return. Every ship in the harbor is accustomed to seeing a blip or two in that area."

Pete wet his finger, ran it inside his collar, and pulled out a few more shards of sharp plastic. "If my estimates are correct, we are currently lying very near, almost in the shadow of that old wreck."

"So, they see us, but think we're part of some old sunken ship?"

"That's what I'm counting on. If I'm wrong, none of us will have to worry about trials back in Moscow."

He removed a larger piece from his bleeding right palm. "Since you're the reason we're laying here, you're invited to a wardroom meeting to plan just how we are going to extricate ourselves from your lovely Russian bay.

"While I make some preparations, I'm going to provide you an outfit accessory." He removed a pair of handcuffs from his rear pocket and dangled them from his left hand. Anastasia rolled her eyes.

"I suspect those blue eyes of yours have entrapped many a man. You are much too pretty to be completely trusted." He rolled his own eyes upward. "Those ex-friends of yours might well be missing us, because I am truly the brilliant tactician my sainted mother believes." He winked at her. "On the other hand, your former countrymen may know exactly where we are and wish you to appear to dramatically escape.

"I am not going to risk my men and this ship by foolishly choosing the wrong door, so whenever you are out of this room, you get to wear one of these pretty bracelets – and my Exec is going to sport the matching one. While you are in the wardroom, at our meeting, I will have this stateroom searched to see if you accidentally dropped anything.

"Lastly…" He had stepped all the way into the room, pulling the green curtain closed behind him and hipped her chair until it and she slid across the tile foor further into the room. "…before we exchange pleasantries in the wardroom, Miss Spy, please remove all your clothes. I am interested to see if my Exec missed anything more than a few freckles and a very sharp knife."

A few seconds later, Asya, wearing only black flats and matching thigh-highs, was turning on her toes in front of Pete. She shivered. It was cold in the submarine, especially naked. A long whistle, accompanied by the shriek of steel against steel, startled her awake. After a few seconds, she realized her coat had slipped from her lap onto the floor. She was curled up in the train seat, her right hand thrust inside her purse, gripping the gun.

She reached down with her left hand and snuggled the coat back up over her shoulders. She then watched through thinly open lids the passengers disembarking and boarding at the Lafayette, Indiana stop. No one seemed a bit interested in either her or the empty seat at her side. After the train began moving, she closed her purse, placed it on her lap under her coat and permitted her body to coax her back to sleep.

It had been a hell of a day.

CHAPTER SIX

"Captain O'Brien, are you okay?"

He had gotten to his hands and knees, but was still quite dizzy with his head trying to frantically tell his arms not to push him back up so quickly. He was trying to remember exactly how he had arrived face down in the snow with his face against the front-right sidewall of someone's Ford pickup. An old lady holding a Starbucks cup was leaning over him. It was coming back. Right. He had spotted Asya. He shook his head, immediately regretted it, but nevertheless lifted himself to his knees. "I'm fine, Sondra. Did you see which way she went?" By pushing against the side of the pickup, Pete managed to make it to his feet.

Sondra shook her head emphatically. "I didn't see anyone. We were talking and you suddenly yelled, 'Astra!' ran out, took a fall on the ice that always forms on the top stoop in the late afternoon." She looked at him apologetically. "I've got a small bag of salt the Mister buys me behind the counter that I usually spread out there myself, but with the excitement of you coming and us talking, I clean forgot. And then you swooped down across the sidewalk like Wonder Woman in the movies." She dug a package of Kleenex out of her sweater pocket and began to wipe his face. "You slid clear across the sidewalk and hit your head against that truck."

She pulled gently at his arm. "Oh, goodness! You have a cut on your face. Are you limping? Did you hurt your leg? We should get you in out of the cold." Sondra was actually leaning on him for support in the rapidly accumulating snow. She suddenly twisted him to meet a woman walking toward them who was taking long pulls on a thin cigarette. "Look, here's Dora!" – and under her breath, she said to Pete, "What a nasty habit. I spend 30 minutes every morning deodorizing the lobby. I quit in 1979 along with Rosaline from over on Richie."

"Dora, I would like you to meet the nicest young man: Captain Pete O'Brien of the United States Navy. He's been waiting to meet the new young woman in 406."

"It'll be a while."

Both Sondra and Pete looked at her questioningly.

Dora flipped her cigarette into a pile of snow next to the stoop. Pete could feel Sondra's pulse of littering-disapproval through her thin linked arm. "As I was getting off the bus, 406 passed me running like she'd seen a ghost." Ms Stroup brushed past Pete and climbed the stairs, huffing words over her shoulder at each step. "Sondra, I've told you before: you would trust a yellow-dog democrat. That girl obviously wasn't that eager to meet your Captain O'Brien." She pushed open the front door and paused to throw her own sally over her shoulder. "And neither am I."

Since Sondra had missed her bus, Pete insisted on seeing her home. After they finally got a cab to stop, Pete talked her into sharing. He had an ulterior motive, which he raised as they crossed over Fall Creek on North Meridian.

"May I ask you for a favor?"

"Sure. I'm a Midwest girl. We do favors for free on weekdays and twice on Sundays. As long as they don't involve anybody that kisses snakes or baptizes in a tent. My papa always drew the line there after his first girlfriend was bit at a revival."

"May I leave you with a couple of notes for Asya? One to slip under her door and one for her lobby mailbox, so she won't miss them? I really want to get in touch with her."

"Seal them and I won't even let Dora read them."

Pete delivered Sondra to her door, shook hands with her husband, wrote his notes and made his train east with an hour to spare. He had come to Indianapolis on an impulse. It hadn't turned out well, but he didn't intend to quit. He finally had a datum on her location. She wasn't just anywhere in the United States. He would rearrange his schedule to make time in two weeks and be back.

As the train pulled out of Indianapolis, the car lights dimmed, and Pete leaned back and thought about the last time he had seen Asya. It had been a brisk morning on Japan's Inland Sea. No Russian submarine would have dared follow them into the Sea through the Shimonoseki Passage. The sun was just above the horizon, already beginning to burn away the morning fog.

The port of Kure, and absolute safety, was less than two hours away. Mooring there would not only deliver Asya, but as the first line went over the pier, it would mark his very last mission as a submariner. He was so very physically tired of the unique life and death responsibility. Once they reached Kure, he was going to dive into a bed and sleep forever. He was completely drained. Emotionally dry. The real glory in submarine missions was in having the guts to try. Fail or succeed, those in the business knew those who tried. They were the ones treated with respect, for success was a fickle mistress, and well known to hobnob with men who did not deserve her.

Pete wasn't sure what others would say about his success on this trip, but he would always have an award he wouldn't wear on his uniform – in this case, the feel of the woman currently trying to get out of the cold wind by burrowing into the side of his salt-encrusted foul-weather jacket. Pete looked down at the top of her head. She came almost to the top of his shoulder. He had had funny dreams about her the last two nights – what would he sacrifice for her if she weren't immediately going into the witness-protection program? Would he give up his navy career for this woman he had met only three days ago…?

Anastasia had refused a cap and the breeze on the open bridge was continually tumbling her hair. In the half-hour they had been exposed to the sea air, she had moved much closer to him. From the bridge, it was a sheer 20ft drop followed by a bounce off an unyielding steel hull into a freezing sea. Pete had dispensed with the handcuffs.

"Peter, you must return my knife."

"Anastasia," he said patiently, "I am not giving you a knife to bury in someone's side. How big a dummy do I appear to you? What if this 'rescue' was only a ruse for you to assassinate an official waiting on the pier?"

He turned his attention back to the red-and-black buoys ahead. It was good to breathe in real air, rather than the artificial stuff they manufactured 24/7 on the submarine. He could actually feel his stress begin to drop, flowing away in the brisk wind. His last run. It would be a relief to pass on the responsibility of command. Swede was right: he had let the grind of command responsibility push his personal life aside, he...

"Will you return it to me in a year?"

Up ahead, the gray stones of the Kure breakwater began poking up through the fog. One careful turn to the left was all this particular landing required.

"I never told you why I spy for America."

Pete leaned down toward her.

"I was living in Moscow. My mother was still in our village. She had been seriously ill for years." Anastasia gazed off toward the shore. "She was finally beyond the aid of any medicines. I had come home to be with her. While I was there, a friend alerted me that my apartment was being searched." A tremor ran through her low voice, "We both knew what that meant."

"What will happen to your mother now you've escaped?"

Anastasia looked up at him. Her eyes were shiny, but clear. "Nothing will happen to her."

Pete was surprised, but he remained silent.

Anastasia shifted her weight so she was leaning against his side and again gazed at the Japanese coastline. "I was with her when the call came about my apartment. We both understood what it meant." Her voice was now halting. "She insisted I run. The Georgians killed my father before he ever held me. I was her only child."

Pete could see her eyes were blinking. "I left her all of the morphine I had smuggled – more than a month's supply."

She paused, and a few seconds became an awkward silence of nearly a minute before she continued. "So, they will do nothing to her." Pete could barely hear her voice above the wind. "I am sure she was dead long before they arrived."

She looked up at him. A tear had left a wet streak that ended near her upper lip. "I do not regret what I did." Her voice was steady as she locked her gaze on him. "And I will someday kill the American who betrayed me." Her soft voice rose: "It must have been someone in your CIA. I was too careful in Moscow. I would never have been discovered." She smudged away the tear and her voice became very matter-of-fact: "I will find him or her. You must return my little knife. It has been in my family for many generations."

She wrapped her long hair around her hand. It briefly veiled all of her face but her eyes as she corralled the strands by tucking them under the collar of her jacket. "I have been reading up. In your Kentucky, you have the Hatfields and McCoys. They are continually killing each other."

"They did for generations."

"In my part of Russia, we have the same sort of vengeance. We call it kun." Her eyes had deepened in color behind the shield of her black hair. "I have sworn to take retribution for my mother." Pete had not heard her speak so coldly. "One day my knife will taste kun."

She released her hair shield and pulled on his jacket. "Promise you will return my knife." She was back on the same subject and Pete let his mind move on to more pressing matters. The sighting of the breakwater had reminded him of his forthcoming checklists. As soon as he met his relief on the pier, they needed to quickly direct the accomplishment of several official checks. As soon as those were completed, there would be a short ceremony to introduce the new commander to the crew, they would need to jointly inventory the nuclear sources, discuss each of the offic...

"Peter, place your arm next to mine."

Pete looked down to where Asya was struggling with her oversized coat, dragging on the unwieldy waterproofed material. They really had nothing aboard for her to wear, and even the smallest waterproofed items were outsized for her.

"Is this some sort of Russian goodbye ritual?"

"Peter, I trust you, no matter what you think of me." She had managed to arrange the heavy green fabric of her jacket so that nearly her entire left arm was exposed. "Please just loan me your arm!"

Checking that the turn into the harbor channel was not imminent and that Ackerman was paying strict attention to the seaway, even if undoubtedly drinking in every word of what was going on behind him, Pete undid his left cuff button and pulled his uniform sleeve back to bare his arm. "This ceremony better not take long. It is chilly out here this morning, Miss Spy."

"Hold your arm tight against mine, Peter. Please. Feel how warm we are together."

The softness of her skin was more temptation than Pete could resist. His eyes closed and he knew he stopped breathing for a second. Then he felt a sting. When his eyes flashed open, blood was already welling from two long straight cuts, one on his arm, the other on hers, and Asya was pressing the two open wounds together.

"Damn you!" Pete struck her on the shoulder and she lurched against the side of the cockpit and fell at his feet. The Officer of the Deck turned toward them.

"Mind your course, Mr Ackerman." Pete said sharply. "Don't run us into the jetty. I can take care of this."

Pete reached down, grabbed both of Anastasia's wrists, yanking her to his chest.

"What the hell were you doing?"

"Peter." Anastasia's eyes were nearly black with intensity. He would have recoiled if he hadn't been tightly holding both her hands. "Your blood is now mixed with mine. We are linked forever. I owe you for saving my life. You owe me my knife."

He could swear her eyes were glittering. "At the moment, it is in my right pocket. And," she continued, "you should change the combination to your safe."

*

As soon as the brow went over in Kure, Pete used the steel ladder on the side of the sail to descend to the submarine deck. He made his way off the ship and over to the small group of officials on the pier. A good-looking man, nearly as tall as Pete and roughly the same build, led the delegation. The man was exceptionally well dressed in a charcoal gray suit covered by an expensive camel-hair overcoat, the collar turned up against the sleet.

"I am Assistant Secretary of State Winsor Asher, Captain. The CIA has asked me to take a package off your hands." He extended his right hand for a firm handshake as he simultaneously showed his State Department credential set with his left. "I understand you and your crew did an exceptional job, Captain. Not only did you rescue our agent, but you also bloodied the Russians' noses. I want to extend our nation's thanks. Did she tell you much about her background?"

Pete just looked at Winsor. He hadn't slept for three days. The mission was over. He would never see Asya again. He was tired.

Winsor repeated himself. "During your voyage, did she tell you much about herself?"

No, she actually hadn't.

Just then Asya ran past Pete and threw herself into Asher's arms. "Winsor, you traveled all this way for me!"

CHAPTER SEVEN

Near the three-mile mark of Asya's early-morning run in Washington Park, a sportscaster on Chicago Sports Radio began interviewing a man who had achieved fame both as a player and as a coach. When asked what he most remembered from his long career in athletics, the airwaves had gone silent. Asya had decided she was in a dead zone, and considered reversing her direction to hear the reply. "What I most remember," the athlete had finally replied, "Is I never dream about coaching."

It was hours later, and she was sitting in the forward few inches of her ergogenic chair using the eraser on her pencil to thoughtfully tap one particular information segment on her computer screen. Her iPod was now tuned to classical music, but the words "I never dream of coaching" were still looping through her mind. She went back to her proprietary spreadsheet and tossed the pencil carelessly onto her desktop.

No matter how intricate and interrelated the flow of trade on the Uzbekistan and Turkmenistan travel routes were to world cotton prices, and how much money she could make for herself and her firm by her unique understanding of the myriad of factors involved, she had never dreamed of making money. Her left hand felt for her coffee cup and she took a sip, her eyes not leaving a column of numbers centered on her computer screen. She pressed a few keys to introduce an algorithm she had spent the past few weekends debugging and shifted her butt back in her chair, remembering old sounds and feelings: her body falling, twisting; the fingers on her right hand flung out, vainly reaching for safety; the Moscow crowd gasping as her fingertips deliberately grazed the top wooden bar only to snap tight around the vibrating lower staff, her muscles visibly cording as she leveraged her downward momentum to thrust her torso back up, aiming for the upper bar.

As her body continued rotating upward, Anastasia would always feel the centrifugal force testing her body. She ignored the burn, focusing only on keeping her legs straight, together, and each finger curled around the wooden shaft. Her years of painful practice provided precisely what judges most valued – strength – and, on her face, the serenity of discipline.

The program finally booted up. She leaned forward, typed two more commands and placed her right hand over her coffee, unconsciously absorbing its warmth as numbers began rapidly filling, tumbling down the screen...

Back in Moscow, her body slowed near the top of its arc, and she unhurriedly shifted her left hand to an undergrip. Steadily – inexorably, to the watching crowd – she halted her long body's swing and shifted into a handstand. Unseen by the audience, the bicep in her right arm began to tremor with fatigue. Recognizing her physical limits, Anastasia sharply shook her head. Her chignon fell free.

As it did, Asya let go the bar and rotated into a twisting somersault dismount, her long black hair now streaming dramatically behind. As her lithe figure whipped through its final rotation, her toes 'stuck' the landing. Quickly using both hands to push back the billowing hair from her face, Anastasia pivoted to face the judges and triumphantly thrust her hands in the air.

Vasilii Gubin, her coach, was the first person to reach her from the sidelines. As usual, his congratulatory grasp around her waist included his thumbs brushing familiarly against the undersides of her breasts, "Preekrasna! Incredible! I cannot believe you do so much with my coaching!"

Still smiling for the judges, Anastasia brought her elbows sharply down along her sides, pushing Vasilii's unwelcome hands away. Stepping a half-pace apart from him, she again raised her arms, swiveling a quarter-turn toward each of the three packed seating areas to acknowledge the enthusiastic crowd. Only then did she extend her left hand to Vasilii.

Together they walked to the sideline to join her teammates and her coach's wife. She knew the crowd loved the image she and Vasilii presented – the slim 16-year-old-girl, with such hidden strength, walking hand-in-hand with her coach. He, at 5ft 5in, was only slightly taller than her. But he had barrels for upper arms and still had the famous 48in chest that, 20 years earlier, had helped brand him as a gymnastics world champion. The crowd's applause followed them to the side of the floor, where the three stood together, awaiting Anastasia's score.

There was the inevitable delay and the crowd sat back down and grew quiet as the judges deliberated. Finally, the scorecards began turning – 9.8, 9.6, 9.9, 9.7 and 9.8 again! First place!

The crowd stood and cheered. Each of the Gubins kissed her on both cheeks and Anastasia took several steps from the team area out into the gymnasium. She waved again to the standing crowd before turning to duck into the tunnel between the stands toward the common dressing room. She needed a few moments by herself. She was mentally exhausted.

She used her teeth to worry a tape end loose from her left wrist and began unwinding long strips as she walked. She needed a scrunchie for her hair. The cold from the bare concrete floor flowed up through her thin gymnastics slippers. The base of her neck hurt from the shock of the landing. She pitched the ball of tape from her left wrist into a waste bin along the wall and got a fingernail under the top tape end on her right wrist. Olympic qualifications finally over! She was so tired...

Two men stood outside the team's dressing-room door, their black fedora hats and long black coats effectively labeling them either as secret police or men from the espionage agency. Each claimed to be the rightful successor to the KGB and most Russians hated both. The taller and older man had a lit cigarette in the corner of his mouth, his left eye slightly closed against the curling smoke. "Miss Khrapunov!"

Anastasia instantly stopped, the balls of her feet sliding nearly a centimeter forward in the thin layer of grit that lay atop the concrete underneath the stands.

*

A swath of Chicago morning sunlight had captured nearly a third of her desk. The desk phone in that patch was ringing insistently. Anastasia blinked and used her mouse to key the screen control. The music in her left ear muted, replaced by her boss's voice.

"Asya, *kochanie*, do you want to go directly from here tonight or do you want me to pick you up at your apartment?"

"Mr Dunajinski. I appreciate our business relationship. But, I am not your 'Polish honey.' This is a business dinner, not a date. I prefer to meet at the restaurant."

"Asya, I did you a big favor." Anastasia felt a cold draft swirl around her. The perception was so real, she opened a drawer in her desk, took out a scarf and placed it over her shoulders. She said nothing. Her pencil teetered on the desk edge and she reached out and captured it.

"I know you've been dating that Alex guy from Washington. But I'm asking you to give me a shot. If, after a few dates, you insist there can never be anything there, then so be it. I'm more interested in making money than anything else." He paused, apparently waiting for her to speak.

In the several months she had worked on the Chicago Mercantile Exchange, Anastasia had discovered that when Adam Dunajinski wasn't actually speaking, he tended to softly hum show tunes under his breath. Her jury was still out on whether or not this particular habit was endearing or maddening. As long as they weren't around other people, she was willing to let it fall toward the cute end of the spectrum. At the moment, while he waited for her to speak, he was somewhere in the middle of Sinatra's version of Baubles, Bangles and Beads. He had given her a job six months ago, when she had shown up out of nowhere. Was she ready to start over again?

"However, I do insist you call me Adam. I'm only five years older than you. OK?"

"OK…Adam."

"Navy Pier at seven." He abruptly shifted songs. The Philadelphia Opera's recording of Verdi's *La traviata brindisi* à la Mr Adam Dunajinski swelled in her ears. Was she going to have to learn to predict mood differences based on music preferences?

She absent-mindedly placed a pencil in her hair behind her ear and noted it stayed too readily in place. She would need an hour to wash it before the 'professional dinner' tonight. What a pain. But her mother had so loved long hair. She pulled the pencil out and leaned forward, focusing on her algorithm results, keeping her left hand balled in her lap, forcing her fingers away from the mouse, occupying her right-hand fingers by twirling the pencil instead.

Her eyes integrated her new screen – 87 percent probability of more than 300 percent returns... Mr Dunajinski only thought he knew everything... On Saturday, Winsor was flying into town for a show and late dinner. Last month, it had been Alex. She had contacted both of them when, after three lonely months, she realized she trusted no one here in Chi Town – including her Polish prince. Too bad Peter had never – ummm – putting the pencil between her lips, she permitted her right hand to descend upon the mouse and caress it to highlight a two-tailed binomal, then both hands on the keyboard to enter the data, a few strokes to add parameters and hit start, and a new blue-green undulation rolled across the screen. A success probability just lower than the magic number of ninety! How could she have missed that?

CHAPTER EIGHT

Although the sun had set several hours ago, some of the DC rush-hour traffic still remained on the roads when the cab pulled to the Wisconsin Avenue curb and stopped. A block of eastbound traffic quickly bunched behind it as two cars fought to merge left into the same space. The normal Georgetown din became amplified as horns were tapped instead of brakes. Ignoring the commotion, a man unhurriedly climbed out of the taxi and made his way across the uneven brick sidewalk to the circular steps. A tall mustached black man in a tuxedo and silk top hat waited there, prepared to open the iron-strapped wooden door.

As he did, the doorman accepted the proffered gloves and cashmere coat with a slight inclination of his head. "Sir, your guest is waiting at the bar. Your usual table has been reserved."

As the member passed the polished mahogany that George Washington had reportedly leaned upon, he directed a soft request to the bartender, "Scotty, Macallan, 18 Years. Neat" and, without further pause, made his way to a corner table in the living room. His guest immediately joined. The two men wordlessly shook hands and sat, waiting to open their conversation until Scotty had delivered their drinks and returned across the room.

The guest spoke first. "Is this safe?"

"You are a student of American history. Where is your proper sense of reverence? This was one of our first President's clubs. Probably his favorite one. Didn't they teach you anything at UCLA?" The member took an appreciative sip of his scotch, and leaned back in his chair, letting the aroma seep into his sinuses before permitting the liquid to slide slowly down his throat. "Why do you think we get all squirrely if an American shows up on the Queen's List? By God, Americans are queerer about tradition than a Peer in the House of Lords! The CIA wouldn't bug this place if it were the last building in Washington."

"I was thinking more about the FBI."

"C-I-A. F-B-I. Po-tate-to, Po-tah-to." The member took another slight sip and grimaced before removing a sheet of paper from his breast pocket. He turned it over and his thumb pressed out the paper's folds before he reversed it again and slid it across the table, so it spun halfway around before coming to rest in front of his guest. It was a graph done in three colors.

"Pretty. What is it?"

"The gross domestic product of China and Russia compared to the United States. Charted for the past 30 years and projected ahead for the same."

The member leaned against the leather back of his chair and permitted himself another small sip while his guest looked at a proposed skeleton for world domination. It has always been the same, from the time of the pharaohs until the present. Power and influence came from the barrel of a gun, whether the weapon looked like a wheat basket during a famine or a medicine jar during periods of plague. Influence was purchased with money. Excess money. Extra dollars than those required to feed populations and fight normal wars. Each of those additional dollars had an extraordinary influence in increasing United States security. But extra money had to be generated. It needed to be wrested from competitors, derived from better and cheaper products – to be sold to lesser powers.

The raw facts were simple. The higher America's gross domestic product, the more available money to pursue freedom's causes. Consequently, the safer the women and children in Iowa, Texas and Kansas. Power could always be foolishly wasted, as Russia did in Afghanistan, America did in Iraq and the China had during the Cultural Revolution, but… His thoughts were interrupted when his guest began tapping the paper with his forefinger.

"Yes?"

His guest put his hand to his mouth and spoke quietly behind his fingers. "The economists I've spoken to don't predict Russia will recover this quickly."

The member dismissively flicked his fingers. "I don't think anyone thought the russkiyes' economy would be so decimated at the end of the Cold War either. Everyone misunderstood how much the Russian standing army had cost. But once the Soviet Union broke apart and Russia privatized its energy assets, market inefficiencies were recovered at a remarkable rate."

"Even with losses to the robber barons and mafia?"

The member barely contained his distaste, "You don't actually listen to what we feed the media, do you? The Russians are doing fairly well. Billionaires and thieves don't steal nearly as much as were wasted by the inefficiencies of communism and the cost of a large standing army. Granted, it took some years for the new situation to stabilize." The member tapped the sheet. "Look at the last five years. These Russian numbers were audited by the International Monetary Fund. Those are not statistical anomalies."

The guest shifted his forefinger from the purple line to the red one. "Your China numbers show the same bias."

The member did not answer, but signaled Scotty for another round and sat back in his chair. It was always best if his guests believed they had convinced themselves.

After a few silent minutes, his guest folded the paper back on its original creases and held it up between his thumb and forefinger, "OK. I can see where someone might make these assumptions. May I keep this?"

The member nodded.

"And you predict the two of them together will overtake us within the next decade?"

The member took a small sip of scotch. The question was too insulting to answer. The answer was as clear as the colors on the paper.

"And you believe it's possible to influence the future?"

The member only looked at him and tipped his glass back again.

Another minute went by. The drone of conversations in the club remained quiet. Scotty came with two fresh drinks and a bowl of mixed nuts and departed with two empty glasses.

"You know I will support you whatever you decide. What are we going to do?"

The member moved the bowl of nuts to one side and leaned forward. "Russia relies on St Petersburg to be its trade window to the West. They have spent billions making it appear to be Western-friendly. Dour Moscow with its robber barons and too-obvious mafia scares off investors, and Russia greatly needs outside investment. Similarly, in China, where, while they don't lack capital, they do need ready market access. They gain the latter from the Hong Kong window, where the majority of China trade flows in and out to the West. Each of these cities has centuries of history with the West."

His guest was a man with a great deal of international experience. "Of course," he said impatiently.

The member drew a second piece of paper from his breast pocket, unfolded it and dropped it on the table in front of his guest. "These are the same GDP projections if those two cities were to cease functioning as trade centers."

"Why would they?"

"Who knows? Plague. Some natural or unnatural disaster?" The member rolled his glass between his fingers. "And if it were an unnatural event, how in the world could such a catastrophe be blamed on someone else?"

"Israel?" His guest's brow had suddenly begun to perspire. He was looking around the room as if he expected Mossad to suddenly jump out from behind one of the 300-year-old wall panels.

"Why stir that hornets' nest? Some days I believe the Jews have better intelligence than we do. I do not wish to challenge them when unnecessary."

"Syria? Iran?" His guest suddenly leaned across the table, literally hissing: "If you wanted to make me fucking uncomfortable, you have completely succeeded. I am not talking any more here!"

"OK." The member stood up. "Let's have dinner and go back to my place. I have it swept every week. There is both a plan and a timetable, but you may find some of the remaining missing pieces interesting."

CHAPTER NINE

It was August and the Washington Nationals were still in the pennant race! Baseball fever was at full throttle in the crowd pouring off the subway at the Navy Yard metro stop. When they had gotten on downtown, Asya and Winsor had made the rookie mistake of standing near the car doors. They were consequently being carried up the street just ahead of a churning sea of red and white. It required nearly a jog to stay ahead of the crowd and also avoid stepping on a child or inadvertently elbowing a parent. The shriller the police whistles, the faster children pulled fathers and mothers toward the sanctuary of the looming ballpark. Suddenly, a mother trying to corral a set of curly-haired three-year-old twin girls jolted Asya on her right hip. The two were identical, wearing matching ivory sundresses covered with pink fish. They had shiny shoes and were intent on displaying their sequined slippers to everyone who had been on the metro. Over their dresses, they wore sequined leather harnesses, which buckled around their waists. They put thumbs under the straps that ran over their shoulders and explained to anyone who glanced their way. "So, we can sit in the first row."

Their mother's only assistance was a slender five-year-old boy, whose thin freckled face was topped by a cowlick that had slipped through the plastic adjustor of his National's ball cap. Like many of the other children, he wore a red shirt, but his had 'Bobbie' printed on his back. The worn fielder's glove on his right hand was obviously his own. He had an eye on his sisters, but the longing glances he cast ahead at the stadium indicated he was interested in getting inside before any more of this unique opportunity was lost. Their mother smiled her apologies at Asya, and Asya tried to give her a bit more space by inching closer to Winsor.

Before she could, Winsor lifted her off her feet and swung her to the outside of the sidewalk, where they permitted this man-made wave to sweep by. They stood for a few seconds under one of the leafy Dutch elms that made downtown Washington passably bearable in the late summer while Winsor used the break to check his mobile phone. It was only a few seconds before Alex and his date, Sunjin Rose, caught up with them. As the two approached, Asya tried to recall what she knew about Sunjin. The two women hadn't been able to talk aboard the metro. Didn't the Secretary of State bring Sunjin with her from California? Hadn't there been a question in *The Washington Post* about her citizenship?

What was Alex saying? "…Sunjin thought the next time we would see you was when you and the other children stopped for cotton candy."

In one of the two men's exchanges to which Asya had grown accustomed, Winsor silently held the envelope with the four tickets high above his head and waved it back and forth, his right hand's middle finger on the side of the envelope toward Alex, which, of course, induced Alex to drop Sunjin's hand and lunge at Winsor's shoulder. They promptly ignored the women and chased each other out into the street between the slow-moving cars. As they did, Asya linked arms with Sunjin and turned to follow the crowd up the slight hill toward the stadium. She decided to work on satisfying her curiosity: "The word 'Sunjin' is a delicate name for a woman. I don't think I've ever known anyone with that surname."

Sunjin laughed. "You've probably known few Korean women with French fathers. There were actually two Sunjins in my Paris kindergarten class! And the other one took my Play-Doh and claimed it was hers!" She pushed her hair back and placed her hand dramatically on her chest. "Oh, the tragedies of childhood!"

They were passing a partially filled trashcan. Sunjin loosened her arm from Asya's, stooped and picked up sections of a newspaper that were falling out and firmly binned them. Part of the front-page headline 'Chechnya Threat' showed around the folds. Sunjin retook Asya's arm. "I thought this outing would be cancelled after that."

Anastasia nodded agreement. "I imagined today was going to turn into a dinner, at best. I had my mouth getting ready for Vietnamese at that place on Pitt Street. I think someone told me they're using sauce made from fish native to the Chesapeake Bay."

"I read that same review." She paused. "Or maybe Scarlet ate there and mentioned that to me."

They had reached the part of the street where the walkers were pushed closer together by the white crowd-control sawhorses. The throng was beginning to funnel toward the main gate. "I guess someone at TSA decided the threat was limited to East Coast flights, so the Dodgers were able to fly into Pittsburg late last night and bus over."

Sunjin leaned into Asya and, as she did, lowered her voice even more. Asya found her accent difficult to reliably understand, particularly given the background of the buzz of excited fans around them who were also streaming toward the gates.

"I know you are…State consultant, so I can…crazy bastards – and all Chechens are truly crazy…my family used to live a block over…in the 15th *arrondissement*…murder nearly every month…someday one of those nuclear weapons…" Asya forced her head closer to hear. She could taste Sunjin's hair in her mouth. How did men ever stand it?

Even as close as they were, it was still difficult to hear. "…the ones that Alex works so hard to track…or even worse, plutonium…" Then Sunjin yelped: "Ouch!" Her head whipped around. "You jackass!"

"What are you two whispering about?" Winsor was immediately behind them, arm-in-arm with Alex. Evidently, the men had been mimicking Sunjin's and Asya's head-together stroll. It very much looked like Winsor had flat-tired one of Sunjin's shoes when the two women had not immediately noticed them.

Sunjin wasn't even trying to hide her impatience at this latest juvenile antic. She stepped in the middle of the stream of fans and turned around, letting her shoe dangle from her toe. "The 15th *arrondissement* and plutonium. Unlike our dates, we were having an adult conversation."

Winsor immediately knelt down in the street, balanced Sunjin's bare foot on his knee as he carefully unlaced her sneaker, slipped it back on and retied it. "My apologies. It was a mistake, I assure you." He looked up and winked at her. "Or if it weren't, it should have been." He bent low, kissing the toe of her sneaker. "There. All better." He stood, reclaiming and linking Asya's arm, and taking the lead toward the turnstiles. "Now, if our little group is going to speak about two such dramatically diverse subjects on our day off…" – his voice took on a jaunty tone Asya suspected was deliberately adopted to annoy someone he knew to be one of his boss's best friends – "…then I will be the instructor, for I speak French fluently, have been to the top of the Tour Montparnasse and more importantly have drunk at the bar where Brigitte Bardot frequently had her afternoon bourbon, so what else is there to be known about the 15th?"

He paused and kissed Asya. His lips were warm and smooth against her cheek. Even when he was in one of his irritating moods, he could turn the charm on as easily as a clerk made change.

"And Alex" – he turned and used the ticket envelope like a conductor's baton to tap his friend on the shoulder – "can talk about the nasty stuff!"

On cue, Alex responded, "Radioactive for thousands of years. Even a worse poison!" His voice began to pick up enthusiasm, "At one time, the KGB's favorite method of assassinating turncoats in the West, because the death was…"

They were almost to the turnstiles. Winsor waved Alex to silence. "Enough, my friend. We have shown our employer's favorite that we too can be adults! Here are your tickets. The goal for today is to have fun. On to section 121!"

Asya mentally shook her head. She was unsure why Winsor was needling Sunjin. She seemed like a nice person. Sometimes her boyfriend seemed to unnecessarily love to walk the edge on relationships. In the crowd, she glimpsed the young mother, her twins and Bobbie. The four were ahead of them on the escalator that led up to the second deck. On the escalator, Asya again fell in beside Sunjin. Halfway up, a klaxon sounded over the loudspeaker system and the fans broke out in applause.

Asya looked over at Sunjin, "Why the applause?"

"Someone for Washington just hit a home run!"

"They use a submarine diving alarm to signal home runs?"

Sunjin gave her an odd look. "That's the local shtick. How in the world do you know that awful noise is from a submarine diving alarm? Not that I doubt you, but I've never heard anyone mention it and I follow the team. I've already been to 10 or 15 games this year. It's certainly a unique sound and I 've heard many people ask what it was. No one else has claimed to know." Sunjin smiled, "Are you a secret watcher of the History Channel late at night when you should be writing reports for the Secretary?'

They had reached the top of the elevator, so Asya simply threw her answer over her shoulder "My Chechens were in Vladivostok" as she stepped off the elevator and then doubled back to take Winsor's arm.

By the sixth inning, the Nationals were ahead 5-0 and the crowd was relaxed. After a beer run, Winsor and Alex had decided to watch the game from the concourse, and obviously discuss something, leaving Sunjin and Asya in the seats. Not the best boy-girl date behavior perhaps, but it was a lovely sunny afternoon, the seats were in the second row of the first elevated section along third-base line, and Asya was in the process of making two new friends. As chance would have it, Maria DeReggi, the mother of Bobbie and the twins, had seats directly in front of theirs, and while their brother anxiously watched for the opportunity to catch a foul ball, the girls spent some time describing to Sunjin and Asya precisely where and when their mother had purchased their dresses, their sequined slippers and their leather harnesses. Since their seats were right behind a dangerous drop to the field, their mother had outfitted them in little harnesses looped to her wrist, and – miracle of miracles to Asya – by gluing sequins to the leather, had convinced them that the harnesses were simply the very best accessories for three-year-olds to wear.

Finally, Maria inserted herself into the endless flow of her girls' breathless narratives: "I know it was crazy, but we'd been planned this outing for months." She glanced fondly over at her son.

"It was intended to be Bobbie's birthday present. Sam wangled great seats for us all up here in the first row. Then, at the last minute, he had to work. As you can see, the twins get so much attention because they're young and cute, but Bob is really my pillar at home. He didn't even say anything when his dad told him he would have to cancel. So, I decided to figure out a way to manage. I was worried about the twins and this –" she gestured at the waist-high wall directly in front of the seats that was the only barrier to a 40ft fall to the seating section below – "so I decided to make harnesses for the twins so they couldn't crawl over even if I got distracted. What was the worst…?"

Anastasia dove past Maria, grabbing the green iron railing at the top of the cement wall with her left hand as she simultaneously seized the tail of Bobbie's shirt with her right, her knees slamming against the backs of the chair row to keep herself from pitching over as she pulled the boy back up over the wall and back into the aisle. She had been watching Bobbie stand to catch a foul ball as she was listening to Maria. It was amazing how fast the ball curved toward them off the bat. Bobbie had quickly lost his sense of spatial awareness, followed by his balance.

As his cap spiraled downward, Maria hysterically wrapped both arms around her son and screamed, "Bobbie, what were you doing?" Both twins instantly broke out in tears. Asya and Sunjin glanced at each other for only a second before each assuredly gathered a girl in their arms. As Asya smoothed the hair of her twin, she noticed the people around them were standing and applauding. Out in center field, their little drama was being captured on the large scoreboard by a camera that had apparently been following the flight of the foul ball. Asya ignored everyone and focused on stroking the hair of her twin, but the people only applauded more loudly. She could see the players on the field had stopped and were also clapping. Finally, a section usher appeared with two gifts for Bobbie – an official major league ball and a replacement National's cap – and, while Maria took the twin from her arms, the usher urged Asya to stand up, raised one of her arms and had her turn to the right and then to the left to accept the stadium's thunderous applause.

It was going to be a long time before Asya attended another ballgame.

"Mom, stand up."

Bobbie was tugging at Maria's hand. At his mother's insistence, he had removed his fielder's glove, which was now crammed into her purse. He was standing very straight, his new cap carefully held by the bill over his chest.

"It's the seventh-inning stretch. It's when they sing."

The ballpark public announcer came on, "And now, to honor America, we ask everyone to join us in singing *America the Beautiful* followed by *Take Me Out to the Ballgame*. The words will be on the scoreboard, so everyone can join in. To lead us today we will have one of America's true heroes: Captain Pete O'Brien of our Navy's submarine force. Captain O' Brien, the microphone is all yours."

A booming baritone rang out to become gradually submerged as 40,000 fans found their collective voices.

"O beautiful for spacious skies…

"For purple mount…"

The music built. The beautiful communal prayer seemed to rise from the very green of the field. It swelled up until it was with the grandstands and then surged upward into the stars. Anastasia felt her chest hurting.

She hadn't let herself react when Bobbie was in danger, but the initial notes from Pete's voice had pushed her buttons. This song was filling her soul. Memories were flashing through her mind – of the Midwest, where she had become an American; of her beloved Steppes; of Peter waiting for her on the bridge of his ship. A tear began to form in the corner of her left eye. This wouldn't do. Asya stopping singing and excused herself, stepping past Sunjin and climbing the aisle against the stream of people returning with beer, hotdogs and Cokes. She couldn't help but wonder if he had been in the park earlier... Fingers touched her upper arm...

She spun around to Winsor's unexpected query: "Ready to leave now and beat the crowd?"

CHAPTER TEN

Pete placed his hands on the eighth-floor window frames and pushed outward until his muscles throbbed. He could shove against solid masonry walls to his heart's content. The historic Fairmont Hotel had withstood more than its share of quakes, and a former SEAL could do his best on the bulkheads. He felt his mind and his body unwind. It was always good to get out of an airplane. Even better, San Francisco was one of his favorite places to be. Down below, foot traffic on the Wharf was beginning to wane. Soon, the usual afternoon temperature drop would begin to seduce fog down from the hills. Wispy moisture from the valley would slip over and follow the trolley tracks down to the waterfront. It was the moment each afternoon when San Francisco's persona shifted from a sunlit American city to one more befitting a shadowy Asian port.

He turned from the window and hung up his suit, leaving everything else in the suitcase. Then he impulsively checked the drawers in the hotel-room desk. It was his ritual every trip. He would search for a local phone book to see if it contained anything different from his computer browser back in Virginia. He ran a thick finger down the column that began with 'Con.' Nope. No Anastasia Conner, not even any 'A Conners.' In fact, only four Conners, one that began with I. There were also two people with the initial M and a lone W. Another empty city or she was using a different name.

Bob said the theory at the Agency was that something had spooked her the very first day. Her boss in Indianapolis maintained he had noticed nothing unusual. He had even passed a lie-detector test administered by the police. Whatever had happened, she had fled the witness-protection program –whether to join a Russian undercover cell or for some other reason, no one knew.

Whatever had happened, she was gone. Pete kicked off the cotton hotel slippers and flipped easily into a handstand, his heels against the wall for balance, doing forty ups and downs before dropping to the floor for crunches. He hooked his feet under the edge of the bed. He had missed his weights workout today and would again tomorrow. He worked until his abs burned and then lay flat on the floor until his breathing returned to normal while thinking through tomorrow's agenda – loose nukes, for Christ's sake. If Russia can't take care of its own nuclear weapons, what the hell is a convention going to accomplish? They are certainly never going to invite us into their country to help! Of course, it didn't matter what he thought. If the Chairman of the Joint Chiefs was interested, and he was, then Pete was going to be jumping in planes and traveling around the world.

Pete rose to his feet, drank a glass of water and opened the window. The sheers flapped in the light breeze of the rapidly graying night. Humidity always twanged his knee, although he tried never to massage it whenever anyone was around. He momentarily closed his eyes, his fingers feeling along the dip below his right kneecap to the long purple scar. He heard a foghorn begin and, by the time the long hoot finished rolling through the open window, he was 15 years younger.

Immediately in front of him, the Russian soldier was pushing open the door of his wrecked Army Scout car. He stumbled out onto Vladivostok's cobblestoned street, his eyes surprised at seeing Pete dressed in ninja black, his left hand frantically trying to unjam the Kalashnikov he was bringing to bear. Pete fired once and the soldier dropped into the fog boiling up from the Harbor. The sound of the gunshots rolled up and down the streets and echoed between the houses. Lights began coming on between Pete's SEAL team and the waterfront.

"Keep moving!" Pete yelled.

As his team turned to sprint the last half-mile, Pete was careful to stay a hundred yards in the rear. It was his job to defend their backs until they got the Russian with the anthrax secrets into their underwater sleds. Then it would be back to their submarine *Grayfish* and safety. At the end of the street, Pete flattened himself against a doorway. Above his head, a dingy wooden mermaid swung back and forth on squeaking metal hinges.

Looking back up the road, Pete could see citizens in nightclothes pulling curtains aside or standing in their open doors. Several hardier souls hurried over to the scout car, which sat on the sidewalk, its radiator steaming. How much longer did the team have before armed respondents arrived – 30 seconds? Less? In fog, everything sounded so much closer. Pete again scanned the six-lane street that ran along the heads of the piers. It was the only remaining barrier between him and the safety of the sea.

He could see Swede was already strapped back into his scuba tanks, crouched with his rifle steadied on the wall, two Predator missile-launchers laid out atop the wall. He was listening to the distant sirens wailing, peering through the fog and scanning the breakwater. Swede would signal when the sleds were safely in the surf and Pete could leave his support position. One siren suddenly shifted in pitch and began to rise.

"Now, Lieutenant!"

Pete began the sprint. Sixty yards to safety. He could do this. He had been on his college track team – both the 100 and 200-meter dashes. Out of the corner of his eye, he saw three pairs of lights turn the corner, one after another. The headlights extended long, trembling fingers in the fog as the vehicles raced across the waterfront cobblestones.

Now he could see beyond the seawall. Both sleds were wallowing in the surf, a pilot and buddy holding each. In front of him, Swede began laying down a stream of fully automatic fire to the left toward the lights of the three cars. One of the other men was pumping out grenades, which he could hear skipping on the stones. A Predator was being counted down. He narrowed his focus down to the seawall. Out of the corner of his eye he saw the first Predator whoosh away. Ten yards to go. He was going to get everyone back.

"Down, Lieutenant! Down!"

Pete closed his eyes as he recalled the excruciating pain as a Russian boat-tailed slug had changed his life. He stepped back from the window. San Francisco Bay had disappeared in the gray mist. He lowered the window to an inch, closed the sheers and swallowed the memory.

"Ladies and Gentlemen, good morning." The bow-tied, white-goateed speaker – from his appearance every bit the tenured professor his program biography promised – looked over the tops of his bifocals at the five semicircular rows of attendees peering up at the podium and the huge screen in the front of the Fairmont conference room. "On this map, the countries with nuclear weapons are shown in red. In green are the two countries that have voluntarily renounced all weapons of mass destruction…"

Pete sat quietly in the audience looking at the projected image. The Cold War had been over before he attended the Naval Academy, but he had always found the numbers astonishing.

"…listed in the order of the number of weapons we believe they now possess. For example, when the Cold War ended, we found that Russia…"

Pete was more intimate with this subject than any bow-tied academic. The US had been unaware that the Soviet Union had possessed more than 40,000 nuclear weapons. Of course, the United States had nearly as many, so…

"…but the arms-control agreements with the United States significantly reduced this danger." The lecturer stopped, stroked his goatee for emphasis while nodding at an acquaintance in the front row. "And in arguably the most important event of the Cold War, our friends from Kazakhstan decided to surrender their nuclear weapons. This one bold stroke significantly reduced the danger of nuclear Armageddon for civilization. We will this afternoon hear from a representative of the Republic of Kazakhstan on that brave decision."

Pete mentally shook his head. While important, the Kazakhstan events had actually been rooted in a major US intelligence failure.

During the Cold War, the Russians had successfully hidden nukes from CIA and military-intelligence satellites. Since the West had eventually won the Cold War and winners write history, this particular breakdown had been lost in the 'fog of war.' From the look of the speaker's charts, it was also not going to be mentioned today.

Pete repositioned his event-stenciled coffee cup and began leafing through his program, stopping at the list of attendees. Although he was the sole representative from the Joint Chiefs, it seemed every other Washington organization had sent at least several big guns to this event. He permitted his mind to drift. When he did so, his thoughts inevitably returned to his own personal elephant in the room.

He absent-mindedly unbuttoned the left cuff of his shirt, pushing up his suit-coat sleeve. He ran his fingers along the thin white scar that extended from just below his elbow nearly to his wrist. If only he hadn't spent an entire career enjoyed the thrill of risking it all! If only she hadn't been destined for the witness-protection program! How could he have missed what he now realized was his one opportunity? The woman to his left coughed, glanced at him disapprovingly and then pointedly looked back at the speaker.

Pete slowly rearranged his sleeve and rebuttoned the cuff. According to the program, the attendees included not one but two Assistant Secretaries from the State Department: an Alex Yates as well as a Winsor Asher. In fact, the latter was the luncheon speaker. Winsor Asher! Wasn't Winsor the name of the guy who met *Grayfish* in Kure? The one she threw her arms around and who had pissed him off? "Well, we're on the same side now," he mused, "and Winsor's a longtime Beltway guy. Wonder if he has any suggestions on how I might find her?"

When the program broke to change rooms for lunch, Pete trailed Asher and Yates into the banquet room. They were both being assisted by a young female aide, and the three were evidently assigned a table up near the dais. It was open seating and Pete quickly followed before the table could fill. He tipped a chair against the table to claim a spot and then circled, introducing himself. He was standing by the aide's chair by the time Winsor unfolded his notes and headed for the podium. The woman gave her official a last pat on the arm for good luck and turned to sit down.

"Here, let me assist you. My name is Pete O'Brien... Asya!"

He clumsily hit the full glass of iced tea that stood at his place setting. It tipped back and bounced squarely against a wine bottle, leaving its sprig of mint free to fall into Asya's salad plate before reversing direction and spinning outward, cascading its contents directly into a dinner plate. There the brown liquid splashed, drenching Pete nearly to his knees. Anastasia didn't say anything. Around them was the buzz of people taking their seats, servers moving between tables and, on the stage, the master of ceremonies tapping on the microphone. Finally, she placed her right index finger in the center of his chest. "You!"

Her voice was not friendly. Pete held himself still. Her finger slowly ran down over his ice-tea-wet stomach until it reached his belt. Her eyes darkened as she grasped his belt buckle and slowly pulled him toward her. She was looking directly into his eyes. "I know this uniform means more to you than anything else."

He was caught up in her eyes. Suddenly, he felt a gush of cold water and ice down his pants. She was smiling brightly up at him. "Maybe this will help dilute the stain." She held up an empty pitcher, released his belt and gently patted his waistband back into place. He could feel the rivulets of water running down his legs into his shoes. She turned away and sat down at the table, her back straight.

He may have spent too much time in the military, but he did know when covering fire was necessary.

...

"Kerstin, this is Pete O'Brien. How are the two of you?"

At her response, Pete grimaced. He had known this phone call was not going to be easy. "Yes. I may have been a little delinquent after the wedding. But it was a lovely..."

There was a rush of words in his ear. Why had Swede married such a badass woman? "That long? You know I do think of you both frequently."

Oh, damn. That was a low blow. She was really bringing out the heavy artillery. He paused to make his voice as sincere as possible, "How old is she?"

Again, that flow of words as if a dam had broken upstream.

"How time flies." He gave up. He couldn't do this. Maybe Swede could, but Pete knew he was only going to make another 15 seconds – "Kerstin!"

"Great idea. Please put him on speakerphone."

"Swede, you bastard! Quit laughing. Leaving me out to dry is not nice."

"OK, OK! Maybe I do need something from you guys, but next time I will be buying dinner and changing your daughter's diaper. Trust me."

CHAPTER ELEVEN

The valet brought Pete's car to the front of the hotel. The doorman opened the passenger door and steadied her arm as Anastasia swung her hips into the convertible's low seat.

It was a beautiful day and he took a minute to lower the top before driving off. She had agreed to come, but he had no idea how she would play it. She appeared practically bubbling. "This will be grand fun! Alex, Winsor and I had been scheduled to fly back to Washington this evening, but something important came up. They ran off without me, so I had a free afternoon."

She was wearing a thin white sweater with a ruffled collar, cinched around her waist with a narrow gold belt over a gray flared knit skirt.

A wide-brimmed black-belted straw hat, tied by a black bow under her chin, protected her from the late-afternoon sun. It also, frustratingly, hid her face from Pete.

Pete concentrated on pulling away from the hotel without hitting the many texting or cell-phone-talking pedestrians. He had forgotten how much he missed hearing the soft, low register of her voice.

She was laughing. "...very mysterious. And you ran off without even one word at the lunch – so impolite!" He risked a sideways glance. Were they recalling different events?

"After Winsor called, I thought I was doomed to spend this beautiful afternoon in my room with a book. How nice of you, Peter, to ask me if I'd like to see your Napa Valley." Maybe she was talking so much because she was also nervous?

He finally located the street he was searching for and accelerated into the traffic flow. He relaxed as he glimpsed the tower tops of the Golden Gate. "Asya, we haven't seen each other since Kure. What happened after you left the submarine?"

She inclined her seat back a bit, settled her shoulders into the leather and eased off her white pumps. The crown of her hat barely reached the top of the headrest. She folded her hands together in her lap and began a story he suspected she had related before: "Your CIA took me to a place in Virginia and questioned me for three or four months. Then they gave me a new name and the witness-protection program trained me for another 30 days." This last statement was accompanied by an involuntary and unladylike snort.

The huge hat rolled toward him and her voice and eyes teased: "How do you like the name Anastasia Conner, Peter?"

Pete knew she had no way to know he had spent a year searching the internet and every phone book he could find for that precise name. The hat shielded her face as she turned toward the eclectic mismatch of 1890-vintage row houses that ran along the highway. "Of course, I don't think you ever knew my real one," she said. They were now passing large, graceful trees. Pete's military eye noted the former Army Presidio parade grounds were not being regularly watered and had yet to be greened by the winter rains. Anastasia appeared absorbed in the picturesque adobe buildings on the grounds of the old fort.

"Oh, Peter, what a beautiful bridge! This must be your famous Golden Gate."

Their car merged with streams of traffic from the other tollbooths and started up the incline to the suspension bridge before Asya continued her story. "The CIA moved me to Indiana, gave me a birth certificate, a social-security number and pictures in little silver frames of two non-existent parents. They found a job for me as a secretary in a company that distributed heating oil."

"You've been in Indiana working as a secretary for more than a year?"

"No, Peter." He heard the frown in her voice. "That is what they intended for me to do. You forget. I already knew someone in your Central Intelligence Agency betrayed me. In Indianapolis, a pair of assassins tried to kill me on my way home from work the very first day. A third thug was waiting at my apartment. I killed the first two, outran the third and sneaked onto a train to Chicago!"

The wheel jerked under Pete's hands and he caught it before they sideswiped the curb. It was lucky they were finally away from the hundreds of men, woman and children who had been walking, jogging or biking across the Golden Gate Bridge this particular sunny afternoon. Jesus! How close he had been! How in the world had she thought he was...

Should he bring it up now? Why not? He engaged the cruise control so he could focus more on his passenger. "You know I was the man waiting for you in your lobby that day in Indianapolis. I'd waited all afternoon. And then I finally saw you and ran after you, but I fell in the snow. I've been trying to find you ever since."

He said it so low, he wasn't sure she had heard, especially with the top down. Maybe he should have waited until they had stopped and he could have focused completely on her. Had she flinched?

Asya bent the brim of her hat back with her left hand so Pete could see her eyes. She was smiling at him mischievously, continuing as if he had never spoken, 'Peter, I bet you did not think I could get a job in Chicago. You're wondering what I could have done to make so much money so quickly.' Suddenly, her eyes were no longer laughing, but distant with remembering, then vacant with thought and suddenly clouded with tears. Her hand abruptly pulled the brim down hard. Had she just registered what he had said?

Nonplussed, he looked back at the road and realized he was only a couple of car lengths back of a slower-moving car. He jammed on the brakes, checked his mirrors and abruptly swung left to pass.

Had she really thought he was an assassin?

He turned on the radio to fill the silence and found the XM oldie station. The sensuous voice of Nat King Cole filled the car. It was one of his favorites. As her silence extended, Pete let the soft fabric of *A Nightingale Sang in Berkeley Square* wrap around him. The past was the reason people drove convertibles – to let the breeze sweep mistakes away. He was signaling a lane change after passing a tandem trailer truck when Anastasia quietly continued her story. "I was valuable at the Mercantile Exchange because of my knowledge of Middle Europe. I developed some unique trading algorithms that proved very successful." Pete turned the radio down. Her voice was not as strong as it had been before.

"But it wasn't the most satisfying work. So, after the business had two good quarters in a row, I took my bonus, sold my algorithm to my boss and relocated to Washington, DC. Two months ago, I found a job as a Russian analyst in one of your 'think tanks.' At the same time, my Chicago boss has kept me on part-time as a – how do you call it? – consultant."

She continued after Pete's quick nod. "In Washington, I specialize in the new republics. The think tank was pleased to find someone who could speak the languages and knows the history between the two areas. We do some contract work for the State Department as well as the Pentagon.

"When not officially working, I help the Republic's embassy improve their trade and relations with America. Since it will never be safe for me to go home again, I help my people from Washington." As if she were tiring of her own story, Asya adjusted the seat controls on her side to elevate her leather seat, crossed her legs, and adjusted her long skirt, "The CIA gave me citizenship. I am now a normal American woman. In a few months, my name will even be published in the phone book. I even made a down payment on a little apartment in Georgetown with my consulting bonus."

What was she doing with Winsor? Simply advising? It had been a year. He mentally shrugged. At least she wasn't wearing a wedding ring. Pete was reluctant to ask, so, for the next five minutes, they drove in silence until they turned off the freeway north of Mare Island and started up the two-lane road to Napa Valley.

At that point, Pete decided he could wait no longer. "Asya, I have something for you." He withdrew a long thin white box from the inner pocket of his blazer. He had not had time to wrap it.

"A present, Peter? How nice." Pete watched her expectantly out of the corner of his eyes. She flirtatiously tipped the box lid aside. Suddenly, her entire body froze. She stared hard into the soft cotton that lined the box. A red flush rose from her neck until it covered her entire face.

After a few seconds, he anxiously asked, "Are you OK, Anastasia?"

She removed it from the box and held it in front of her, balancing the haft of the knife on the tips of her right hand's three longest fingers. She exhaled and the knife slowly rotated back and forth a few degrees. As it swiveled, sunlight caught on the inlayed gold and jewels in the bolster.

Pete knew that item well. For the past year, it had traveled everywhere with him, even with all the TSA requirements – in his briefcase during official Navy travel, in checked luggage on commercial flights. Keeping it close had seemed the right thing to do.

There was more traffic on Route 29 than he had remembered. He accelerated around a truck, found a half-mile of open road, and again looked over at his passenger. Her face was strained. She was whispering, apparently to herself. He leaned toward her to better hear "…know if I am OK, Peter?" Her voice gained strength, "Sit back, watch the road and let me tell you a story." Pete obediently pushed against the steering wheel and pushed his butt firmly back in his seat.

He sensed rather than saw Asya whirl and then felt her arm lash across his right thigh as she drove the knife deep into the leather between his legs, "I am *not OK!* You *bastard!*"

CHAPTER TWELVE

Pete looked down with astonishment at the knife and then over at her. He glanced up at the road ahead. His eyes widened and he literally stood on the brakes.

Asya didn't bother to check what was happening on the road. She was furious with Pete. If he crashed and killed them both, then it was karma. Her right hand was pounding on his bicep. "I waited for you!" She knew she was shouting. What did he expect her reaction to be? "Why do you think I returned to Washington? How hard did you try to find me? Your precious Navy! I waited more than a year!"

She pushed herself back in her seat. The scene in the Indianapolis apartment lobby had become so clear in her mind the moment he said it was he that had been there. She could never forgive herself for allowing the earlier events to affect her so!

Why had she not recognized those broad shoulders, the way his head dipped a bit to the left when he was leaning down to talk to someone? Why had she been so focused on escape? If it had not been snowing so hard, if she hadn't truly despised that pig boss, if she had not just killed those two and been so – alone – and yet he really had come for her. They had lost a year – two! Damn him to ад for slipping!

Asya swept the hat from her head, throwing it down in the floor. Her stomach had been hurting ever since he had told her, and she could feel tears coursing down her cheeks. She was having difficulty seeing, which made her even angrier. He had no idea how much they had missed. Her new start in America had been…had been…sullied! She wanted him to hurt, too. She flung the words at him like bullets: "I waited for my knife and my submarine captain! Your word as an officer – hah!"

He was braking again, this time pulling off the road. Before he could place the car in park, Asya grabbed his arm, leaned close and brought it hard between her breasts. She whispered as she drew his eyes into hers, "What do you really want to know, Peter? Do you want to know about Winsor? How about Alex and Adam? I date all three. Two nos and a yes, my Peter. Maybe one and a half and one and a half."

She enjoyed the look of pain that crossed his face. Good. He was the one who had slipped in the snow. He was bigger. He was faster. He was the damn SEAL. He should have been able to catch her easily. The past year was his fault. In fact, how in the world had he missed her at the ballpark last week? Hell, she had been on the scoreboard! He had only sung, and his little ditty had given her a headache that lasted all weekend! "Winsor and I live in separate houses in Georgetown. I don't think he truly loves me, but yes, Peter, I fuck him."

Anastasia put her hand on Pete's chest, and shoved him back in his seat. She then reached between his legs and retrieved the knife from the foam, sliding it back into its leather sheath. She would never, ever tell him, that even in her angriest moment, she had rotated the blade midstrike to turn the razor-sharp edge away from his groin. God, he gave off manly smells. He was lucky she did not bury her nose in his chest!

She leaned away from him, her back flush against the cool door, her shoulders still trembling with suppressed anger, looking at the sheath and knife in her hands. A truck went by, then another, and the convertible rocked for a few seconds in each of their wakes. "And now you return my knife. First Vasilii, then the CIA, and now you. Two deliberate betrayals and one case of indifference." She let her voice descend to a conversational level.

Pete wisely chose to remain silent, simply sitting with his hands on the wheel, staring into the bright sunshine. She wondered what he was thinking. Ignoring him, she raised her skirt and buckled the returned sheath onto her left thigh, casting the leather she thus replaced over her shoulder and into the back seat. The old harness felt supple. Like familiar old boots against her skin. The bastard had even kept it oiled! She slowly slid the knife back into its rightful place.

Pete chose that very moment to pull back into traffic, and she could not resist goading him once again, "Drive on. Show me your Napa Valley. Share with me how you were so smart to lure my friends away. Drive on. Talk or be silent. But do not *ever* ask me again if I am OK."

CHAPTER THIRTEEN

After their little roadside tête-à-tête, Asya had chosen not to speak again and Pete couldn't think of a damned thing to say. Their journey had covered 20 miles since the incident Pete had mentally labeled as 'the dagger event.' Which meant Pete had now walked through two famous wineries, and followed the requisite number of charming guides elaborating on hot days, cool nights, California oak barrels and constant-temperature granite storage caves.

During the second tour, Pete had reached for her hand, but Asya petulantly pulled away. Although they continued to walk side by side, several inches of cool California air had separated them. At the sampling tables, she tasted the whites and Pete silently watched her sip and chat up the vintners. Back in the car, the winding miles between the vineyards were spent in silence, the acres of individually tied, hand-pruned, irrigated and carefully nurtured grapevines uncommented on.

Luxurious English ivy marked the third place they stopped. Long, shiny strands matted each wall of the original family home as well as the tasting and sales building. The ivy luxuriously ran over the stone archways, clung to walls along the edges of the fields and climbed the working sheds. Strands had even begun to cover the cottages that sat on the highest ridge of the property. A truly restful place, Pete thought, as he stepped out of the car onto the crushed white granite. Every time he visited Napa, he felt as if his soul had been refreshed. Though, of course, he'd had better days.

By the time he had reached the passenger's side, Asya had already joined the group queuing at the showroom door. Pete shook his head. No matter how she acted, she now knew he had been trying to find her. Christ, what was he supposed to have done, pick Chicago out using a tarot deck? Think of shadowing Winsor? She, of all people, should know mistakes were made and life had to move on. He called to her back, "I'll be in the car. Join me when you're done."

She didn't indicate she had even heard.

Forty-five minutes later, Asya returned, slightly swinging two cardboard boxes. The labels indicated each contained two bottles of the winery's premium cabernet sauvignon, which she carefully laid on the floor of the back seat. "For Alex and Winsor," she unnecessarily explained, before permitting Pete to assist her into her seat. She put on her hat and carefully tied the black bow under her chin to hold it in place. He backed the car without comment and turned toward the main road. Before reaching the asphalt of Route 29, he spun the wheel to the right and the convertible made its way through the crushed granite up the hill to the bungalows as Pete watched his companion's profile out of the corner of his eye. No flinch yet.

Pete backed into the parking place in front of the last cottage. He stopped the car and swung his door open, stretching for a moment before walking around to Asya's side, removing a single bottle of premium wine as well as a corkscrew and two crystal balloon goblets from the trunk on his way, the glasses and wine fitted between the fingers on his left hand. When he arrived at her door, he slipped a room key from his coat pocket. He dangled it in front of the windshield, saying only, "For me." All he could see of her was the brim of her hat and two small hands folded together in her lap.

The air in Napa Valley was very still for a long minute. Even the bees near the car stopped flying. Was she sensing the beauty he saw in this picturesque valley? He heard a breath of wind, perhaps the forerunner of an evening shower, softly stir the ivy leaves on the cottage behind them. Did she feel even a fraction...?

Her shoulders rose once and then dropped. They lifted again. Her long pale fingers reached up and slowly undid the bow on her hat before she laid it carefully in Pete's seat. She flipped down the visor and looked in the small mirror on the back, running each index finger across her eyebrows. She shook her long black hair once, arching her neck back to look at the way it fell around her ruffled collar before flipping the visor back up. Only then did she quietly ask, "Are you going to open the door, dear Peter?"

Inside the cottage, after he had opened the wine and poured two glasses, Pete stood looking through the window sheers. The green of the valley was soothing, as was the dry heat being pumped by the afternoon sun. He could see moisture rising from the grape leaves. When he heard the bathroom door click open, he turned and extended the wine. He hoped she didn't notice that his hand was slightly quivering. She was completely nude – as pale as bond paper. The shadow from the windowsill deepened the natural darkness between her thighs.

She shook her head at the offered goblet. "I have had enough wine. We only have this afternoon. I wish to remember." She closed the distance between them and rose on her tiptoes. Her fingertips pressed softly against his cheekbones as she tilted his head down so that her tongue could tease his lower lip.

Pete put the goblet on the windowsill, bent his knees and abruptly picked her up. She continued to focus on his mouth and perversely pushed her breasts against his chest. Pete shuddered from the warmth of her flesh. Before he fell down, he needed to find something to lie upon.

He knew the room shadows were different, but couldn't recall how it had been earlier. They were lying on their backs, touching from shoulders to heels, her hand in his, fingers loosely linked on his chest, their breathing slowing together, when she asked, "And just what did you do to lure Alex and Winsor away today?"

The last thing he wanted to do was talk about other men. He wanted to spend the time locking away every second of this afternoon in his memory – her teasing, their laughing...

A finger poked in his side. "Peter, tell me!"

Pete stared up at the ceiling. The sun was much lower than when they had entered the room. The soft, mottled shadows on the wall gently moved as the sheers shifted in the late-afternoon wind. He was going to have to remember to put the top up on the convertible before they went back. "I had a Russian friend call and tell him there were nuclear weapons in Kazakhstan for sale – and that there was an offer already on the table from some Chechens."

Asya abruptly removed her hand from his, rising up on her right elbow and partially turning to face him. As she did, her black hair framed her high cheekbones and fell partially across her full breasts, obscuring the heart-shaped birthmark he had first seen when he had ordered her to strip in his *Grayfish* stateroom. "Kazakhstan?"

"Yeah," he distractedly replied. "I don't think one in a million people even know where that country is, but they were talking about it yesterday in the lecture." He leaned over and kissed her left nipple before continuing. "So, I figured the whole thing sounded crazy enough that two State Department guys would be very interested."

Asya put her free hand under his chin, raising his gaze from her breasts up to her eyes. She shook her head slowly. "You fool, dear Peter. I am not Russian. I was born and grew up in Kazakhstan. And both Winsor and Alex know the Kazakhs very well."

She closed her eyes and her lips tightened in a thin, wry smile for a few seconds before her eyes opened. "Peter, whatever will I do with you?" She looked at his body sprawled out on the bed for a few seconds and Pete felt a tingle. She shook her head side to side, and slowly ran her left hand through her hair, before placing it on his left hip, her fingers splayed out, her fingerprints burning into his skin. "You get aroused whenever we speak about Winsor or Alex. Was your plan today to screw them or me?"

Pete sat up and leaned over her, grasping her arms just above her elbows. She had a surprising muscular development for a woman, but his hands still wrapped more than completely around her biceps. He watched her eyes blaze with defiance and then soften as she obviously dialed back her impulse to physically resist. Of course, that inclination activated an avalanche of his own Neanderthal genes. Very deliberately,

Pete straightened his arms as he slowly rolled back flat on his back, spreading his legs and digging his heels into the side of the mattress to lock his body to the bed.

Effortlessly, using the brute strength built from years of working with steel bars and cast-iron weights, he swung Asya up into the air. As her body left the bed, he saw her abdomen muscles ripple. He held her at arm's length over him. Her lower lip curled. She was holding her torso and legs straight out, apparently effortlessly, her eyes coolly fixed on his. He marveled for a few seconds and let himself enjoy her body – she truly must have been some athlete – before he focused on the moment and began slowly lowering his arms while losing himself in the exquisite lines of her high cheeks and dimpled chin.

Within seconds, his upper arms rested flat against the bed and, while he could feel the heat of her body over his, she still trembled a few centimeters distant. Their nipples were the only part of their bodies that were touching. He raised his head and waited. After a few seconds, she lowered her chin. Slowly, deliberately, Pete teased her lips with his tongue and began wetting her full bottom lip.

By the time he had reached the far corner of her mouth, Asya's eyes had closed. He lowered her to fit about him as he whispered in her hair, "I have wanted you from the moment I first met you in my room."

The temperature dropped sharply as soon as they left the Valley. As the car started down the grade to Sausalito, Asya removed her hat, pulled a scarf from her purse and fastened the silk around her face and hair. On the incline up to the Golden Gate, she finally spoke: "I won't see you in Washington, Peter." He was shocked out of his memories of the afternoon. "What?"

A soft hand caressed Pete's right arm, "No, dear Peter. You waited too long to return my knife. You still have your career with your Navy. I have established new relationships and built new ties. I must do my work for Kazakhstan."

"Asya, I must…we have…"

She removed her hand and returned it to her lap, settled her shoulders back into the leather seat and stared down the road. Her voice was low, but clear and controlled, "Peter, we must breathe, nothing more – the rest is by choice. We both made choices. Now we have loved." She paused a second and then her voice was firm: "Do *not* call me in Washington."

Neither of them said anything more until Pete pulled up in front of their hotel. Then Asya extended her right hand as if to grasp his shoulder, saying quietly, "And Peter" – Pete leaned toward her for a kiss, but her strong arm kept his face six inches from her own, unhurriedly blinked her long black eyelashes like a Monarch butterfly – "don't forget to pay Avis for the seat you made me ruin."

Taking Alex's and Winsor's wine cartons from the back seat, she accepted the assistance offered by the Fairmont doorman and lightly stepped from the car.

CHAPTER FOURTEEN

Official Washington was not built on a capricious design. The edifices, which house the President, the Secretary of the Treasury and the Secretary of Defense, not only stand side by side but also are surreptitiously connected. The East Wing of the White House is joined to the Treasury Building by a secret underground passage (built when South Carolina might be tardy with her taxes and it could be necessary to check on the available silver coins and gold bars available to meet national obligations some late night). On the opposite side of the White House, there was an awning over the passage to the building where the President met with his Generals and Admirals as well as his Secretary of State. Of course, since this was the War building, there was in addition a very secret tunnel for candid discussions.

This arrangement (armies at the Commander in Chief's right hand and his money man on his left) was the perfect set up to fulfill the needs of a young nation. However, during World War II, the complicated logistics of the fighting caused the War Department to seek a more expansive site for all the specialists needed. The President and his Secretary of War were in a hurry. In fact, the same man placed in charge of constructing the new building for Defense would later be entrusted with overseeing the top-secret development of the atomic bomb. General (then Colonel) Groves was a man who got allegro results.

The new airport had just been built across the Potomac River on reclaimed marsh. There was a pentagon-shaped piece left unused. Politics pushed the new building into that space and Groves poured cement night and day. While this has always been seen as a marvel of achieve-ment, in fact Colonel Groves inadvertently empowered the Secretary of State. While the Secretary of Defense retained the tremendous political power inherent in spending a disproportionate chunk of the country's greenbacks, he was now and forever after isolated on the "Virginia side of the river."

The countries twenty-nine other smaller agencies still claimed the DC side of the Potomac, and with proximity to the President brings power. At the moment, two of the younger State Assistant Secretaries were demonstrating one of these power perks by taking an hour from their desks to walk to Casey's for a coffee and Danish. They both had time on their hands. Their early ninth-floor Monday meetings were over. With all the schedule disruptions other people were experiencing from the forecasted overnight snowfall, neither Winsor nor Alex had any other meetings until noon.

Winsor easily dodged a spray of snow and water from a passing solitary taxi, "Have you spoken to Asya lately?"

"Taking her to the Kennedy Center tonight." Alex had no intention of volunteering anything more. Although Winsor had originally intro-duced Anastasia to Alex and infrequently the three of them attended events together, Alex well knew he was competing with Winsor for Asya's attention. He had wished more than once that he had met Ana-stasia first. He was hoping his move to the White House…

"…a bit distracted on the telephone yesterday."

"I haven't talked to her in a couple of days." Internally Alex gri-maced. He had been busy getting his new task force together and turning duties over to Winsor. He was reporting to the White House, actually the Executive Office Building, in only a few more days. He would telephone Asya at her Think Tank as soon as he could get away from Winsor. Maybe she would like to go to the Norwegian Embassy event next Saturday.

"She and I are attending the dinner the Norwegian Ambassador is having before the cattle call Saturday evening. Want me to get you an invitation? That new Schedule C down in the Latin America section was certainly casting come hither looks your way all morning."

Crap! "No. I appreciate your interest in setting me up, but I need to be in New York this weekend. The President asked me to assist our representative in crafting a position on the Chechnya's."

Winsor chuckled, "I think you should rethink moving over to the White House. You would make a great Welcome Lady here at State. Maybe you could get one of those little library carts and wheel it around to each new employee's desk. Stock it with maps of the area, Girl Scout cookies, 40%- off coupons for local events, the newest in trashy novels and prophylactics printed with your cell number. Size extra small, of course, so you don't run afoul of the Districts truth in advertising laws. I understand they are quite harsh!"

Winsor sipped his coffee and eyed the barista, "I could give you a box of mine for comparison. Don't want the foreign nationals we have in the Department to think poorly of all of us Americans. I have the State Department Mission printed on mine. All four paragraphs. You could use them side by side for show and tell…"

Alex raised his cup threateningly, "Where do you want to wear this coffee? On your vest or in your crouch?"

Winsor pushed his chair away, stood and tossed his empty cup and Danish wrapper into the trash receptacle, "Enough fun. If you walk me back so I can get in my safe, I'll share the paper I recently wrote on Chechnya and what I saw as our options there. You might find it helpful in your new role."

Alex followed Winsor out of Casey's and back up the hill.

He picked up and waited for a dial tone. There are certainly lots of classified items in government that have no reason to be classified, but the fact that it is possible to covertly call anywhere in the world from a State Department Office on 'C' Street isn't even considered classified. Too bad.

Here we go. The country code was burned into his cortex. The city code was the first four digits written in his scheduler in the comments section on the day on which he had first met Asya. She would be horrified if she knew. The actual telephone number was the last five digits of a series that ostensibly connected to a McLean flower shop.

His left-hand ring, middle and index fingers started the Buddy Rich riff from *West Side Story* as he waited for the connection to be made. The NSA tracked calls from practically all other telephones in the world, including 10-second messages delivered via throwaway 'burners' from the backstreets of Bangladesh. He chuckled to himself, the fingers of his left hand segueing to gently keyboard the music he had fallen asleep to last night. The only numbers in the world free from surveillance were the couple of thousand in this building, as well as a few Navaho smoke signals out in New Mexico. Of course, those nosy pricks in Maryland might inadvertently pick up a conversation on a twisted satellite-relay bounce. Even if they did manage to subsequently trace it back to a blocked number, they would discover this particular call originated from the desk of one of the schedule Cs – which would be an unfortunate loss for both of us, because she is seriously good-looking, interested in her career here in Washington and there is at least one entry in her personnel record that has real blackmail possibilities. It is amazing how many doctors inadvertently hook patients on Percocet. Her mother is also an attractive woman. He looked up to check his door was still tightly shut.

His fingers had returned to drumming. God, he hated satellite delays. It was even worse when the call was encrypted… A series of three beeps told him the connection had finally gone though. He forced his mind to clear. It was a trick he had practiced since childhood. He imagined himself floating above and slightly behind himself, looking down – calm, at peace with the world, in control, with no cares… there… He cast his voice lower and let the guttural stops roll slowly out of his throat, "Abdulbek, you may want to send someone else to lead next week's activities. It's a trap. The UN has Special Forces prepared to come down all over your ass."

Despite his calm, the reaction over the wire caused him to press down on his desk so hard he feared the white whorl of his fingerprints would set in the varnish. He struggled to keep his voice from rising.

"That's not our agreement. I tell you some things and you send money. I don't tell you how I know. You don't question how much." He forced his voice further down the register. "Abdulbek, you know my account's address. Hit send to Switzerland or this is your last call." He hung up and stared down at his still trembling hand. He pressed down on the table even harder until the trembling finally stopped. His thumb and entire wrist ached. He dry-swallowed two of the four pills he kept stowed in the small silver box in his watch pocket and then roughly shoved his left hand in his trouser pocket. He held it there for 10 minutes until the pain eased and his fingers slowly unclenched.

The snow was spinning down harder. An early departure today would be in order.

CHAPTER FIFTEEN

Asya shrugged her coat off her shoulders, catching it on her left arm to free her right hand to unlock her front door. As she turned the key, Alex's fingertips ran down the exposed skin on her nearly backless dress, stopping at the tab of her zipper, which he flipped once up, then down. She held herself motionless until his fingers stopped. She then answered his unspoken question: "Alex, I enjoyed the play as well as the dinner, but I've developed a migraine. I need dark and quiet."

"I like the dark." His tone was playful as his index finger again unlatched the nylon tab.

Asya turned and ran the fingers of her right hand along his hard jaw before softly kissing him lightly on the cleft of his chin. "Not tonight, Alex." She let her hand drift further down until the heel of her palm firmly pushed against his chest. "Not tonight," she repeated and turned away, pushing the door firmly closed and immediately throwing the deadbolt. She knew his feelings were hurt, but she needed to deal with her own problems.

She stood with her back against the door while her eyes adjusted to the dim light. When she had left, she had turned off everything except for the recessed light that shone down onto the black granite counter in her kitchen alcove. From where she now stood, the reflection of that one beam was neatly centered in her living-room window. The very window that looked down over Georgetown, out over the Potomac River, across the Key Bridge and into the dark woods of Virginia where Peter lived. Asya took a deep breath, kicked off her shoes, closed her eyes and let her mind float, following the light, until it reflected against the window and, like a moth, followed the beam back down to the counter where she drank her morning coffee. Down onto the engraved crystal bowl given her by her teammates at Dunajinski, Inc – OK, probably completely picked out and paid for by Adam, who still sang under his breath, and yes, it was a habit that did turn out to be very annoying over the course of a full evening – but the bowl remained the most aesthetic thing she owned, so she always liked to think it had been a gift from the team. What a complicated life!

A furry tail brushed against her right ankle, ran across her toes and curled around one ankle. Someone was tired of being alone and wanted to be picked up.

The bowl on the counter was beautiful. A true work of art. It currently held a bouquet of lilies – the national flower of Kazakhstan. She would have to remember to add a quarter-cup of cold water to the bowl before she went to bed. The apartment was terribly dry during winter.

A new spray of lilies, always bound with an ivy sprig, had appeared on her doorstep every Thursday since the week after she returned from San Francisco. There was no note. Only droplets of water still fresh on the leaves. Keeping her back firm against her front door, Asya slowly slid down until she sat flat on the wood floor and the impatient Siamese could climb over her knees and claim a spot on her chest. Pitti-Sing began purring into her neck. Two paws, claws carefully retracted, kneaded at her dress.

Life had once been simple. She had only worried about making the Olympic team and possibly facing a firing squad. Now, three men were interested in her and another desired more than she wanted to give. The reflected light in the window flickered. She placed an irritated cat on the floor, rose and hung up her coat. A cup of tea before bed would be good. She filled the kettle with fresh water and turned on the gas burner. Striking a long wooden match, she first lit a cone of white sage that sat ready in a white porcelain dish. Then she lit the gas burner, before blowing out the match and absent-mindedly stared out the window while the water heated. From where she stood, she could watch the tourist riverboats churning up the river. Their navigation and deck lights wavered on the ripples created by the strong current. All the boats were currently headed upstream to dock in Georgetown and discharge their evening's charges. The first boat was mooring. The captain and crew were assisting passengers at the forward prow. People were disembarking in pairs. All couples, several with children. She knew from experience there would have been more children in the earlier boats.

The gentle hiss of the kettle brought the memory of the surf and pulled Anastasia back to the white beach near their home. She was again a child. There had been a storm the night before and the high waters were insistently tugging at the sand. She and her mother were walking barefoot, avoiding the small clumps of drying seaweed and occasional nests of tangled driftwood. They had come upon a beautiful starfish. Anastasia had run toward it. As she did, one of its arms moved. Anastasia had cried, "Mother, it's still alive!"

Her mother had tucked her skirt high in her belt, carefully worked her long fingers into the moist sand beneath the starfish, and walked out into the surf. When the waves swept over her thighs she had lowered her clasped hands into the water until the sand and the starfish dissolved back into the sea. Anastasia could still remember standing on the beach sobbing while her mother left her. Her mother had hurried back, gathered the child to her breast, and soothed her, slowly stroking her already long black hair. She said, "Sometimes, a person needs to be brave, Anastasia…"

The light bulb in her kitchen alcove softly popped and died, leaving a wisp of smoke and a graying filament. Now the only light in her apartment was the glow from the Georgetown street lights below. The kettle whistle had become insistent. Just like Peter. He had begun by calling once a week. She had ignored him and it had escalated. The past two Mondays when she arrived for work, there had been a steaming *venti latte* in the middle of her blotter. No one in the office admitted to knowing who had left it. They were not an observant lot. None of them would have lasted a week in Russia.

This past Monday she had arrived an hour earlier at her K-Street think tank. The coffee was already there, but she could have sworn she saw him duck into one of the elevators. On Wednesday, she had received an anonymous ticket to *Giselle* (third row!) for the following evening. Pete had slipped into the aisle seat beside her just before the curtain went up. His fingers had stroked the back of her hand throughout the first act. As soon as the intermission curtain came down, he rose and moved swiftly up the aisle. She had remained in her seat and prepared a scathing speech for when he returned. But his seat remained empty for Act Two. He made her want to tear her hair out! Of course, she knew the *Giselle* lovers met in a winery. And she was certainly aware it was one of the most romantic Russian ballets of all time. What did she think she was – a Kazakh peasant?

He was somehow slipping behind her shield. Even worse, she was unsure she was resisting as hard as she should. She had 'star 69ed' his number the last time he had called – her traitorous right index finger had almost called him back. She had even Googled that nightingale song he liked so much. Nice lyrics, but never had there been any nightingales in Berkeley Square! Only a country of twitchers would dream up such a song. People had been going off to war. Instead of focusing on survival, someone had instead written about two lovers meeting. It was daft. Like Alice falling down a rabbit hole or what's-her-name being carried off by a tornado. Asya poured hot water over her kava tea and cupped her fingers around the steaming cup. It proved some people are a bit off. The Brits are crazy about birds and Peter is simply loony.

The heat felt nice. The tea and the sage provided a pleasant smell in the alcove. She could feel both scents curling into her sinuses. Pitti-Sing leaped to the counter and pushed against her shoulder.

She hadn't even realized she had a headache. Like Peter's pain when they had been aboard *Grayfish*, the ache was low, nearly in the back of her neck, rather than her head. She leaned forward to massage the pain, the ends of her hair nearly falling into her tea. This was clearly tension-related. She needed to find a way to relax more. She sat back on one of the tall stools and pulled the cat into her lap. Possibly she should take up yoga. The company had a Sanskrit weekend coming up in a month. Or maybe she just should wait outside the Pentagon some morning, beckon Peter over and thump him between the eyes with the haft of her knife.

Snow was being forecast for tomorrow. When Alex walked her back after dinner, the first winter flakes had already begun easing their way earthward. Peter was a tall, lanky man. It would be awkward to catch him as he fell. He was also heavy. He well knew she was much smaller than him. How could he possibly resent it if she stepped aside and permitted him to land face down in the soft snow – on the Pentagon steps – for all to see? Perhaps, as his body slipped by her on the way down, she might pluck that white hat of his out of the air, the one with all that lovely gold visor braid, and give it a short spin on her finger? Her upper lip bent up at both corners as she pictured the scene. If he truly cared for her, he shouldn't mind.

She sipped her tea as she reflectively scratched behind the cat's ears. Pitti-Sing stood on her lap, balancing and arching her back against her fingers. Asya's smile broadened as the tea warmed her stomach. She could feel the tentacles of her headache begin to loosen. Maybe she wouldn't need to learn yoga or waste time on a Sanskrit weekend after all.

CHAPTER SIXTEEN

Across the Potomac from Asya's dark window, Pete rolled over, swiping blindly at an unwanted noise. His fumbling hand finally located his cell phone. Eyes still closed, he relaxed back into his warm bed, "O'Brien."

"Boss, its Swede."

Pete had been expecting to hear the voice of the Pentagon Duty Officer with yet another report on the unfolding Middle East drama. He sat up and switched on his nightstand lamp – "Swede? What time is it?" The arc of the light caught a relatively bare room. There were no curtains or pictures to break the monotony of the walls. Instead, a series of maps was taped everywhere, and pamphlets, monographs and books on tactics were stacked on the floor up to the height of the window.

"11pm here in San Francisco." The map nearest the bed, the only one readable in the weak light he had turned on, showed Israel's elongated borders. It was highlighted by the yellow pins he had inserted to mark new housing construction projects.

Correctly anticipating Pete's likely response, Swede quickly added, "Boss, I'm not drunk. Don't hang up, we need your help."

Pete leaned down and closed the box of colored pins at his feet, "OK. What's up?"

"You remember Yuri, my neighbor down the street? The one who helped us run that scam on the guys from State?"

"Of course."

"Well, Yuri's currently back there in DC. He sometimes consults for the Defense Threat Reduction Agency, and he ran into a guy who convinced him some Kazakhs are shopping nuclear weapons on the world market."

Bad news, but there was always more evil than good walking around the world. Swede certainly knew that. Pete swung back into bed, plumped his pillow and doubled it under his head while Swede continued.

"He couldn't find anyone at DTRA to pay attention and he couldn't even get past the gate guards at the CIA. Then he thought you might be willing to trade something for that favor he did."

Pete had considered clicking off the light. Instead, he plugged in a set of earphones so he could speak on the phone without using his hands, swung his feet back to the cold floor, and went to the dartboard hung on the back of the closet door. Ever since he had come back from San Francisco, the board backing had been a city map of Astana, the capital of Kazakhstan, the coldest capital of any country in the world. He was not waiting for that fact to come up during a bar bet. He pulled out his steel-tipped darts and stepped back to the worn black line taped on the hardwood floor. "Doesn't this story sound at all familiar to you, Swede?"

The first dart settled securely between the tiny concentric metal circles – triple 20. You can never keep a good darts player down. Even on two hours sleep. He had a meeting in four hours in his office to evaluate an analysis on the Middle East his staff had prepared for the Chairman of the Joint Staff. He had worked with his team all weekend on this project, not leaving the Pentagon yesterday until after 10pm, but he owed Swede at least a hearing, which was why he was on his feet instead of lying in his warm bed. His second dart bounced off a wire and buried itself at an angle in Lake Balkhash. Not good. At this rate, he was going to lose more than his money in that lake. "Didn't we run this same game ourselves just last month?"

"Yuri thinks this is real. His wife is Kirsten's best friend at the hospital..."

The reason for the call suddenly became clear. Some men had no good sense where women were concerned. Swede had always been one of those. A good man for the first five years Pete had known him – a fighter, a risk-taker, a man who understood what had to be done – and then he had become completely irrational as soon as he met Kirsten. He had even left the Service.

However, he literally owed Swede his life, so Pete also owed Kirsten. Which meant – he ran his hand over the inch-long stubble on his head. He had been letting it grow out in favor of a more sophisticated 'Washington look', but he still needed to shave his face every morning, "All right, I'll chase this rabbit for you. Where and when does Yuri want to meet?" Last dart – on the way – good! No – single 20. I am going to get my butt kicked next Friday night at Army-Navy.

"They say they have to see you before morning. Can you get into Georgetown within the hour?"

"Right across the bridge."

Thirty minutes later, Pete made a U-turn in the light snow that was beginning to fall. He parked at a deserted curb, turned on the overhead light and looked again at the address he had carefully written on his hand. Something was wrong. The address matched a darkened photo-and-copy shop. He tried Swede's cell phone, but the call went immediately to voicemail.

He stepped out of the car, looking up and down the street, alert for any signs of activity as he buttoned his Navy overcoat. He had decided to take the extra 10 minutes to get into uniform. He suspected he was not going to get the chance to change his clothes before it was time to be at work. And, if Swede's report were real – it probably wouldn't hurt to look official.

At the moment, there was no traffic and no people on this thoroughfare that would be clogged in three or four hours with traffic into the District. It was so late, even the Georgetown students were asleep. Anastasia had an apartment somewhere near here – he knew because he had given the flower shop her address. Probably one of the new ones that overlooked the river. Three or four inches of snow was being forecast for the next 24 hours, which, if true, given the haphazard way DC approached clearing the roads, would make for sketchy driving tomorrow. The snowfall rate appeared to be picking up and the wind dying down. Big flakes were now swirling around each streetlamp like a swarm of Philippine moths.

It's too quiet, Pete thought. There is way too much psychic energy on this block for half past two in the morning. Just then the copy shop's door swung partially open and a pale hand motioned him in. OK, here goes nothing. Pete crossed the street, looking carefully at the figure in the entrance. His early-morning doorman was obviously Chinese, wearing a cotton ch'ang-fu, the traditional pre-Revolution Chinese kimono-sleeved robe. The gown hung nearly to the floor, slit in front and back to permit walking – and fighting – without falling flat on your face.

"Follow me." His English was surprisingly unaccented.

The guide stepped inside, lifting up a hinged section of the counter and slipping under it, patiently holding it up until Pete followed. The man parted two black curtains behind the counter and stepped through. Pete lowered the bar flap, tucked his cap under his left arm and followed into the dark. As he pushed the curtains aside, two hands in his back shoved him violently forward and the space suddenly flooded with light. He caught his balance and swung around only to painfully crack his right fist against the metal door that had silently slid shut behind him.

"Please stand still, sir, while the machine checks for weapons."

Pete rubbed his reddening knuckles. He was standing in a cage about four feet wide and eight feet long. The walls were at least 14 feet high. A speaker grill attached to the top was the apparent source of the instructions. Two unsmiling men dressed in Western clothes stood on a gridded metal platform that formed the top. Each was holding what looked like a 16-gauge shotgun.

After a few seconds, the wall in front of Pete clicked ajar. The voice from the grill politely instructed, "Please proceed, sir. Take the elevator to the second floor."

Pete didn't hesitate. In for a dime and all that.

When the elevator door opened, he was in another brightly lit wide passage. In contrast to the entrance, rich silk tapestries hung every five to ten yards. Along the hallway, large blue-and-white porcelain jars gleamed atop polished mahogany pedestals. A thick rug, predominantly blue, but bordered with bright gold, covered the floor from wall to wall. In the very center of it was sculpted a multicolored village of bent trees, laden oxen and big-headed peasants.

"By all means leave your shoes on. Our friends made these rugs to walk upon – they are very rugged – and already several hundred years old. As we proceed, the rug will tell a story."

The smiling speaker was coming down the hallway toward Pete, his hand outstretched. His creased face and wrinkled eyes told of a man in his early sixties, about 5ft 9in, 180 pounds, Pete would guess. He was neatly groomed, in a Western suit, hair graying around his temples, wearing thin gold-rimmed glasses. Definitely not Chinese features, more like Northern Russian, with high cheekbones and European skin coloring.

"My name is Rafi Parzarev, Captain. I am the President of Kazakhstan." His English was surely better than Pete's Russian. His left hand gestured back down the hallway. "Is this not an interesting place? Our Chinese friends secretly built this completely inside another building. They call it a 'safe house,' I believe.

"I cannot show you around, I'm afraid. They are not so happy

I even asked to bring you here tonight, but…" He shrugged dismissively. "If you walk with me, I will buy you breakfast for coming out into the snow this morning."

Pete followed President Parzarev down to the end of the hall, where the latter pushed open a set of French doors. Inside the room were two small tables and chairs. There were no windows, pictures or other furnishings. Several men in Western suits stood along one wall. They all looked uncomfortable. Yuri, Swede's friend, was one. Three of the others were men Pete judged to be non-diplomats, given their muscular necks and the bulges under their ill-fitting dark coats.

The President turned to the person sitting at one of the two tables – a slight man who appeared to be at least in his eighties or nineties. "Captain, let me introduce you to my best friend and the only Kazakh citizen who was ever a member of the old Soviet Politburo. Dimitre Kuntameyev, this is Captain O'Brien."

The old man nodded, but did not offer his hand. His eyes were milky from cataracts, his hair long, sparse and disheveled. A scraggly beard, white except where it was stained a nicotine-yellow near the corners of his mouth, clung irregularly to the bottom of his lower lip as well as the very tip of his chin.

"Please call me Pete, Mr President."

"Good. Pete. I am Rafi and my adviser is Dimitre. And this," he gestured toward the men standing against the wall, "I believe is your good friend Yuri from San Francisco." Pete wasn't positive how good a friend he was, but given how uncomfortable Yuri appeared, Rafi and Dimitre must be very powerful men. Pete extended his hand. Yuri gripped it hard and murmured, "Thank you."

Pete was trying to decide if he should read anything special into the expression in Yuri's eyes when Rafi impatiently tapped him on the shoulder, "Now we sit down and talk. I think we will have an early-early breakfast. How do you like your eggs?"

In the next half-hour, while two of the thick-necked men tried to set the table without their holstered guns giving someone a concussion, Rafi talked knowledgably about America and events in Moscow since the end of the Cold War, as well as the impact in Asia of the US decision to disengage from Iraq and Afghanistan. Dimitre said nothing. He sat smoking, holding each butt between his thumb and middle finger, the lit end toward his palm, drawing each cigarette down to less than one half-inch in length. When it reached that stage, he would peer intently at the cigarette as if he were surprised, bringing it into the least cloudy part of his vision, and then immediately select a new one from a long silver case and ignite it from the old butt, flicking the latter to smolder in a large cut-glass ashtray sitting in the middle of the table. The other men, including Yuri, stood or lounged against two of the walls. No one else smoked or moved to sit at the table.

Pete tried to pay attention to everything. He still had no idea what this evening – actually, morning – was about. Didn't look like anyone was intent on killing him. That part was good.

When platters of eggs, ham and rice were brought in and Dimitre was given a clean ashtray, which the latter immediately commenced to fill, Rafi stood and shooed the standing men, including Yuri, from the room. As he closed the door behind them, Rafi's shoulders visibly slumped. He walked back to the table and stood behind Dimitre, one hand on his friend's chair. Without glancing back, Dimitre handed him the silver case. Rafi took one, closing the lid with an audible snap. He lit his cigarette with a silver lighter from his pocket, blowing a long stream of smoke toward the ceiling. He examined the burning end reflectively for a moment before he turned back to Pete, "We realize you do not know us, Captain, but we have heard a great deal about you and we find you are our last opportunity.

"Dimitre and I have been in America for three days. We have a terrible problem. We have recently found a large hidden cache of old nuclear weapons. Kazakhstan doesn't have the military force necessary to protect them. If the Russians find out they exist" – he silently shook his head – "I fear they may use it as an excuse to retake our country" – his jaw tightened – "and rape our gold, oil and grain resources again. If the Chechens learn about them" – he dismissively threw his hands up to the level of his shoulders – "who knows what those crazies will do?"

He ground his cigarette out as he held Pete's eyes, "We must have America's help! We have talked to senators, congressmen and important officials, but no one can get us access to your President!" His voice rose with incredulity, "Some we talked to are men who have run for President themselves!" His shoulders slumped, "None of them has been able to help." Rafi looked at his watch. "It is 3.15 in the morning. In only 13 more hours, Dimitre and I have to depart America. We took a great risk to leave Astana at this time." Dimitre nodded his agreement at these words, which was the first move Pete had seen that had not centered on a cigarette.

Rafi was beseechingly holding out his hands. "You must help us, Captain O'Brien. You must help."

CHAPTER SEVENTEEN

As the flight attendant answered questions and distributed headsets, Anastasia leaned close to Pete's ear and indignantly whispered, "I am *no* man's personal assistant and I am certainly not *yours.*"

He shrugged and reached down under the seats for a thin, battered black folder. Like passports, some things still needed to be on paper. Flipping back the scratched brass catches, he extracted a set of official orders personally signed by the Secretary of Defense. His thumb and index finger riffled through the pages while he pretended to search for a paragraph he had personally requested be inserted. He loved the suspicious look on her face. It was certainly well founded. Once he found the tabbed page, he ran his ring finger slowly down the margin before stopping at the section highlighted in yellow. He was wondering how long he could draw this out before she snatched the papers right out of his hands. "Here it is," he said. He wished he needed glasses so at this point he could pretend to search his pockets for them. "In addition to the other provisions of the contract, Ms Anastasia P Conner will act as Captain O'Brien's assistant and interpreter on a matter of national interest. By the way, what does the 'P' stand for?"

Anastasia's new blond hair swirled as she angrily twisted her face away from Pete and stared out the window. She appeared fascinated by the men loading the baggage. He took a deep breath. He still believed it had been a good idea to seize the moment. How many times did anyone have the opportunity to ask the President of the United States for a favor? And the results were OK so far. She was aboard the airplane and the passenger door was closed, wasn't it? Perhaps it had been a little tenser than he had expected. It was surely a damn good thing that knife was checked!

Of course, he had his own good reasons to be on edge. While Rafi and Dimitre had both been pleased with the White House meeting, Pete had been listening very carefully – and he understood American English much better than either of them. The American President had made no firm commitments –only generalities – a deliberate nuance he had confirmed to the small group that remained once Rafi and Dimitre had departed the top-secret meeting. "I won't believe anything until someone I trust has put an eye on these things and tells me they truly are nuclear weapons."

The President had looked around the Oval Office. General Jack Monroe, the Chairman of the Joint Chiefs of Staff, a man 20 years Pete's senior, with graying temples and a dozen more age wrinkles in each of his cheeks, nodded his agreement, and the President had continued, "Russia and China are special countries. Both can do real damage to the United States, so there are never black-and-white answers when those two are involved – and they each border Kazakhstan."

The President frowned. "I'm sure President Parzarev has his own political reasons to push for immediate action, but until we better know the facts, I intend to keep my powder dry."

The Secretary of Defense was thoughtfully rubbing his chin as he interjected: "I also assume you want to keep this very close-hold for a while." The President nodded his agreement and the former Senator from Indiana who had made a name for himself by his interest in defense procurement issues, continued, "Rather than arousing a lot of official interest, why don't you send someone like Pete over there under the cover of something like reviewing their military training. He's junior enough not to attract too much attention, and Rafi already knows him.

"Pete ought to be able to fly under the radar sufficiently to 'put an eye on' any weapons. Since he's on the Joint Staff, he has the big picture. That will help him develop a Kazakhstan situational assessment you can use to bounce against what you are getting from your country team and that new group the Vice President is establishing."

The President had nodded, "That works for me, particularly since he dragged this particular dead cat through my door…"

Which is when Pete had decided to ask the President for a favor.

And here they were, held up for another 48 hours, after the National Security Staff had raised a concern that Pete might attract unnecessary attention if he were to accompany the two Kazakhs on the same commercial flight to Astana.

President Parzarev had eagerly agreed with the delay. The extra time would provide him with an opportunity to begin to rally the necessary political support to invite the Americans in under some pretext. While many of his party still hated what Moscow had done to Kazakhstan during the Communist regime, those events had been some time ago. Just as Americans had forgiven the British for burning Washington in 1812, the millions of deaths of White Russians were now generations ago. Most Kazakhs were more interested in their common ancestral heritage. Even more importantly, China, Russia and Kazakhstan would always be next-door neighbors, while America, no matter how supportive, was a long way away.

The delay also gave the Secretary of Defense the chance to call the chairman of Asya's company and request her temporary assignment to DoD for three months. Since arrangements in the company had already been made to assign her to Alex's task force in the White House, they were more than willing to cooperate. As was Anastasia, who until she arrived at the airport, was ignorant of Pete's involvement.

After he had studied maps of the region for several hours, Pete had become belatedly worried about the danger this trip might pose to Asya. The two of them might well venture close to the Russian border, and he had rescued her from those clutches not too long ago. After considering the options, he had called in a chip from Bob Farrell. (Actually, he had taken the precaution of calling Sandi first. When she had heard about the Indianapolis fiasco, Sandi had maintained Bob owed him; on the other hand, Bob, especially two weeks ago, after Pete had ignored a called 'Let' at racquetball and clobbered him across the thigh, had said the two were quits forever, which was another reason Pete had called Sandi before Bob).

Whatever, Bob had come through like a champ and had arranged for Asya to receive a makeover, which had eaten up half a day, as well as a new appropriately well-worn and multi-stamped passport, the faded back cover of which looked like it had been stored for a few summer months in a Texas truck's glove compartment. She was now a brown-eyed blonde. She looked like any number of good-looking women of Scandinavian and German extraction who annually migrate from the upper Midwest into the excitement of our nation's capital.

With all of the stimulation of her official and unofficial modifications, Asya had neglected to follow up on the details of the official party make up. When she and Pete met in the check-in line at Dulles, she had initially been shocked. Then an angry blush had begun to creep upwards, beginning at the V in the neck of her white blouse, and seeping pinkly into her cheeks.

Pete handed his passport into the check-in clerk and lifted up his luggage as well as Asya's. "We're together."

"We are definitely *not* together!" She spoke as if someone were choking her. Pete looked at her with concern. "I don't even want to be near him!"

No, it wasn't a health problem. She was just really, really pissed.

The clerk held out his hand for her ticket and passport. He scrutinized them carefully before handing both back to her, "I'm sorry, madam. These are government seats that have already been assigned. You have the window in 28G and the gentleman is on the aisle in 28E. The middle seat will not be assigned."

The dialogue continued through security.

"I can hold it." Pete reached out and took her heavy coat, while she struggled to slide her passport into her purse and simultaneously tuck a computer under her arm.

Anastasia snatched it back, dropping her purse, which promptly popped open, spilling some of the contents. "You can do nothing for me!"

Along the walk from the Aero Train, which whisked them under the runways to a set of tall escalators that would lift them three stories to the concourse and their gate, Pete had asked, "Do you want a book?"

"No." She deliberately chose a different escalator than the one he was riding and without turning her head in his direction, said, "I don't want a book. I want to know why one of Winsor's or Alex's people isn't here instead of you."

When he didn't answer, she abruptly turned right at the top of the escalator and entered the bookstore, proceeding directly to the mystery section. When Pete joined her, she hissed while scanning the shelves, "Kazakhstan doesn't even have a military!"

"Yes, it does. Have you read this one?" Pete showed her a reissued copy of *Hunt for Red October*.

Anastasia glanced at the cover. "Sophomoric and boring. The movie was better, but only because of the Russian captain, Sean Connery. He was a submariner a woman could respect."

"I read in an interview that Sean said he based his character on an American officer he met."

Anastasia raised her right eyebrow in momentary interest and then, remembering she was angry, rearranged her face back into a scowl and wordlessly slotted *The Hunt* back in the wrong rack. She subsequently selected several mysteries, seemingly at random.

When the plane lumbered off the runway and the steward had given them each a glass of wine, Pete reached over and placed a hand on Anastasia's left forearm. He imagined his fingers could feel the faint scar he knew was beneath her long sleeve. "We need to talk. Please move over here." He wrapped his hand around her thin arm before she could pull away, "Enough games, woman. We have work to do and you need to know what has happened during the past week. Move over here. I don't want anyone to overhear."

Asya shrugged her arm loose from his grip, raised the armrest between the seats, undid her seatbelt, slid partially over into the middle seat and looked defiantly up at Pete. He leaned his head down toward hers. She made a moue of distaste, turned her face away and closed her eyes. With his left hand, he moved her long blond hair back and temporarily tucked it behind her near ear, before putting his mouth an inch away and whispering, "Anastasia, this may be dangerous. I admit I probably shouldn't have asked for your help, but you wouldn't speak to me. You were dating other men and you were driving me crazy."

He paused. All he could think about were the delicate hairs around her ears. Her eyes were screwed tightly shut. Pete pulled his lips back an inch and whispered, "I knew I needed help. What we do or fail to do in the next week could make a real difference in the world."

Perhaps it was his imagination, but it seemed as if her jaw relaxed. Pete decided it was time to tell her everything that had happened, beginning with that extraordinary evening in Georgetown.

He did so, but she refused to open her eyes at any time during his story. After 10 minutes, he lost patience. "Asya, I told the President that America had to do this. I told him it was like the boy standing on the beach picking up starfish after a storm and throwing them back in the water. A man walks by, takes in the seemingly endless numbers of dying creatures and says to the child, 'What in the world are you doing, son? You can't save them all.' The boy looks at the adult and then leans down, picks up another starfish and throws it as far as he can out to sea, saying, 'I just saved that one.'"

She let her eyelids drift open, but still looked past him at the movie that was playing in the back of her seat.

Encouraged, Pete continued: "I obviously don't know what we'll find in Kazakhstan. I think the first task is to evaluate if Rafi is honest. Then we have to find the place where he said the weapons were found – he said a man-made cave in the mountains – and see if this is all some sort of ruse."

He had been mentally organizing what information the President needed ever since the Oval Office meeting. "Along the way, I think we wouldn't be doing our job if we didn't make some sort of judgment about what's going on in Kazakhstan. When we get home, we're going to have to produce a report. The President is going to want our opinion as to whether Rafi is playing the United States off against China."

Pete looked out the window as he mulled over his thoughts. They were at 35,000 feet now, and the clouds had closed off the view of the ocean below. "We know he is using us against Russia, and the President thinks he can deal with that because of his personal relationship with Vostrov, but the real question is: what are Rafi's ulterior motives?"

Pete glanced down at Anastasia, "I could visit the cave by myself and make an assessment of the nuclear weapons, but I can't do any of this appraisal stuff without you. You're the one who understands the people – both Russia and Kazakh – and speaks their language."

"As well as German, Turkish and Uyghur," she said.

She was finally participating! Time to wrap up his pitch. "Your new country needs your help, Anastasia, as do I."

Asya was slowly nodding agreement, but she surprised him when he heard her say, "And Kazakhstan and Rafi need my help too."

"Have you ever met him?"

"Peter, Kazakhstan is my specialty and Rafi has been President for decades. I follow his career closely."

Pete lowered his voice, "I liked him during the two hours I talked to him, but we can't get carried away. The CIA says that when he was a young man, he was thrown out of the Politburo for taking bribes, and there are reports he has continued that practice." Pete had spent his two days being briefed by Bob's people and reading Kazakh history in the CIA library.

Anastasia looked Pete directly in the eyes for the first time since they had reached the ticket counter. She placed her hands on the table in front of her and wrapped the fingers of her right hand around one of the glasses of wine the flight attendant had delivered. Her voice was sarcastic, "That was Dimitre who was thrown out, and most Kazakhs believe the charges were trumped."

"Trumped? You mean 'false'?" Perhaps Pete had skimmed the material a little fast.

"Yes, trumped!" With this declaration, she threw back her wine with a flourish and appropriated his glass of wine too.

They both said nothing while the airplane engines were throttled back from the climb and slipped into the monotonous whine of a long high-altitude flight. Anastasia had made no move to leave the center seat. However, it was probably still a little early to think about licking that pale-pink earlobe that lay there so close to his lips.

"Peter," Anastasia said, finishing off the last of his wine, and gazing into the empty plastic glass, "is our trip top secret?"

"Yes, it is. I am not even sure the Secretary of State knows what we're doing."

"Then perhaps you should have informed me sooner." She spoke as if she were lecturing a child. "And I wouldn't have asked Winsor to feed my cat or Alex to water my plants while I was gone." Anastasia gave a quick glance up at Pete though her long eyelashes with her last words and then firmly closed her eyes, "I'm going to sleep, Peter."

She reclined her seat. As her face settled into repose, Pete watched her face muscles relax. She was truly a beautiful woman. Now that he had time to carefully study her, her nose did not appear quite as sharp as Pete had remembered. He also noticed a small birthmark above her upper left lip, as well as a tiny white scar on her chin. As he watched her, he could feel the bands around his chest loosening. He hadn't realized how tense he had been in anticipation of their meeting today.

In half an hour, Anastasia was deep in sleep and she had snuggled her head against Pete's chest. He adjusted his blanket so it covered her shoulders, and allowed his own eyes to close. At least she's here. No more unanswered phones. In a way, this trip was like a grander ticket to the ballet: she would now be part of the cast, about to enter upstage left...

Some hours later, the plane hit turbulence and Pete's eyes opened. Asya was back in her assigned seat, curled up against the window, an open book face down in her lap. She was expressionlessly watching him.

CHAPTER EIGHTEEN

"What do you really know about Kazakhstan, Peter?"

"I had trouble finding it on a map two days ago."

Asya nodded at what she had expected to hear. "We have six more hours on this flight. We need to make you smarter."

She positioned a pillow between her and the cold skin of the airplane and drew her legs up into a yoga position. She smiled sweetly at him, beginning with the same briefing she used to introduce Central Asia to audiences who were willing to pay think-tank rates: "My ancestors belonged to the Greater Horde, who conquered the area that includes the lands north of Iran and the oilfields west of the Caspian Sea." She was going to make Peter regret that special assistant crap and those 'official' orders.

"…the Russians, when they tried to take over our country. My clan also fought the Chinese, who, in the 1800s, were aided by Swedish soldiers of fortune…"

She could see Peter still seeking a comfortable position in which to listen. He had angled his long legs under the center seat, trying to straighten them. From the gleam in his eyes, it looked as if he had made the mental connection between the Nordic-warrior comment and her own pale complexion – he should have seen her mother! He was still rooting around in his seat like a nesting boar.

"Peter," there was a frown in both her face and her voice, "are you going to be attentive, or do you want me to go to sleep? You said this was important for America. I am trying. You must too."

She kept her face stern. "You also need to be closer. I am not going to continue to yell across the plane." There was no way she could manhandle him the way he had her, but he was definitely going to be the one to move this time.

Anastasia began to speak again as soon Pete settled in the center seat, "After the fall of the Tsar in 1917, the Bolsheviks moved south to occupy our fertile farmlands and rich mineral mines. One of my great-grandfathers was a renowned White Russian leader against these cruel invaders. He died on the battlefield, as did my great-grandmother. My grandfather was brought up in a state orphanage.

"The Soviets took our land, plowed our grazing fields, stole the iron ore from our hills, poisoned our water with nuclear fallout and our air with their space-launch center. Of 20 million original Kazaks, Stalin killed or starved nearly four million to death." She tried to keep her voice dispassionate as she tolled the terrible numbers every Kazakh child knew by heart. "Another million fled to China. After Stalin died, the policies did not…"

Pete signaled the flight attendant for two more glasses of wine and Asya drank half of hers to soothe her throat. "Kazakhstan is nearly the size of the western half of your United States, with lots of beautiful desert and miles of grassy plains." This part was always easier. She closed her eyes and pictured the land. "Our mountains are higher than your Rockies.

About half our people are Sunni Muslims, a few are Russian Orthodox, like me… Our ancestors were nomads who lived their lives on the land, close to nature, so religion is not…"

She paused while dinner was served. Pete stayed in the center seat and she felt the heat from his thigh warm her as they ate. After the dishes were cleared and coffee was served, she spent another hour describing the political players they might expect to meet in Astana and Almaty. Finally, the reduced oxygen levels in the cabin took effect. Asya yawned for the third time in as many minutes and wearily pushed the armrest down between the two of them. She pulled her blanket up around her shoulders, and closed her eyes. The headache that had been bothering her for weeks was nearly gone. Tomorrow she would be home for the first time in years.

CHAPTER NINETEEN

The plane changeover in Frankfurt brought with it a three-hour layover. While Anastasia curled up with one of her mystery novels in a chair near the departure gate, apparently oblivious to all the terminal's speaker announcements and the foot traffic, Pete was not nearly as nerveless. He felt driven to do something. He decided to check in with his office. After his staff assured him the Pentagon was managing to get along without him, he asked to be connected to the other major game in town.

"Bob, Pete here. Anything going on at the CIA I might be interested in?"

Farrell's voice was cool, "Since I'm not permitted to know exactly what you're doing, Pete, how the hell would I know?"

"Give me a break. You know I was directed to report only to the Secretary."

Pete imagined he could hear Farrell's molars grinding as his friend decided whether or not to add any slack to Pete's inhaul line. Finally, he heard an audible sigh, "I thought you might call today. Let's see if anything I pulled from the morning message traffic might interest you. Sandi sends her best, by the way." There was a few seconds' pause, accompanied by a faint rustle of papers. "Our German desk reports that a good-looking blonde, accompanied by an ugly Navy captain, is in Frankfurt, apparently headed for Kazakhstan. The information was passed here by flash traffic to see if the captain had permission to travel to that particular destination."

"You can't spy on me." Pete was indignant. "I'm an American citizen!"

"Who is not currently within the United States, Pete. Besides, our informant seemed more interested in the blonde. Did you know she is 103lb and appears to be a 34B?"

"You will never know."

"Oh, we have a good analytic shop in Frankfurt and they are directly tied to the airport's imaging equipment, so I think that's close."

"Why don't you have them analyze Sandi?"

A repressed chortle came through the speaker, "A little sensitive, are we?" Bob's voice turned more serious as he paraphrased a dispatch for the unscrambled connection: "In Astana, our Embassy reports a member of the right wing gave a strong Parliamentary speech yesterday. The topic was the importance of Kazakhstan maintaining its 'historical' good relations with its Russian neighbors, with emphasis on the 'mistaken efforts' of some officials in reaching out to the West. He called on citizens for 'extra vigilance' against letting the West rape the 'rich, virgin lands of Kazakhstan.'"

"What the hell does that mean?"

"Kazakhstan is normally one of our quiet zones. Their President is powerful, and he keeps it that way. If I were to guess, I would say these are surface cracks indicating some domestic tremor. As you may or may not know, the migration of Russians into Kazakhstan during their days in the Soviet Union produced an internal strain. They now have a majority of ethnically Russians in the northern areas near where the Ural Mountains dip into Kazakhstan, but no representation. Dimitre Kuntameyev has Kazakh voting organized like Daley did Chicago."

"The Russians have no voice?"

"Got it in one, Pete, my man! The government is entirely Kazakh and the Parliament nearly so. If I were to guess what is currently going on, I would say some expatriate Russians think they smell an issue and are doing their best to politicize it. To confirm that, I would have to talk to our people inside and this isn't yet at the level where it's worth risking blowing them."

"Kazakhstan doesn't sound like the most stable place in the world."

Bob snorted. "It's a hell of a lot better than lots of the places you and I once thought were great for a night on the town." His voice took on a formal tone. "By the way, my fine Washington ear is picking up the sense that the Secretary of State's nose may be slightly out of joint. Someone told me she suspects the President is contemplating developing some policy without 'properly consulting' State. You wouldn't know anything about that, would you?"

Pete knew he was making a mistake with his friend, but the President had been very specific about limiting who was to have knowledge of his real mission. The President's list had not included State or the CIA, "If I do, you'll be the first to know. I still remember the briefings you gave a shirttail SEAL the first time he was about to go into Indian Country." Bob was silent and Pete could hear the ice forming on the phone line. He quickly added, "I know who my real friends are, Bob. But they just announced our flight. Please give my best to Sandi."

Back in Langley, Bob hung up his black phone and picked up the ringing red one. He had so many special phones on his desk, it was sometimes difficult for his administrative assistant to find places to stack the folders she brought in every couple of hours. A red phone for State, white one for Defense – he wondered if he should order a special striped blue one for the Director. "Bob Farrell."

"Bob, Alex Thainton here. How is life today in snowy Virginia?"

Bob tucked the receiver between his chin and his shoulder as he leaned back in his chair. "Just perfect, Mr Secretary, and how the hell is the weather in your neck of the woods?"

"It was extremely cold in Ontario last night, I can tell you, but the evening might well have been worth it. I came across some information I think you will find interesting..."

Bob hit the latch that remotely closed the door to his room and shifted the telephone to speaker. Oh, Alex, you are as smooth as your good friend Winsor. Bob always found it easier to think devious thoughts with both his hands free and he suspected this was going to become that kind of conversation. What information was Alex really after today? Bob hadn't gotten to and stayed in a CIA corner office through both Democrat and Republican administrations without having a well-developed spidey sense. Currently, that force was tingling at a seven on its way to an eight!

By the time his heavy door had eased completely shut, Thainton was well into explaining the status of Canada's latest plan to build more nuclear submarines. Bob began drawing squares on the pad of paper in front of him. "Why in the world was Alex even in Canada?" he was pondering. "Wasn't he supposed to be leading that new VP task force on Kazakhstan – what a coincidence! I wonder if he has been brought into a particular loop that I have not…" Bob placed anchors in the center of each of the squares he was drawing – fouled anchors – which he would like to chain around the neck of a particular Navy captain he and his wife well knew.

The Canadian nuclear-submarine thing was a proposal that periodically arose, fanned hot by Canadian patriotism and American and domestic-industry self-interest, only to always wither on practical and fiscal grounds. Alex was involved in a fishing expedition this morning, and not even a terribly imaginative one. Bob wondered if he should be insulted. He knew what Sandi would say. But she did not really understand the role of a civil servant. One had to be a political appointee to be offended in Washington.

What was The Honorable Mr Thainton's real game? Had he heard Defense was playing in a sandbox reserved for State – specifically one assigned to the Honorable Winsor Asher and tentatively promised to his own new task force? How might he have been alerted – by someone in State? In the White House? The Pentagon? Pray not from a source in Bob's own office?

The latter was not inconceivable. Asher had friends from his previous duty here at the CIA. He might well have found out that two people had recently obtained visas for Kazakhstan in record time and nudged Alex to trawl the waters. This meant a leak in Bob's office. And leaking to a political was just as bad as giving something to a spy. Both were the actions of whores.

Now Bob was going to have to find an excuse to flutter the prime suspects in his own office – nothing like a lie-detector test to separate the sheep from the goats. He simply wouldn't tolerate rats in his own nest. Obviously, someone had been induced to show his true colors, probably by Winsor – he bet it was that Executive Assistant who had that worshiped the ground Asher walked on. As if Bob didn't have enough on his plate having to construct some devious crap to catch a piss-ant!

He used his fingers to massage his temple. From a purely bureaucratic perspective, both Alex and Winsor were using their State time well. They were moving up fast. Either one would make a terrible enemy. But if Bob betrayed Pete, Sandi would cut his balls off.

There needed to be a way to contain this as much as possible. The boys over at State must have Asya's and Pete's names already. If so, only confirming what they already knew would probably be safe. Maybe that was the answer…

Over the telephone, Alex was still giving a word-for-word replay of his Ontario-submarine discussion. Bob hit mute, yawned and reached under his desk to buzz his AA for coffee. Wherever this conversation was going was obviously important to Alex. What was the CIA position going to be? He hoped this was not about Kazakhstan, but having just gotten off the phone with Pete, it seemed too much to ask. Coincidences don't just happen in Washington; they are very carefully planned.

Pete had implied this was a classified mission, but Alex had the highest security clearances – perhaps not all the compartmented ones – and Central Asia clearly fell within his and Asher's area of responsibility. Everyone knew the two of them were close. Christ! Winsor was even friends with the President of Kazakhstan, and Alex was about to be!

His AA soundlessly pushed the door open and brought him a fresh mug of coffee. Bob mouthed, "Thank you."

Of course, his wife would be appreciative if he could give either Winsor or Alex the slightest professional headache. Sandi's distaste went back a half-dozen or more years. Bob had then been relatively new in a supervisory role at the Agency. Winsor and Alex had attended one of the weekend summer cook-outs Sandi had planned at their house. During clean-up that night, Sandi informed Bob that neither of the men was welcome again. She had refused to discuss any specifics. Since she had once served as his agent, and he knew her kill record, Bob might not know her reason, but he was damn sure about her feelings.

He leaned back and took a sip of his coffee. The main spring in his chair slightly squeaked as Alex Thainton continued circling, "...I shared this information with the Secretary this morning and she was very interested." Bob pressed the button unmuting the telephone as Alex continued, "She asked that I personally bring you into the loop, saying how much she values your perspective..."

Decision time.

CHAPTER TWENTY

A Rolex like the one on his left wrist sold for $40 in the Philippines; at least it had last year, when he was haranguing the seller down from his original asking price. Similar timepieces were available on nearly every corner in Olongapo, along with the other knock-offs, the Pateks and Cartiers, along with a few Breitlings. The vendors were inevitably long-haired pretty boys, tailored shirts open to their waists, wearing tight pegged pants and long jackets, even in the sweltering heat. Inside the black velvet linings of the street merchants' jackets, the watches dangled in neat rows. Interspersed were what appeared to be genuine Thai gold chains and cloisonné baubles. They were selling dreams to the tourists and sailors – as were the young women on the street competing for the same $20 bills.

But this Oyster Rolex, with 12 quarter-carat diamonds marking the hours, was actually an original. He had paid $68,000 for it in Zurich, slipping $300 to the security guard who stood outside the door to the little shop on the circle. He had made twenty-seven international trips last year. A collectible watch on the arm of a man carrying an American burgundy-colored diplomatic passport was a foolproof way to bring undeclared currency back into the United States. In fact, the sale of a single Breitling – one that a Boston jeweler had particularly desired – had covered his Georgetown Club dues last year.

Lately, he had begun wearing this Oyster, because it seemed to lengthen the times between episodes. Of course, the diamonds would chip the hell out of his desk if a bad spasm occurred – and since all the desks on this floor had once belonged to a figure in American history – the lazy bastards in maintenance would have quite a refinishing project, but it was not like they ever did... Was the call finally going through? No. Not yet. It was always amusing that any of his co-workers thought he would wear a knock-off...ahhh...

"Abdulbek, good to hear your voice. I'm so glad you took my advice last week...

"I am sorry to hear that... Your sister's son... Did he live?

"No. I realize you had to... Yes.

"Abdulbek, the responsibilities of leadership always rest heavily on those of us..." He paused and listened attentively for a long 15 seconds. His left-hand fingers had already started quivering and he pressed the tips hard against the polished wood, concentrating on keeping his voice level. "I believe people understand." He let some enthusiasm sift into his voice. "I have some better news for you: you are about to become a legend."

One of the bezel diamonds lightly scored the desk surface and a thin twist of shellac curled up. It immediately shattered into three white shreds that his little finger impatiently flicked off the surface.

After clearing airport immigration and customs in Astana, Pete and Asya hailed a cab outside the terminal. As they slid into the back seat of a 21-year-old Ford, Pete suggested, "Let's drop by the Embassy and pay our respects. Then we can get cleaned up and relax for a bit. Will you please tell him," Pete looked at the notes he had taken back in the CIA library, "Furmanova Street?"

Anastasia gave him a deadpan look, "I can, but we would consequently have a very long walk. Furmanova is where the Embassy was located before the capital moved from Almaty. The Astana Embassy is on Ak Bukak." Her right eyebrow quirked slightly up before she tapped the driver on the shoulder and spoke in a language that seemed much fonder of consonants than seemed appropriate.

From the end of the telephone conversation they could overhear, the Astana defense attaché didn't appear terribly interested in meeting two newly arriving Americans. Finally, Pete placed his military identity card squarely in front of the receptionist, an attractive young woman wearing long, dangling bronze earrings. She read his rank and particulars into the phone and in less than a minute, the American attaché, a young Army Lieutenant Colonel, appeared. He led them to his small office, fetched a second chair for Anastasia, and asked his administrative assistant, a diminutive girl of about high-school age, to obtain coffee for the three of them.

"We only got the notice that you were coming yesterday, Captain, and I haven't had the chance to update my 'visiting fireman' brief. I can give you an oral summary of what is going on." He appeared to remember his boss, "The Ambassador is down south or I'm sure he would have liked to have seen you."

"That's fine, Colonel. We just wanted to check in so you know we are 'in country.' My personal assistant and I are here at the invitation of President Parzarev to review their military modernization. She is very familiar with Kazakhstan and we were well briefed before we left Washington. A quick update on any important events of the past week will suffice."

The attaché appeared puzzled. "That's great, Captain, but why are you *really* here? The Kazakhs have a very small military – mostly ground with a sprinkling of air forces. They don't even have a coastline."

Pete smiled to take any sting out of his words, "Colonel, I think you have been absent from the United States much too long. We have transitioned to fully Joint back home. All the Services are co-operating much better these days." Right, Pete thought. Full co-operation between the Services was achieved during blue moons on alternate leap years.

He kept staring at the Colonel so he would realize that this was simply none of his business. Pete was senior to him, and any Army/ Navy rivalry nonsense was going to stop right here. Fortunately, the Colonel was one of the few American military officers in Kazakhstan, so the question wasn't likely to come up again, particularly since the attaché appeared to be putting up only a mild protest in the event any senior Army officer ever enquired. He wasn't really interested. Pete knew that, because the Colonel had spent the last several seconds shifting in his chair to see if it were possible to find an angle to see down the front of Anastasia's blouse. Five minutes after they left the room, he wouldn't be able to recall Pete's name.

Pete raised a hand and passed it between the attaché's eyes and Asya, "Why don't you quickly run over the highlights?"

The Colonel started, and then, either unable or unwilling to adapt a long brief into a short discussion, launched himself into a canned general overview of Kazakhstan. After the first 10 minutes, Pete had trouble staying focused. When you added up their back-to-back flights, he and Anastasia had been in the air for more than a day. Perhaps they should have taken a nap before they visited the Embassy... He felt the toe of her shoe nudge the back of his right leg and bit the inside of his lip. He knew his eyes had drifted shut.

"...picked up in the past few days, Captain. President Parzarev has not been seen in public for about a week and his opponents appear to have interpreted that lack of visibility as a sign of weakness. They have significantly increased the level of their critical rhetoric." The colonel shifted in his chair, apparently still fascinated by Anastasia's chest. "We don't know why he isn't on television tamping down the unrest. Parzarev is usually Johnny-on-the-spot at getting himself on channel K-1 at the first hint of any disquiet."

Asya's hand came over to rest on Pete's arm. He looked at her and she shook her head. Apparently, Pete was to ignore the fact the Colonel was sexist as well as stupid.

The Colonel apparently sensed Pete's annoyance and looked his way. "Moscow fuel shortages are already occurring this winter. Russia is unhappy about having to pay full price for Kazakh oil. At the same time, a significant portion of the Kazakh population would just as soon be part of Russia, and Russian industry needs Kazakh raw materials. In fact, the Ambassador had a survey done and it looks like pro-Russian sentiment in this country is running as high as 40 to 45 percent."

The Colonel shook his head dismissively. "Boy, was President Parzarev angry with the Ambassador over that survey. You've certainly come at an interesting time."

"Well, interesting times are all a military man can ask for, aren't they?" Pete had dealt with this fool as long as he could. He rose, flexing his right knee, "Now, let me have your telephone number and hopefully we won't have to bother you for a couple of days. Where have you put us up?"

"Sir, you are both at the Radisson Hotel. It and the Ritz-Carlton are the best hotels in town. Both are normally chock-a-block with oilmen, but the Ambassador keeps a suite at the Radisson for our VIPs."

Anastasia's room at the Radisson was typical of Western European hotel accommodations. It contained a single bed, folded comforter and one flat pillow, along with a narrow-curtained window and a poorly lit bathroom crowded with a toilet, bidet and shower. Immediately adjacent, accessible from both the hotel hallway as well as through a door that opened directly into the suite, Pete's much grander accommodation included a large living room with an outside balcony, the latter already dappled by new snow, a dining area, bar, small kitchen, giant bedroom with a king-size bed and an equally large bathroom with a sunken tub. Pete observed Anastasia looking covetously at the tub and felt a twinge of guilt. "You take this bedroom and I'll sleep in yours."

"No," she half-heartedly protested...

"Yes. I'm more comfortable with small rooms...must be all that time aboard submarines. And I never use a tub. Just don't open the front door to anyone and our secret will be safe."

Pete picked up his suitcase and disappeared down the hall into the smaller room. A few seconds later, he returned, wheeling her luggage into the larger room. "If you leave the adjoining door unlocked, I'll have access to the common room and will make coffee in the morning for both of us."

CHAPTER TWENTY-ONE

A minute later, Asya heard the faint sounds of Pete's shoes hitting the floor and his bedsprings complain. She went to the balcony and drew back the heavy curtains.

Large snowflakes were still drifting down. Despite the bitter cold, she had always loved this city.

She pensively looked out over the afternoon skaters on the frozen Ishim river as her mental muscles slowly unwound. She could feel her tension gliding away, along with the brightly scarved athletes. A low noise startled her. She half-turned and listened carefully for a few seconds before relaxing. Peter was already snoring.

Turning back to the river, Anastasia watched the dual effect of the snow and the shadows from the gathering dusk as they worked their magic to soften the city. Americans were fond of saying you could never go home, but here she was, and she had a big beautiful tub waiting for her. There were some downsides. Peter had no idea of the dangers Kazakhstan posed He was so naïve. Her image in the glass shimmered slightly as she tried to rationalize her feelings.

He definitely was a man, but it would definitely be better if he didn't always blunder straight ahead like a *muzhskoy*. The concept of using a feint or misdirection, or simply waiting for a more opportune moment were as foreign to him as an all-vegan diet. She feared her native land was going to eat him alive.

She slowly twisted her head back and forth as she continued to study her reflection in the glass. Her long hair swayed and rearranged itself around her shoulders. She knew he thought he was falling in love with her, but the more she considered it, the more she was convinced her initial impression had been correct. He was a nice man, but, like a shooting star, their moment had come and gone. He would be a good memory for her old age. Now Alex...or perhaps even Winsor...

As the snow swirled before her, she felt faint surf sounds begin to build in her mind. She let her eyes drift closed. After a moment, her pulse began to slow. She remembered. She could almost see a wave rise from the flat sea near her home and begin to swell. Within seconds, the water crested, crashed, rolled toward the beach, rose again as it neared the shallows, foaming white for a few seconds before curling over onto the back of the retreating surf. She leaned forward and pressed her entire forehead against the cold glass. The succeeding wave pushed up onto the beach, scattering brown and white sandpipers before it while leaving a trace of froth, as well as a tiny irregular ridge of sand to mark its furthest advance. Except for the skittering birds, the beach was deserted.

The beach had been empty that fall day eight years ago, when Anastasia got off the train. She had left Moscow straight from the gymnasium. She had removed and stashed her shoes and socks beside her traveling bag on the blowing white sands, wrapped her coat around her and began to walk into the wind. Her face was raked by the blowing sand. Her soul felt exposed and raw. She had decided during the train ride to accept the FSB terms. She would buy life for her mother. But, Anastasia would make sure her sacrifice was a full-valued one. At the Olympics, she would find a few hours away from the team's keepers. She would somehow contact the American CIA. They should be interested in a woman who both worked for the FSB and despised them.

Asya still held the image of that afternoon in her mind's eye. She could hear the fading waves and the cries of the birds overhead as the wind blew her qualms away with the sand.

In the Astana hotel room, she pulled her face back from the glass, opened her eyes and looked sightlessly down into the late-afternoon traffic. It had been at the Olympics where she had first met Winsor. Handsome, debonair Winsor, dispatched by the CIA for the Games to fish for potential recruits. He had made a 17-year-old girl a woman – and a spy. She blinked once. The past was the past. But was it also the prologue?

Peering at her reflection in the window, she ran her forefinger along her eyebrows, rearranging the fine hairs into their normal smooth curves. Winsor had been her case officer at the CIA. Even after he changed jobs to State, he had insisted on flying halfway around the world so she would have a friendly face to meet in Kure. He also introduced her to Alex.

She leaned back away from the cold, watching her features shimmer slightly in the window's uneven reflection. She could still remember Winsor's frustration when she had refused him during their Tokyo stopover. Winsor never knew about her experience aboard the submarine. He had not even acknowledged the Navy captain who had driven his ship into the teeth of the Soviet fleet to enable her to escape. The man who had given her new hope.

Tired, Anastasia leaned her head back. Her hair fell loose as she rotated her shoulders and neck to relieve the tension of the day. The surf sounds had faded. All that remained was the silent snow, falling in the dark beyond the windows. She frowned. She enjoyed Peter. She felt calm when they were together. And, for one afternoon, he had made her feel cherished. Nevertheless, his Navy would inevitably call him again. He had once walked away from her. And he did not know her the way Alex or Winsor did.

Asya's eyes darkened and her pupils contracted. She reached out and touched the cold glass directly in the middle of the image there. This woman was responsible for her. No one else. Never again. Peter had done her a favor by tricking her into traveling with him. Perhaps it was time for her to return to Kazakhstan for good.

But what would she be coming home to? Her mother was dead. Asya's hand slowly fell to her side. Her finger had left a fogged smudge on the cold window.

The brown in her eyes deepened as she continued examining her reflection. She lifted a curl of unfamiliar blond hair up from her shoulder, and then leaned forward, pushing the hair back on her forehead. I must make sure I am not showing any dark roots. She grimaced at her reflection.

First, I will eat. She crossed to the telephone on the living-room desk, gave her order in Kazakh, and then, not bothering to keep the annoyance from her voice, repeated her choices in Russian. That done, she chained the front door, entered the grand bedroom and began undressing. She had time to bathe before room service would arrive.

CHAPTER TWENTY-TWO

"Help!"

Pete sat up reaching blindly for the telephone. His fingers found only an empty nightstand. Where was he?

"Peter!"

He rolled out of the small bed. His bare feet soundlessly hit the cold tiled floor, toes gripping the slick surface for better purchase. His swinging arms found the door to the suite and he used a hand on the doorjamb to propel him even faster across the carpeted living room. He was fully awake. The door to Asya's bedroom was ajar. Two large men in jeans and identical brown leather jackets were inside, standing with their backs to the living room. One was holding a gun, the other was standing in front of Asya, his right hand grasping the top of her robe, the fingers of his left shoving her backward. She was trapped between the thug and her bed.

The man holding her pulled his hand back and cuffed her across her cheek. "*Blyad*!" She crumpled back onto the bed, her robe falling open to expose her right breast and the incomplete hair-coloring job.

Pete reached the men as she fell. His left hand, fingers stiff, arced down, striking the gunman's arm as solidly as he had ever hit any pile of boards. The gun discharged as it flew out of the man's hand.

As the room rang from the noise of the gunshot, Pete pivoted and put his entire weight behind a left cross to the gunman's temple. The man fell against Asya's lamp and nightstand table and rolled heavily, face-first, onto the floor. He began shakily trying to rise to his hands and knees, but slipped and fell flat.

No time to ensure he was finished. Pete turned his attention to the man who had struck Anastasia. Her assailant was already shuffling forward, thick arms bowed out from his body, his hands vertically finned – a style Pete immediately recognized as honed from misspent years on wrestling mats.

Pete took a short stride forward and hit the man in the nose and the chin, and followed with a right elbow to the throat. The man absorbed both fists and the throat shot, only shaking his head, before rushing forward with a series of short steps and a scream. "Aee–heah!"

Pete dipped down and stepped directly into the charge, his own long arms slipping under the man's armpits. As their chests met, he clasped his hands behind the man's back, arched his spine and let the Russian's momentum somersault them both over. He could smell grease, stale onions and this morning's vodka on the Russian's breath. As they rolled, Pete held the man tightly to his chest and drove his own forehead against the bridge of the man's nose, picturing the nasal bones splintering and being driven back into the brain. The sudden dead weight in his arms announced success. Pete immediately unclasped his hands, pivoted on the back of his head, arched his back and rolled, throwing the heavy weight off him and against the bureau. The dresser gave off a loud crack and pitched crazily forward as one side of the mirror shattered.

Was that five or seven years of bad luck?

Oooff! His breath was driven out of his chest.

The other Russian had leaped onto his back as Pete was trying to get to his feet. The man already had both arms around his neck in a hammerlock grip. He apparently hadn't found his gun, which was a good thing, but that hold would eventually have the same results if Pete couldn't break it. The Russian was going to try to drive his head down against his chest. If that happened, it was a sure prelude to a broken neck.

The only escape was to get his shoulders turned inside the assailant's grip or to throw the man over his head. To do either, he had to be on his feet. Pete arched his back to avoid losing any more ground while he forced himself first to his hands and knees and then to his feet. The Russian was focused on keeping the hammerlock tight and increasing the pressure. Pete drove his left elbow back against the man's side to open a couple of inches and obtained only a muffled "oomph" in response. No gap opened between their bodies.

The clasped hands behind his neck continued to squeeze inexorably. Pete's chin was now almost at his chest. He gritted his teeth and focused on keeping his neck and shoulder muscles tight as he reached back over his head with both arms. If he couldn't go inside, he had to take the man over the top. Forcing his right hand further back, Pete's fingers brushed the gunman's coat collar. In response, the gunman forced his neck to bow down another quarter of an inch. Pete's right-hand fingers grasped the collar. He pushed to get the same hold with his left. The gunman forced his head down another bit. Pete's left fingers slipped on the assailant's smooth leather jacket.

On the other side of the bed, he saw Anastasia stumble to her feet. He watched her eyes clear and then widen. She reached beneath her robe, unsheathed her knife and clasped the blade between her teeth. His chin was about to touch his chest and Pete could feel the gunman begin to come up on his toes. Which way would he shift his weight? Right? Left? Pete had to out-guess him or he was dead.

Suddenly, Asya took two steps back, shed her robe and dove toward the bed, both arms raised. The mattress depressed beneath her hands and she sprung up – vaulting over both Pete and his assailant, her nude torso twisting as she disappeared from Pete's view.

"Aieeeee."

He felt the gunman's arms loosen. Pete immediately let go of the collar and spun to his left, leading again with a hard elbow between their bodies and driving his right forearm up into the man's throat as he completed the turn. Maybe this time it would work. It did! The gunman, blood spurting from his mouth, toppled over backward and lay still.

How did I do that, Pete thought?

"Peter, get him off me."

Looking down, Pete realized he could see a clean-shaven leg beneath the gunman's body. He rolled the man aside and found Anastasia, one breast splattered with blood. "You're hurt!" Pete pushed the body aside and reached for her.

Asya ignored him, standing up with a lithe gymnastic move. Leaning over the gunman's body, she pulled her dagger out from where she had driven it into their assailant's back. As she calmly wiped the blade clean on the back of the man's leather jacket, she muttered, "And that, dear Peter, is how we execute a Tucked Tsukahara with a half-twist." She walked around the bed, found and donned her robe and carefully belted it before she again met Pete's eyes, "I thought they were room service. I was careless. Now what do we do?"

"What do you think they wanted?"

Anastasia moved to the end of the bed, and picked up a small gray bag, unceremoniously dumping its contents on the bed. Green duct tape and several short pieces of rope tumbled out as well as a very large folded white laundry bag. She raised one eyebrow. "I think their intent is obvious. Fortunately, they were surprised to find a woman in this room. I had time to yell and retreat."

CHAPTER TWENTY-THREE

When Pete and Asya departed the Radisson the next morning, the streets and sidewalks had been cleared of the previous evening's snowfall. Powdery drifts remained in some alleys, sliced through by the occasional bicycle-tire tracks. Cutting through the square in front of the Presidential Office, they wended their way around several dozen pre-schoolers tumbling breathlessly in the snow.

As they walked, Peter reached down and took Anastasia's left hand, and, when she didn't immediately pull away, slipped their clasped hands into his right coat pocket. She knew he was resisting the impulse to protectively put his arm around her. He was learning. Maybe she would only have to tap him between the eyes every other month.

"I care about you, Asya."

She glanced up. "Which is why you practically kidnapped me to bring me here and then let that bad man beat me up. I have a mark on my stomach." Without letting go of his fingers, she withdrew their hands from his pocket to gesture. "It's that wide."

She looked away so he could not see the twinkle in her eyes. "After you went to sleep, I joined you in the same bed. I slept with my arms around you. You didn't even turn over, much less wake up!"

She knew he was frowning. "It was only for the cameras, Peter. I thought it best if they believed we were dissolute Americans." They were at the marble steps that led up to the President's office. She had him off-balance. It was only fair; he had kept her askew for the past month.

Nure's office befitted a head of state. The ceiling was 15 to 20 feet high, and an imposing crystal chandelier hung in the center of the room. A large stone fireplace, containing a huge banked fire, took up much of one wall. The rest of the room was edged in warm wood. Below the chair rails, dark mahogany panels were inset into the walls. The same rich texture framed each door and window. Two couches, separated by a low wood coffee table, formed a conversation area in front of the glowing red coals. Finally, against the wall behind the President's desk was a large Kazakh flag, spread out to show its distinctive blue sky and golden sun.

There were no papers on his workspace, only an immaculate green felt blotter, along with a jeweled letter opener and an antique writing set. The latter was fashioned in the shape of a terracotta peasant and his kneeling yak. A quill sloped gracefully out from the ink well unobtrusively recessed into the back of the yak.

"I'm sorry Dimitre cannot join us, but it's a busy day in Parliament. Please take a seat in front of the fire. You met my assistant, Boris Valikhanov." Nure indicated the man who had helped Pete and Anastasia with the police inquiries the previous evening. Boris's eyes were tired. He looked very much like a man who had not made it home last night.

"Boris, sit with us and tell my guests what you have found out, and perhaps…Miss…Conner will translate for the Captain."

Boris gingerly sat on the edge of the couch nearest Rafi's desk, removed a small notepad from his pocket, balancing it carefully on the black bag he held in his lap, and began to read from his notes. Despite his mincing manner, gold wire-rimmed glasses, and the long brown hair that hung nearly to his collar, Pete noted that, for a secretarial assistant, Boris had a surprisingly thick neck and broad chest. Last night, he had been wearing an overcoat and scarf, and Pete had missed the muscles.

Anastasia translated as the assistant spoke: "Boris says the Russian Embassy here in Astana has reported that two of their trade representatives are missing. The descriptions match the thugs who broke into our room." She paused and cocked her head for a second before continuing: "The Russian Second Secretary has not yet viewed the bodies."

Boris turned a page and read some more: "The police hope to better understand the incident after they've had time to review any other records."

A young woman in a pleated skirt wheeled in a coffee service and poured four cups. Rafi motioned for her to leave the cafetière, took two lumps of sugar and offered the bowl and its miniature silver tongs to Asya. He quietly sipped his coffee until the woman departed. After the door whispered shut, Rafi spoke: "Boris has determined that the Astana police have, without proper authority, been monitoring that particular suite for some time. I am very disappointed in this news and am scheduled to meet with the Chief of Police later this week. I will also apologize to the American Ambassador when he returns from his travels."

Asya stared into her coffee while her mind ran down several tracks. Had there been a camera in the bathroom? How could she have let her delight at being home overcome her professionalism! She should have known the Kazakhs would be monitoring any room the American Ambassador frequently used.

Rafi was speaking again. "...afraid they will find the camera and recording tapes blank. Boris convinced the hotel manager that the President of Kazakhstan had a more pressing need than the police for 'other records.'"

Rafi carefully put his cup down in the saucer, removed his glasses and wearily rubbed his face. He turned to Pete. "I did some wrestling myself when I was younger. The backward roll is difficult to bring off, especially in coordination with that lethal head butt. Even Boris was impressed. Did you bring their gun with you? My doorway monitors did not detect it when you passed."

It was currently disassembled and the pieces duct-taped to Anastasia's waist, but neither of them thought that was information worth sharing, so Pete replied without glancing at her: "No, sir."

"Well, given the control our police prefer to maintain over private weapons, perhaps it would be best if, later today, a passerby found it in the snow. Otherwise, the Lieutenant will never rest. I know you probably feel you need some personal weapons, and though we Kazakhs feel differently than you Americans about guns, since you are under my personal protection, Boris will provide you with an official replacement." Rafi's gaze swung to Anastasia. "I assume you would also like more firepower than that old knife."

Anastasia nodded.

"Good." Rafi looked into his coffee. For a long minute, the only noise in the room was the crackle of the fire.

Finally, he spoke: "My reading of the events of last evening is that one of my enemies knows something is 'up', as you Americans say. The problem might be Russians or it might be Chechens. It could even be the Chinese. I can't believe a Kazakh would betray us, but I may be mistaken. The intelligence Boris has gathered indicates the threat originates with our Asian friends. Whatever the case, I think it best you practice deception."

Pete interrupted: "Mr President, my experience is that speed is always essential. Last night was sufficient proof for me that someone doesn't want us here. That alone gives credence to what you told my President. I suggest Asya and I proceed immediately to the weapon-storage location you discussed with him."

Rafi showed no indication of rising from his chair. Instead, he took a leisurely sip of his coffee. "I understand your feelings, but my political intuition advises me against that approach."

"But…"

Rafi paused for a second and put his glasses back on, carefully fitting the wire rims over his ears. His voice had become weary. "Dimitre and I are still gathering support. We need another couple of days."

He shook his head. "It is safe. There are only a very few of us who know the actual location of the weapons." Rafi looked around the room. "Even Boris here, who is practically my alter ego, only knows the general area." Boris, who had been rising to leave the room, stopped when he heard his name spoken. Rafi was obviously focused on his own internal thoughts, nodding to himself. "I suspect the Russians don't even remember when and how these nuclear weapons were 'misplaced.'"

He drew a deep breath and continued his monologue. "I think it's best for me to keep everyone, including you and your lovely assistant, in the dark for a bit longer. The closest city to where you will want to be is Aqtobe. Boris has plane reservations for you to fly there tomorrow morning, but he also has tickets on a train departing Astana this afternoon.

Rafi impatiently waved away Pete's attempted objection and his voice became firmer. "You are now in Kazakhstan, Captain. This is my country, and those missiles are also mine until the very moment I decide to give them up." He reached over and toyed with his letter opener, his voice getting darker. "Don't tempt me to change my mind." A tone of peevishness had entered his voice. "I don't think your President would be pleased. Undoubtedly there are others who would offer much more."

Suddenly snapping back into the genial-host role, Rafi sat back in his chair, clasping his hands together on his desk. "A guide to the cave will meet you in Aqtobe – but only in Aqtobe. I recommend you travel by train, and Boris will have a couple of his friends use your hotel room tonight." Rafi paused. "Is that agreeable with you, Captain?"

Pete visibly swallowed. "I gave you my recommendation, Mr President, but, as you say, it is your country. Asya and I will be on the afternoon train." He thought for a second and then pressed again: "In the meantime, I would like to know your best guess as to who attacked us. Who else knows why we're here?"

"No one, not even Boris." From the finality in Rafi's voice, Pete gathered that he not only had no ideas, he was weary of Pete asking the question.

Rafi was continuing: "I don't know where the leak was from, but for your safety, it's essential we get you both out of town as soon as possible." He allowed his gaze to float up to the chandelier for a moment, apparently reflectively tallying votes. "In fact, I think we are going to need at least three days, so it is best if you are on the move and away from the capital." He pulled off his glasses and rubbed the bridge of his nose. "Perhaps we should advertise your train trip as an inspection tour of our Air Assault Brigades."

Pete's impatience may have shown in his face, for Rafi used the arms of his glasses to point at him. "If you make one or more inspections, Captain, it only enhances your cover story and makes it easier for me to maneuver you to the vicinity of the cave. A good place to start might be in Almaty, with the 38th. The commander there is a graduate of your West Point and speaks excellent English. You can skip the 37th, because the commander there only speaks Russian and Kazakh…"

"If my cover is so important, Asya can always translate for me…"

Rafi stood, literally brushing the front of his suit and Pete's suggestions to the floor. "No, we need to balance maintaining a cover with the actual danger. It's best if you both get out of Astana as soon as possible. Last night's attack implies your presence has gathered more attention than I had expected. Perhaps it's better to announce you are going to visit the 35th Brigade that is billeted near the Caspian Sea. That way, when the train gets to Aqtobe, you can disembark, sneak a look at the cave and fly directly home from there. All of this should generate sufficient random movement to confuse anyone trying to track your travels." Their audience was obviously over.

"Dimitre and I need three days, Captain. Perhaps while you are not inspecting, Miss Conner will serve as your tour guide to our ancient land so you are not bored." The President turned to Asya and bowed slightly at his waist. "You are a lovely young lady. I hope to see you again in Astana."

She responded by slightly inclining her own head. "You may." She gave him a smile that, from experience, Pete knew she intended as more of a challenge than a pleasantry. "I hope the Russians haven't received replacement 'trade representatives' for their Embassy by the time we return."

Rafi nodded. "I think it will take the Russians time to identify acceptable replacements. Their Embassy may remain short-handed for a while."

They all moved toward the office door. As Rafi held it open, he shook Pete's hand, but held on to Anastasia's for a second, saying, "I understand your Russian is excellent, Miss Conner. You will be able to have many fine conversations with the Russian soldiers who are assisting us in training our troops in the 35th Air Assault Brigade. If your skills need refreshing, perhaps you can practice on the train with Boris. He is a former Spetsnaz."

Spetsnaz – a former Russian SEAL. That made things much clearer for Pete. Years of training focused against Americans. Lots and lots of extra muscles. And eyes that dwelled much too long on the way Asya's skirt shifted when she walked.

Not the best companion for a relaxing trip.

CHAPTER TWENTY-FOUR

"Boris, *mon друг*, it's good to hear from you. I understand you have visitors from my country." The member was sitting at his table in the Georgetown Club. After another drink, he intended to order the London broil, rare. The club was one of the only places in town that could be counted upon to start with a filet-mignon cut… Damn these phones! Even at the speed of light, there was a noticeable reception delay as electrons were relayed from satellite to satellite…finally.

The right side of his mouth pulled sardonically down as he listened to the eager report. "You've done well, my friend. This may make up for failing to alert me when your charges left your country!" He could hear the intake of breath on the other end of the line. The man was right to fear him – and wrong to think he ever forgot a mistake. "I don't care if I were in the Kremlin!" His voice was low, but intense. "You have this number. You found me tonight. Next time, make sure I know!" He shifted his voice to a conversational tone. "I also heard you nearly lost your guests last night."

After a few seconds, he broke up the flow of words in his ear. "You are not my only source in that godforsaken country of yours. What I want to know is what you plan to do now." He turned his face further away from the bar, cupping his free hand over his mouth and the phone. It would be just his luck to have an amateur lip-reader in the room tonight!

In a few seconds, he interrupted his caller. This conversation had already taken much too long. "Just make sure they don't get off the train. I have other plans for that material."

He ended the call and signaled Scotty for another drink. After it was served, he thought for a second, looked up a number and dialed, again listening to the switching sequence as the links ran back to the seventh floor of the State Department and began their electronic hop eastward. A few seconds later, it began to ring with the rough burr common to Eastern Europe. After the third chime, it was picked up in silence. The member smiled. He didn't need an answer – only one person ever possessed that phone. "Abdulbek, I have another job for you. I hope you manage it better than the last one." He held the phone tight against his chest, anticipating the reaction.

"Fuck you!" The words were shouted 8,000 miles away, attenuated by who knew how many switches, muffled against his suit coat, and still distinctly heard two stools down in Georgetown Club bar. He smiled an apology to a bow-tied man at the nearest table who had half-turned in his chair toward him.

Time to bait the water. No one values something unless they have to pay dearly for it, and an enraged king salmon never sees the hook.

Before he could begin, Abdulbek had already begun yelling again and the member put his hand over the phone. "I wasted two of our best agents! Do you know how long it takes to get a Chechen inside a Russian embassy? How much it costs? This is…"

The member did not tonight have either the time or inclination for this conversation. He interrupted: "I am on the track of something that will make everyone recognize the true *konakhalla* in Grozny. The one leader of all of Chechnya!" He paused and lowered his voice to ensure Abdulbek clearly heard the whistle of the swinging chum bucket. "I have learned of weapons-grade plutonium that is available in Kazakhstan…" He was interrupted by an impassioned plea and listened carefully for several minutes before casually replying, "Yes, of course, my friend. For the right price."

The member muted his phone and took a sip of his scotch. His fingertips were tingling as he pictured the puzzle pieces coming together. One or two more and America would be guaranteed to be on top for another 50 to 100 years – and his personal Swiss account would have another $5m or $10m of those new bills. The ones with all the pretty anti-counterfeit metal ribbons woven into their fabric. He unmuted the phone and clamped it to his ear. Abdulbek had nearly worked himself into a lather – and precisely the right place.

CHAPTER TWENTY-FIVE

A local train swooshed into its Astana stop with the familiar shriek of metal brakes clamped against iron wheels. Down other tracks, the black snouts of either diesel or electric locomotives poked out into the weather. Snow was beginning to stick to the metal of the engines that had cooled, while rivulets of water ran down the sides of others.

People were bustling nearly everywhere. The atmosphere was one of pent-up energy. An unintelligible voice announced arrivals and departures, and the air was spiced with wisps of exhaust from a throbbing diesel locomotive idling outside the covered station. Anastasia wrinkled her nose at the faint acrid odor as Pete took a deep breath. The smell reminded him of the engines aboard a submarine.

At a car marked *npnBaTHo*, Pete took Asya's arm and helped her up the steep metal steps where there was a car steward waiting – an older man with graying hair that almost reached his collar. He wore a loose red tunic over black pants topped by a white shirt. The latter had been washed until it was tinged yellow around the collar and the cuffs.

The carriage was entirely empty. Apparently, Boris had reserved the whole thing for their party. They thus could choose from any of the two-dozen leather and metal reclining chairs, all angled to look ahead and slightly out of the large side windows. There was also a set of oak benches on either side, each equipped with flat leather cushions.

The benches faced each other across a wooden-topped table and made a conversation area. The rear of the car was devoted to four sleeping rooms. Each sleeper had two leather couches, again, like the oak benches, facing each other as well as the center of the small compartment. Pete and Asya had been assigned the two rooms on the left side of the car, and Boris and his men were assigned those across the passageway.

The car steward showed them how the table between the couches could be folded up via an ingenious set of runners and slid down flush with the wall beneath a large draped window. Once the back of either couch was folded down, the two narrow beds above it could individually be pulled forward out of the wall, one above the other. As each unfolded, it brought along, like a snake mechanically striking from its cave, a light aluminum frame that supported privacy curtains.

Above the uppermost bed was a storage space large enough for smaller hand-carried luggage – adequate as their suitcases were stored in compartments beneath the car. The washbasin alongside the door could also fold back and disappear into the wall, faucets and all, as the steward demonstrated. In the corresponding niche opposite the washbasin was a narrow closet. Since there would be only one of them in a room intended for two, there was lots of room.

Anastasia hung her coat there and reached back for Pete's. "The steward says he will store the rest of our luggage when it arrives from the hotel, and, unless we're sleepy, it would be better if we sat in the traveling area. You may want to keep your scarf. Sometimes there's a breeze in these cars."

Pete reached in his pocket and Asya shook her head. "Don't tip him now. He will be with us all the way." She took his arm. "Come, Peter. Let us take the tables on the left so we can see Lake Balkhash on the way to Almaty."

They watched the people rushing by the windows until Boris, accompanied by three muscular assistants, boarded and immediately commandeered two sets of seats in the front of the car. Before their group had completely settled, the train jerked once, twice and then slowly began to pick up speed. Within seconds, it was sliding out into the snow.

Leaving the station, Pete was stuck by the number of new buildings. Each apparently held some portion of the hundreds of thousands of people who had followed the government from Almaty. A few older tenements were equipped with railed terraces. Despite the cold and the intermittent snow flurries, white clotheslines strung the length of the terraces held drying garments.

"A casino," Asya said, pointing at a building topped by a large sign announcing 'Zodiak.' "I can't believe how fast Astana has turned into a major city."

"Where in Kazakhstan were you born?"

Anastasia adjusted her woolen scarf around her neck. "Balkhash, Peter, on the huge, mysterious, beautiful lake that is half fresh water and half salt, about as far from Moscow as my uncle and mother could get." Her eyes gleamed for a moment and a smile touched her cheeks. "We will pass it on the way to Almaty, but it may be too dark to see anything."

Pete nodded, and she continued.

"After the Russians killed my father, Uncle loaned Mother the money to start a little shop that sold meat, cheese and bread. It was like one of your delis, except our shop was so small that only three or four people could fit in at the same time."

"I thought it was terribly difficult to buy food anywhere except at the government stores until the late 90s?"

"Kazakhstan is rich grazing land for large herds of cattle, sheep and goats, and our fields of grain and cotton have always helped feed and clothe the Russians. A great number of Russians were forced on us and we were owed for what they did to our Steppes." She raised her right eyebrow, inviting him to fill in the unsaid blank. "So, Mother always managed to keep something in the shop and the two of us ate anything that was spoiling." She paused. "It became easier for Mother after I left for training in Moscow because she had only herself to feed and, of course, once Rafi privatized our economy, almost everything in Mother's shop was completely legal."

"Of course" – her mood and voice darkened and the next words tumbled out – "the Russians still indirectly influence *our* country and they are *not* to be trusted!"

Pete glanced at Boris and his associates across the aisle. They all appeared to be busy and not ostensibly trying to eavesdrop, but there was no sense in tempting fate by encouraging Asya to elaborate further on either what had essentially been a family black-market business or her obvious hatred of Russia. "Speaking of trust, do you have any idea who might have sicced those Russians on us so quickly? Seems to me it was most likely Rafi. I wonder what his game is?"

"Peter, I trust Rafi, and he promised us that no one else in Kazakhstan knew we were coming."

"But who else could it be? We'd only been in the country for an hour or two. It can't be someone from our Embassy. You saw. The attaché was surprised to see us. You say the Russians in our room were after me. But they obviously didn't start out to kill us, or the one with a gun would have fired. It looked to me like a straightforward kidnapping that went south. Who does that leave? I don't understand."

Looking across the aisle at their fellow passengers, Anastasia lowered her voice so Pete had to lean closer to hear. "Peter, if Rafi discloses what he intends to do before it is a *fait accompli*, there would be much unrest. Many people, especially most of the Russians who settled here during the occupation, are still very loyal to Mother Russia. They want to remain close in every way to our northern neighbors. At the same time, they do not especially like Americans." She sighed. "The Russians are not our only threat. The Chinese watch us like a hawk and there are many other strong Kazakh politicians. I am sure at least some of the latter see themselves as Rafi's replacement – he has been on top for a long time.

"The very presence of an American military man, sent here by the President of the United States, might well be all the proof necessary to convince some that Rafi has gone too far in aligning himself with the Americans...

"Oh look! The town where I attended my first national gymnastics competition!"

"Which I'm sure you won."

She laughed, "I was eight years old, Peter. I barely placed in the top 10!" But Pete heard pride in her voice that belied her words. "However, it was my first train ride as well as my first time away from Balkhash."

Asya's voice became more wistful, "And two years later, I was on another train like this on my way to Moscow." She turned toward the window. "I am suddenly tired. I think it will be too dark tonight to see anything as we pass Lake Balkhash. I think I would like to nap until it's time for dinner."

Pete decided he was indifferent to listening to Kazakh conversations. On the other hand, he was more that eager to examine the weapons with which Boris had furnished them. He tucked Asya's scarf around her and walked back to his room.

Sliding the door to his sleeper closed, Pete carefully engaged the flimsy lock. From all appearances, they had slipped away from Astana without attracting any undue interest, but it made him twitchy to be trapped anywhere, even aboard a moving train. Defensive positions were not his cup of tea. He pulled the table stored in the wall up and out, and laid out the weapons from the blue bag Boris had earlier thrust into his hands. At first glance, the bag contained precisely what Pete had requested. There were two guns, extra clips, two holsters, a cleaning kit, oil and a whetstone, as well as a sheathed knife with the distinctive Spetsnaz hilt. He was surprised anything from those old equipment briefings still stuck.

Thankfully, weapons' training was something that had lodged somewhere in his brain and taken root. While the guns were both 9mm, and Boris had provided a full spare clip with each pistol, Pete remembered from somewhere that the clips weren't interchangeable. One pistol was a Glock 15, weighing a little over a pound, and the other a slightly heavier Tokarev TT-33. He picked up each one and sighted it for a moment before spreading out a room towel on the table to prevent the parts from rolling with the sway of the train. Then he field-stripped each handgun, placing each component carefully on the white terry cloth.

Honing his new knife on the oiled whetstone, Pete contemplated the two similar but different assemblies spread out before him. When he fully understood what he was seeing, he moved some of the functional components around until like was lined up alongside like, and turned his attention to the clips. Removing the bullets, he placed them in separate small groups on the towel. With one finger, he rolled each bullet.

Choosing one from each pile, he used the tip of the knife blade to pry the steel slugs loose from the brass cartridges and shook the gunpowder out, building two small gray-black grain pyramids on a piece of paper he had torn from his address book. Wetting the tip of his index finger, he dabbed one of the piles and placed a few grains on his tongue. Making an involuntary grimace, he repeated the process with the other cone, before twisting the paper into a tight wisp that he set off to the side. Well, well, well. A short extractor spring in the Tokarev and a bent firing pin in the Glock to ensure the Tokarev would instantly jam and the Glock would misfire. The powder seemed real enough.

Is Rafi maneuvering to have us killed, or is someone else issuing Boris his orders? Why would he do that, after taking all the trouble to get us here? Pete took the cleaning kit and began brushing, oiling and wiping components as he recalled conversations and facial expressions over the past week and replayed them in his mind.

An hour later, having made his own slight modifications and dry-fired the Tokarev, Pete strapped it into his shoulder holster. It was time to return to the party. He had been involved in hungry business. Maybe there was some dessert left. As he arched his shoulders forward to settle the leather beneath his coat, he again considered the two Russians in their hotel room last night. Why had Anastasia been so certain they were interested in him and not her? Because the bag was so large?

Even more importantly, why hadn't she returned from dinner?

He unlocked and slid the berthing compartment door open. Anastasia was sitting across from Boris in the traveling car. She was laughing, facing Pete, her head cocked slightly to the left. Her long hair caressed the white wool scarf carelessly wound around her neck. Her right hand was lightly resting on Boris's wrist.

When she looked up and saw him, Pete forced himself to keep his face blank as he stepped back inside their room and closed the door. Easing the table back into the wall, he extinguished the light in the room and stood in front of the window. He spread his legs and bent his knees to absorb the rolling. He clasped his hands behind his back.

He had stood on the bridge of his ship for hours just like this, balanced against the roll of the waves, thinking about risks to America, looking out into the blackness. Now he was thinking about something apparently beyond his ability to affect.

The darkening Kazakh Steppe was different than being at sea. For instance, consider the manner in which light behaved at night. On the water, lights slowly got brighter as ships chugged closer. One could think about the potential danger and make plans. On the Steppe, as the train sped along, one or several lights would suddenly appear, only to wink out just as abruptly when the track thrust the train down a hill or around a bend. Asya made Pete feel like he was no longer in control.

Pete was not sure how much time had passed, for he was lost in the growing darkness beyond the window, but his shoulders tensed when the door behind him slid open and a few molecules of perfume teased his thoughts back to the here and now. It was the same scent she had worn in San Francisco. He could feel another curve approaching. He wondered if he would be thrown off the track this time.

Pete closed his eyes.

Behind him, he heard the door-latch click and then the secondary snap as she engaged the lock. Asya did not turn on the light, but instead, moved to stand beside him in front of the window, balancing herself against the sway of the train, so close he could feel the heat of her body. Minutes stretched by as the train wheels clicked over the track welds and the lights of civilization rose and sunk into the Steppes.

"Dear Peter, what will I ever do with you?" she finally said, with the same harsh tone she used when talking about Russians.

Pete said nothing. He clasped his hands even more tightly behind his back.

"You will never make it as a spy, Peter. Your face speaks louder than a...a...a bassoon."

Her voice became more impatient than harsh. "Didn't you understand, Peter? I needed some time to charm Boris. I needed to gauge how loyal he is to Rafi.

"Should I have left that up to you, with no Russian language and your open craving to see if American SEALs are stronger than Spetsnaz?"

So? He had wondered if he could take Boris. Of course he had! Big deal! Didn't she realize that was the way men thought? It was like the simple act of walking down a street. He had no idea what women looked at when they did so, but with every stride, he was always covertly observing every beautiful woman while conceiving a plan of attack against every male.

Some men might have a glass jaw that one good punch would destroy, while others might require a single-arm drag and a one leg pick up before they could be subdued against a wall. Constantly thinking about these things was simply part of who he was. Long ago, Pete had given up on finding a woman who understood this, so he opted to merely reply, "*Hable Español.*"

"Very good, Peter, but so few people in Asia do, and it's '*hablo*' for 'I speak.'"

"Languages are not my thing."

She exhaled a sigh. "But they are mine, Peter, which I thought was why you dragooned me here."

"Actually, I just wanted to see you again."

"*Der-mo!*"

"What does that mean?"

"It has many Russian connotations. In this case, 'No shit.' But I didn't want to see you!"

"Why?"

"Because I had already decided what to do with my life, Peter, and it did not include you."

Pete focused on her reflection in the window, with the dark steppes beyond the glass. "But I like you," he said. In the black mirror-like surface, he could see her eyes widen.

"I know, Peter. Everyone aboard this train knows that." Anastasia shifted closer to Pete. Her shoulder brushed his arm.

"And I may foolishly be falling for you – even though I had to save you from that big bad Russian in Astana."

Pete turned slightly toward her so one breast pressed warmly against his chest, "I could have taken him."

"Peter!" exasperation flooded her voice as she pivoted in front of him, tossing a loop of her scarf over his neck. "Don't you ever listen to what a woman is trying to say? Lean over here!"

Hands still clasped behind his back, Pete bent forward until his lips were a quarter of an inch away from hers. Anastasia stared back, and then the point of her tongue flicked between his lips and she yanked down hard on the scarf.

It was a while before Pete remembered to explain why – simply for safety's sake – he believed they should share a room tonight.

CHAPTER TWENTY-SIX

Asya had taken over possession of the working pistol at 4am, when Pete had awakened her to assume the guard. She had read her book for several hours, but at the moment, she was amusing herself a different way. She was planning to check her traveling companion's reaction time. She knew he prided himself on both how soundly he slept and how immediately he awoke. His body was presently sprawled entirely across one of the bunks, one leg nearly touching the floor. It was no wonder he didn't have a girlfriend! Not only did he sleep like a rhinoceros, he snored as if he were somehow personally involved in pulling the train. She was more than curious to see what happened when he came out of a dead sleep. She placed her mouth close to his ear and whispered, "Change of plan," quickly leaning back as she did.

His sweeping leg would have kicked her across the compartment if it had made contact! The rest of his body lay still. His eyes were now wide open. He was rather quick.

"I got a text from Rafi while we were passing through Saryshaghan. The 39th Brigade Commander is on travel. The President suggests we bypass Almaty and proceed west toward Aqtobe. I informed him of our suspicions about Boris. Rafi will have some men loyal to the Presidency meet us in Aqtobe." She gave into temptation, stepped forward and let her fingers curl a tuft of chest hair that was escaping the blanket. "Rafi recommends we watch Boris carefully and wait for him to act. I agree."

She knew Pete wouldn't agree with waiting. On *Grayfish*, his favorite sayings had been "speed is life" and "inaction is action." She suspected her fingers on his chest were not playing exactly fair, but her loyalties were a bit divided.

Several hours later, their train had chugged several hundred miles and a couple of thousand feet higher up into the foothills of the *Tien Shen*. After adding a locomotive in Almaty, the train turned west to parallel the Silk Road made famous by Marco Polo a thousand years ago. Rather than watch the sights, Pete began studying a map showing major and minor train routes. He reasoned anyone would have had to move the missiles by rail and was trying to become familiar with the likely terrain in which they would be operating.

Asya watched him trace altitude contour lines for a while. She supposed he was worrying about how the United States was going to smuggle the plutonium warheads out of Kazakhstan without butting heads with the Russians. Or maybe it was just the allure that geography had for certain men. She had dated several military officers. Each and every one was anal about maps. She had given one boyfriend a special compass, a lenstatic-something, as a birthday present once, and when the time had come for the two of them to part ways, he had actually asked if she wanted it back! It made her so mad that she had wasted time on him, she almost said yes.

Along the train, the river glistened from reflected sunlight and brought out the colors in the water. Dark blue ripples in the deeper portions marked particularly large rocks, while rifts of white along the banks showed sunken snags. She read her book, occasionally waving to the pilots aboard the working tugs that were struggling south against the current.

Boris and his associates were sitting two rows in front of them. They seemed occupied with a card game. Her book wasn't particularly interesting and Pete had finally folded his map. She decided it was time to force-feed him some more information that might improve his general knowledge about Kazakhstan. "All our major railroads eventually lead to Russia. In fact, the width of our railroad tracks is the particular broad gauge you find only in their country. The Soviets built the roadbeds to ship our food north to feed Russian workers and to transport our raw iron and aluminum to build Russian jobs." She knew it was difficult to hear over the creaking of the train, but something else also appeared to be bothering Pete.

She was just unrolling her spiel on the subject of widespread plutonium contamination – with emphasis on the areas of Kazakhstan where no one now lived and certainly no crops were growing – when she became conscious that he was in severe pain and recognized the cause. "Migraine?"

He only closed his eyes, as if even nodding were too painful.

She suddenly appreciated how bright the car was, especially with the light reflected up from the water. "Why don't you lie down in our room? Please, come. I will make it dark for you and be right out here if you need anything" And maybe, she thought as she stood and took his arm, this will be an opportunity to learn more about Boris without you interrupting.

By the time she had pulled down all the shades in their cabin, put a cold washcloth over Pete's eyes and returned, she was the car's sole occupant. Apparently, Boris and his associates had gone to lunch. Asya pulled the window shade by the bench part way down; made sure the Tokarev was invisibly tucked into the folds of her skirt, and curled up with her book.

She had nearly completed a chapter before the four men returned, each bringing an apple and a bottle of vodka. As she had hoped, Boris joined her at the table, taking a seat across from her.

"American sick?"

His Russian had an accent she still couldn't quite place.

"He has a headache. I'm sure he will be fine."

He unscrewed the top of the vodka and wordlessly extended the bottle to her.

"No, thank you." She bookmarked her novel and put it on top of the table. "I didn't get a chance to ask you last night: how did you come to work for Rafi?"

Boris just gave her a tight smile and kept the bottle extended. Asya carefully pushed the book to one side. The dynamics between the two of them had definitely shifted since dinner last night. He had been pleasant yesterday; now he was almost behaving like a cartoon character, complete with squinting eyes and flaring nostrils. Behind him, his associates were watching the two of them instead of talking or playing cards.

She tried again. "I am from the Lake Balkhash region. Did you say where you were born?"

Boris tipped the bottle back, unpleasantly gulping a swallow, and extended the neck again. "You are a Russian girl – take Russian money, Russian Olympic training. Should never have lain with American lice…" He shook the bottle. Vodka sloshed out and ran down his meaty hand onto the table. "Drink! Will make it easier!"

The associates had risen to their feet and were now lounging in the center aisle, hips braced against chairs in opposition to the rolls of the train, all avidly watching the two of them. She now knew how a mouse must feel when the cobra began weaving its body back and forth. The fingers of her left hand wrapped more firmly around the pistol in her lap. She would be the last mouse Boris would try to swallow!

Boris crookedly smiled and slowly reached across the table. His fat index finger flicked the top button of her blouse. Instantly, the long nails on her right hand fingers raked him hard across his cheek. He reared back and just as quickly she regretted not using the Tokarev.

She tried to raise the pistol and the barrel caught in a fold in her skirt… Boris was moving faster than she had ever imagined he would… She might die, but she would have tried… It was never too late… Boris was reaching for her across the table… The gun sight was still wound up in the fabric of her dress… She would never make it… Pete's hip bumped her own as he slid into the bench.

"I thought you might like your sunglasses, dear. What in the world is the matter with our drunken friend?"

Boris was ignoring her. Every fiber in his body was now focused on the SEAL. The white stripes on his left cheek were slowly blooming into four pink streaks, the spilled puddle of vodka on the table rapidly evaporating.

Wordlessly, Boris handed the vodka bottle and his wire-rimmed glasses back to one of his associates.

The Russian closed his eyes and rolled his thick neck back and then to either side. He fluffed his long brown hair up from his shoulders and let it loosely fall. Asya realized his over-developed muscles made his neck seem but a stubby extension of his chest. Finally, his lips curled against his teeth in a smile. She was reminded of a gorilla at the Washington Zoo she had once seen catch the eye of a tattooed biker in the audience. The resultant display had been the same, except the gorilla had added a foot stomp. She glanced at Pete. He didn't seem impressed. He was simply sitting quietly, watching the show.

The smile was growing on Boris's face. It was now wrinkling the skin around his black eyes. "I think we contest for afternoon delight." The Washington Zoo gorilla had been broader in the chest, hadn't spoken English and she didn't think had quite as much hair.

"Contest?" Of course, Peter was not about to let any challenge slide, no matter how stupid. SEAL against Spetsnaz? Bring out the trumpets. She should be selling tickets. Or running up and down the aisle in a short cheerleader's skirt. Peter had been looking for this for days. Never mind what she wanted. Never mind what Rafi had asked. At least his migraine seemed to have eased. Why had the Tokarev caught on her skirt? This problem would have already been solved.

Boris continued to smile. "Spetsnaz and SEAL. I kill SEALs, but only with guns. I not beaten one with my hands – and such a nice prize!"

Boris turned his head toward Asya while forming his lips into an exaggerated kiss. "I like reward of girl who hates Russians."

This situation was going downhill fast. Maybe she should ruin Peter's fun and just shoot Boris in the balls? Of course, they had only one gun between them and she would have to then get it above the table in time to kill all the associates. Would it catch on her skirt again? Did Peter have a different plan?

"What sort of contest are you proposing?" Pete said.

If he had a plan, did he ever intend to let her know?

Boris unbuttoned his right cuff and began rolling up his sleeve. "Arm fight, like Russian."

Pete raised an eyebrow as he rolled up his own right sleeve. "Arm wrestling?"

Her palm was sweating. One little clue was all she was asking for. Colonel Mustard with the pipe in the ballroom? Miss Scarlet in the kitchen with the candlestick? She surreptitiously wiped both hands on her skirt before again grasping the Tokarev firmly in her left hand. She felt for the safety with her thumb and then mentally slapped herself. Being around Peter made her head mushy – only American guns had safeties!

Boris nodded. "Arm fight." He placed his right elbow in the middle of the table, his hand up for the clasp. "Winner takes *blyad*."

"I think I've heard that word before." Pete kept his eyes on Boris. "Anastasia, what does it mean?"

"Whore." If they lived, would Peter forget she supported Rafi's request to give Boris some slack? That hadn't been her best advice this week. And she had sort of flirted with Peter this morning to get him to support a delay. Would he be critical of that as well?

"Well, Boris," Pete inclined his head toward the associates, "does a brave Spetsnaz need all this help, or can he handle me by himself?"

"*Speenye!*"

The associates drew back a few feet from the table. Asya noted that the one on the right had a mole on his right wrist and looked eager to reach beneath the left side of his jacket. Asya wondered what he was carrying there. Probably nothing she would care to see him pull out. Maybe she would shoot him first and count on Peter handling Boris. You have the trained military mind, Peter, she thought. Do you have a plan, for God's sake? Give me some sort of indication before I go crazy and just shoot you! In a few seconds, it is going to be Miss A in the Club Car with the revolver! She knew she should have signed up to take that yoga class.

Pete put his right elbow on the table next to Boris and wrapped his hand around the Russian's. "On three, Boris? You count." She felt the wooden bench slightly shift as Peter set himself. Was he relying on telepathy? If so, it wasn't working. She hunched down a bit on the bench and stole a look under the table.

"I count in Russian." Boris put his left fist on the table. "*Adeen.*" The pinkie came out. "*Dvah.*" Boris' ring finger shot out from his fist.

At his count of two, Pete swept up his left hand, holding a razor-sharp knife, from under the table and pressed the tip an inch into the soft flesh below Boris' jaw.

"Three, my friend."

As soon as she felt Pete's left hand begin to move, Asya raised the Tokarev, chambered a round, and pointed the heavy pistol in the general direction of the associates. Boris took a quick breath to speak and Pete pushed the knife up another quarter-inch. A rivulet of blood spurted and began trickling down Pete's left arm as he ordered, "Don't take the chance, Boris! You will be dead before any of them gets a gun out. Maybe her gun works. Maybe we found and fixed the bent pin. Maybe we altered the spring. Maybe she will successfully shoot all three of them. Maybe not, but you will never know because this knife will be lodged deep up in your brain before the first echo dies away."

Damn, but he used a lot of words. She translated his general intent. They got the drift. The associates immediately put their arms in the air. She motioned them to turn around. Boris's eyes were clear. He had either instantly sobered up or had never been drunk. Asya suspected the latter.

Boris arched his back and tried to rise from the oak bench, but Pete kept the knife tip pressing into the flesh below his chin and leveraged his body down with this right arm to keep him in his seat.

Pete spoke out of the side of his mouth to Asya. "OK, sweetheart. Now stand up on the bench, leap down behind and hold the gun on them from the aisle. If anyone moves, shoot. At your first shot, I will drive this knife home. Boris, you are going to put your left fist flat on the table and then press your forehead beside it. You need to move very, very slowly. This has to be a team effort, or my hand will slip."

Now he was sharing. Big deal! She felt like elbowing him in the side, but decided it wouldn't be good for his image with Boris. In fact, it might not be very good for Boris at all, so she followed his directions and scrambled over the bench to stand in the aisle.

Pete and Boris continued to engage in a staring contest until Pete twisted the knife a few degrees. The trickle of blood down his arm increased. Finally, Boris blinked and his head began moving downward.

"*Pégale* in the *cabeza*, Asya – hard!"

Anastasia stepped forward, rose up on her toes and whipped the gun barrel down on the back of Boris's skull. As the barrel struck, Pete pulled the knife back, extracted Boris's gun from his jacket in the same motion and slipped out of the bench so he also was standing in the aisle.

Only momentarily stunned, Boris shook his head and started to rise until Pete pushed the round end of the Glock hard against the crown of his head. "It's *your* gun, not mine. You're too strong for me to do anything but kill you if you raise your head. Your choice."

CHAPTER TWENTY-SEVEN

While Anastasia kept guard, Pete tossed their escorts' cabin. It was a fruitful search. They found ten knives, three Glocks, two Kalashnikovs, and a disassembled sniper rifle. Pete confiscated them all, as well as Boris's locked black bag and eight cell phones. Pete trashed the cell phones after removing their SIM cards and batteries – dropping them between the tracks about one each minute – and shoved all the weapons underneath their table in the middle of the car. Unable to raise Rafi for any better guidance, Pete had Asya instruct Boris and his team to sleep in the forward-most defanged cabin.

Several hours later, when the train slowed for a water stop in Aral, the false dawn was breaking. A few minutes later, the engine chugged out of the station, and Pete raised the Glock in a salute to Asya, now standing on the platform with their luggage. He waited until she was well out of sight before he knocked on Boris's door with the butt of his Glock. "Come on out, Boris. I want to discuss something."

Boris began to slide the door open, and after three inches, Pete stopped its progress with his boot. Boris looked the worse for wear. He had cleaned up the blood on his head and chin, but both of his eyes were blackened like a raccoon's. Boris gestured through the crack. "I wish apologize. Too much drink. Sorry." Then he noticed the string that ran back toward the oak bench. Pete saw his eyes make the connection between the string and the door handle.

Pete retreated a few feet and indicated for Boris to open the door a little wider so he could see the entire arrangement. "Do you like this? I am afraid I might fall asleep before we reach Aqtobe, so I arranged a wake-up call in the event you or your associates decide to do something stupid."

Boris looked at the Kalashnikov duct-taped to the top of the oak table. Pete had disassembled the Russians' second rifle, using its barrel and stock, along with the back of the second bench, to form a tripod to position the weapon. The machine-gun muzzle was pointed directly at Boris's cabin.

Pete walked backward until he reached the tripod and held up the string. "I've set this on automatic fire, Boris." Pete watched Boris trace the string with his eyes. It hung from Pete's hand and ran along the floor before arcing up to the stateroom door's outside handle.

"After you close the door, I'm going to pull this nice and tight, and tie it to the trigger. If you open the door while I'm napping, I'm afraid your room will suddenly become very drafty.

"Do you understand the English word 'drafty,' Boris?"

Pete watched Boris coolly evaluate the setup before the latter slowly nodded.

The train was beginning to gently sway as it gathered speed on the outskirts of the small town.

Pete nodded with Boris. "Yeah, I also thought of that Boris," he said conversationally. "If you open the door really fast and hard, the string might cause the gun to pivot and point up, and then you would only have to be lucky enough to avoid the ricochets. So, I have taped a knife here," Pete pointed down to a blade, "to cut the string after it activates the trigger. I also filed the sear to make sure this gun won't stop firing until the magazine is empty.

"By my rough calculations, if you open the door, within three seconds, there will be approximately thirty rounds headed in the direction of your room. I won't be able to stop them," Pete said apologetically, "as much as I might want to."

Out of the corner of his eye, he saw a large stone church lurch past the windows. Asya had said the cathedral marked the last major Aral street intersection. Next would be a hayfield. At the moment, the grade was a bit uphill and the train was still traveling slowly enough that Pete could hear each distinct click as the wheels passed over the welded section joints.

"I figure some of those bullets might even bounce on something in your room and make it back to this end of the car, so I thought Anastasia" – Pete gestured down toward the oak bench hidden from Boris' view – "and I would just lie down here where we would be protected." Eventually, Boris would make a hole in the berthing compartment wall to see what was going on and there needed to be a reason he wouldn't be able to see anyone.

"I tipped the steward $100 and asked him to stay out of the car for a couple of hours until we reach Aqtobe." For the size of that particular American bill, the old man had also been happy to post signs warning everyone to avoid the private car due to a contagious-disease quarantine and had taped over the car door windows.

"We need piss."

"You were in the Army, Boris. That's what sinks are for. Don't forget to run water afterwards so the trap doesn't smell."

Under his feet, Pete could feel the train beginning to pick up speed. According to Asya, the hayfield was nearly the last property in town. There would be one last sweeping curve before the train was up to a speed of more than forty klicks. By the time the grade descended through the next meadow, they would be traveling at more than 120 and he would be verily screwed.

Pete kept his voice laconic. "Close the door, Boris, and return to your card game."

The door slid closed and Pete quickly looped the string around the trigger, leaving a small catenary before the line would bear against the knife blade. He tied the line off to a bench leg and slapped duct tape over the knot to hold it securely in place, then moved to the window and looked back toward Aral. Not a vehicle in sight. The road that ran alongside the railway was deserted.

Sometimes, you just can't get the timing of these things down as precisely as you might want, Pete was thinking, as he opened the forward car door and placed his right foot atop the short railing there.

He glanced back through the window at their compartment, shoved the Glock tightly into his shoulder holster, and grasped the handhold to pull his body up and out between the cars. The gap was actually a little narrower than he had expected and his knee protested as he wedged his body in the opening. He suppressed the treacherous thought that he might be getting a little old for this.

As the train swung to the right, the space between the two cars on his side widened by a few inches and Pete seized the moment, pushing himself between the gap. Tuck and roll was what he had been taught. Just tuck and roll, and pray all the rocks were small and smooth.

CHAPTER TWENTY-EIGHT

Pete had showered away as much as possible of the dirt and shale. He was now lying face down on the bed with a towel over his butt. Asya, swaddled in a hotel bathrobe after her own shower, had pulled a chair up to the bed. While she plied Q-tips, hydrogen peroxide and iodine from the downstairs drugstore, she brought him up to speed on what had happened during his nap. They both knew she was trying to distract him. She finally decided the tough part could not be put off any longer and began using tweezers to pick the rock fragments from the flesh.

Pete took a whistled breath in through his teeth. "Damn! Were you a gymnast or a coal miner?" He unlocked his jaw, looking away from her and out the window. "Did you call Rafi while I was asleep?"

There was no skin left in the section of his back where she was working. She continued using the tweezers, dropping the stones on the floor so they could both hear the little clink. She knew he had turned away so she wouldn't see how much he was hurting. She kept one hand on the short hairs on the back of his neck, massaging her fingers firmly against his tendons. "You are nothing but a big baby, but I think I'm done."

She felt him relax a bit. She let him take a normal breath before she leaned over and poured hydrogen peroxide over the area, watching it bubble whitely, keeping her hands on his bare waist and speaking distractingly louder than necessary. "Yes, I called him. He emphasized that he regrets Boris's unprofessional behavior. He also wanted me to tell you he needs another two days – he is having some troubles with the right wing of the Party."

She watched Peter take several short breaths as he worked to get the pain under control. "Unprofessional behavior, my ass! Did you tell him Boris was going to kill you?" She bent over and pressed her forehead against his shoulder. It seemed warmer than before, which was to be expected. His body was fighting infection. But the rocks and sticks were out. She decided to flood the area with hydrogen peroxide again, spray with antiseptic and bandage it loosely. They would have to find a doctor in Astana who had antibiotics. She couldn't clean any more.

"*Da.*" Her voice was calm. "I also found a wrap for your knee, Peter."

She pushed the towel down and began to gently dab the abrasions on his butt with hydrogen peroxide as she talked. "Rafi understood, and I think he believed me. But for the moment, his men have been unable to locate Boris." She paused while she took a Q-tip and carefully swabbed a long, deep scratch in iodine, "You should have jumped from the train much sooner. It goes much too fast once it is out of Aral. I was worried before we finally found you."

"Boris wanted to chat." He flinched, and she kept her fingers pressed into his hips while he involuntarily arched his back and breathed deeply a couple of times "I have another question. Why does Rafi keep making assurances and you keep believing him? It seems to me that Rafi is close to being at the center of most of our problems."

"I think our biggest problem is you need to get better soon." She taped a bandage over his back to cover the raw wound and put several long strips of tape around his sides, leaning over as she did to brush her lips across the skin in the small of his back. "No. Do not move." She carefully laid a sheet over him. Sitting up, she rested her warm hand on an unscratched portion of his shoulder to keep him still. "You are the one who met Rafi in Georgetown. You trusted him. It was on your recommendation that he met the President."

"They have metal detectors at the White House. I had machines to compensate for my mistakes."

Asya placed her index finger alongside her nose. "He passes my personal sniff test is all I can say." She tossed her hair, "Rafi said he was sending his son, who is one of his assistant ministers, to be our new guide. He will be flying in later today."

Pete tried to sit up, "Then we have some time…" A grimace raced across his face..

She nodded agreement, "To carefully examine Boris's black bag after I get you some more aspirin."

Half an hour later, covered by a light blanket, Pete was lying on his stomach, watching as Asya arranged the room's small writing table. She completely cleared the surface and spread out a newspaper. Then she adjusted the lamp, bending the gooseneck so the single bulb was focused on the middle. Taking a step back, she cocked her head while she reviewed her preparations, nodded once and crossed to the dresser. There she removed and donned a pair of thin rubber gloves from the drugstore bag.

Finally, silently humming, she placed Boris's bag on the newspaper. It was nice to again practice something associated with spycraft. She had been too long pretending to be a secretary or financial analyst or other things she was not. As her fingers began the process of searching for a Boris misstep, endorphins she had forgotten about began to seep into her body. It was a good feeling. As if she were pushing herself to reach for the second twist on the high bar. She would make it or fall. She had so enjoyed being a spy – the danger, the high stakes. Her body could still remember each corner she had driven in the race for her life through the night streets of Vladivostok.

She reached beneath her skirt and unsheathed her knife, ignored the bag's lock, and slit the fabric all the way alongside the zipper. The quiet rip was music to her ears. She unceremoniously upended the bag onto the newspaper.

"Two sets of handcuffs and a black scarf," she quietly announced to her audience of one, whose half-open eyes declared he was fighting sleep. Putting the handcuffs to one side, she held the scarf up in two cupped hands and blew into it for a second before letting it drift down atop the handcuffs.

"Another Glock." Her thumb depressed the top bullet in each magazine, sliding it out a half-inch before pushing the cartridge securely back in. "Two full clips." She began a new pile with the gun and the magazines.

"A box of condoms." She used the point of her knife to slit the box open and pushed the colorful foils aside with the back of her hand. After carefully flattening the cardboard and examining both sides, she shoved it all into the trash pile. "No unusual markings." She was not going to open each one and form a balloon to ensure nothing was hidden inside. She had some standards.

"A small tube." Her knife again did its thing and she flattened the tube, placing her forefinger in the pale gel and rubbing it against her thumb. "Some sort of lubricant." She cleaned her fingers on a corner of the newsprint and kept her eyes away from Peter. Spies didn't blush. He was probably asleep.

Tongue carefully tucked in her cheek, she used the tip of her knife to slice each seam of the bag. Such a disappointment. Slicing a seam didn't provide the same satisfactory rip. Unless it was a Louis Vuitton, they just didn't sew seams with the right tension. A leather notebook, nearly six inches on the long side, tumbled onto the newspaper.

Her pulse leaped, but the professional in her kept her hand steady as she ignored the notebook for the moment and crumpled the bag liner before smoothing it out flat on the table. She closed her eyes and spread her fingers over each square centimeter before running the thin cloth seams between her forefinger and thumb. She opened her eyes, still ignoring the notebook and held the cloth between her and the light. She turned the bag inside out, scrutinizing the liner carefully. Satisfied, she dumped the bag and the liner in the wastebasket; placed the notebook, Glock and clips on the seat of the other chair and gathered up the newspaper by the edges. Before she crumpled the waste together, she paused, looked over at Pete, whose eyes were again drifting shut, and used two fingers to retrieve the black scarf and shift it to the small stack of keepers. He did deserve some sort of reward. He had not said a word about how she had induced him to give Boris some slack. It was all she had thought about while she was treating the horrible injuries on his back. Of course, all bets were off if he couldn't resist saying 'speed is life' for at least another week. She was so tired of hearing that phrase. If he slipped just once, she would blow her nose on that scarf.

She stripped off the rubber gloves, dropped them into the wastebasket, and arched her back, which was always where tension initially affected her when she sat for long periods. She retrieved a new set of gloves and returned to the table with a pad of paper and some pencils. Spreading the notebook out flat before her, she sharpened a pencil and began deliberately leafing through the notebook. As she had expected, it was in code. She looked up to share with Pete, but he was already softly snoring. Pete was *not* patient. He would make an awful agent.

Speaking of spies, she had come to the conclusion that Boris' accent was most probably Chechen. When he had gotten excited during that gun/knife thing, she could have sworn she had heard Grozny diphthongs. How had he ever become a Spetsnaz in the Russia she remembered? Surely Rafi would know? She would have to remember to ask.

She drew a matrix on her pad of paper, entering the Cyrillic alphabet across the top and numbers to thirty-three down the side. How surprised she had been the first time she had learnt that the English got by with only twenty-six different symbols. Again, using the pencil's eraser, she began slowly flipping the pages back and forth. The only noise in the room was now the occasional kiss of paper against paper, Pete's snores, and, while she simply raised her pencil in the air to mark the points when the cymbals clashed, the notes of *The Internationale* she was humming to herself.

Two hours later, the snores in the room abruptly halted and Anastasia made a tick on the paper to mark her place. "So, Peter, you want so much to be with me, and one of the first chances we have to be together, you promptly go to sleep?"

"I was not asleep!"

"Peter, you snore like an elephant. Everyone on this floor knows you were asleep."

She closed the notebook with a flip, "Get up, giant pachyderm! My hands are shaking and my mind is cloudy. I am making no progress. My stomach thinks my throat is cut. Let's eat."

She had already shoved her chair back and removed the glove from her left hand. As she stood and tossed the notebook on the desk, the pages fluttered, dislodging a slip of paper that extended like a crooked tab. She had already turned away from the table, but the stub was too tempting. She used her gloved fingers to extract the slip. She raised it until it was even with her eyes as she simultaneously pushed her hair back with her ungloved hand. Damn, she was tired. Code-breaking was exhausting. She needed a glass of wine.

Pete was swinging his legs to the floor. "Have you found the key?"

"No. But we do have a telephone number."

He had slipped into his shoes and was struggling to button his shirt. Asya moved over to help him.

He abandoned his collar button and unbuckled his pants to gingerly tuck in his shirt. "Do you recall Kazakh telephone numbers well enough to recognize the city code?"

She waited until he slipped his belt tongue in the final loop before handing him the paper slip. "I think this is more a job for your friend Bob. It's an American number. In fact, it has a DC area code."

CHAPTER TWENTY-NINE

A loud knock on their door forestalled Pete's reply. He looked at Asya and she shook her head. She wasn't expecting anyone. Picking up his Glock, Pete moved stiffly toward the door, while he motioned her toward the bathroom – lying down in the bathtub would be the safest… He clenched his jaw; he could already feel the bandage on his back shift and the newly formed scabs breaking free.

Asya snatched up her own *Glock* and beat him to the door, taking a position on the hinged side. Her feet were shoulder-wide apart, arms raised, both hands grasping her gun with the muzzle raised in the ready position.

Damn, she was stubborn.

He looked through the peephole – a tall man with a black briefcase. It certainly wasn't room service but no obvious weapon. He began nodding to Asya as his lips began counting, "one…" Her head synched with him at two. On three Pete flung open the door. As the door swung in, the man brought up a pistol from where it had been hidden behind his briefcase, his eyes searching the room, *"Preevyet*? Anastasia?" He spotted Pete's intentions a tenth of a second too late.

Pete's left hand struck the stranger's gun arm toward the floor, and he rotated his *Glock* so it augmented his right fist just before his knuckles crushed into the side of the man's jaw. Perfect timing, if he were to be his own judge. The man's eyes rolled straight back in his head as the strips of tape on Pete's back gave way. Damn that hurt, but probably a fair exchange.

Pete looked down at the body. In his professional opinion a *Glock* was better than a roll of quarters any day of the week. The US Mint people would simply have to start doing more for their fighting customers or their roll sales of quarters were going to plummet. Pete stepped across the body and looked both ways down the hotel hallway. Empty. He dragged the man completely inside, closed the door, and ejected the round in the chamber as well as the clip in the man's Glock before tossing both on the bed. Asya took a couple of steps back to keep her own weapon trained on the apparently unconscious body while he did a quick pat down. Nothing tucked into ankle holsters or the small of his back. The adrenalin in Pete's body was rapidly dissipating and the pain was beginning to roll in. He was going to have to ask Asya to retape his back. However, the first order of business was to get this particular bandito secured. Pete rolled the unconscious body over.

"Rishael!" Asya dropped her gun and fell to her knees; placing her hands on either side of the stranger's face. Frantically her thumbs pushed back his eyelids and her fingers fluttered around his throat feeling for a pulse.

"Is that Kazakh for – I know this man?" Pete tried to ignore his building pain and mentally recall and replay the man's words.

"He is Rafi Parzarev's son, you fool. His name is Rishael. He is our new escort."

Whoops.

"Get me a cold wet washcloth." Asya glared at Pete.

Looked like the Asya Conner Memorial Clinic had just acquired a new 'first patient.'

Asya ran the cloth over Rishael's forehead and then gently bathed behind his neck. The man didn't move. She leaned over, placed her fingers on the man's forehead and began soothingly speaking to him. When Rishael finally let out a low moan, Asya kissed his forehead.

"Peter – a pillow." Her voice was demanding and cold.

Pete sat helplessly on the bed for the next ten minutes while Asya knelt on the floor conversing softly with Rishael. Whatever they were saying, the man surely seemed to enjoy attention. Must be a Mommy's boy.

Asya seemed to know a hell of a lot of good-looking men. This one had dark black hair that probably just touched his ears when he stood, but lying flat on the rug as he was, he looked rather like one of the Marx brothers. Harpo came to Pete's mind.

This Rishael was probably about the same build as Rafi, maybe a little taller, six-one or two, with high cheekbones and one of those long aristocratic noses. He also had a glass jaw, so he should stick to soft occupations, like being the President's son. Unfortunately, it was evident he and Asya knew each other well. Maybe she liked the sophisticated touch more than she did mucking around. Pete fingered his own nose, the one that had been broken several times and had developed a tendency to wander off in the direction of his left ear.

Rishael was wearing an expensive blue suit. However, Pete noted with some satisfaction, his red and gray striped tie was no longer neatly centered in his collar. A fall will do that to ya. Rishael's heavy five o'clock shadow and bushy eyebrows, on skin nearly as pale as Asya's... Pete was certainly no expert, but he could see how Rishael might be considered handsome by a limited number of women.

At the moment, one of those was helping him sit up. Anastasia was kneeling beside him on the rug and anxiously watching his every movement. While Pete was positive Rishael was milking the situation for all it was worth, Pete nevertheless leaned forward from the bed and extended his hand, "Tell him I am terribly sorry, Asya, I thought he was a bad guy."

"It was my fault," Rishael said in perfect English, "I shouldn't have been waving my gun around."

Great, now the bastard was being magnanimous!

Rishael ignored Pete's hand, instead wrapping his arm around Asya's waist as she helped him to his feet and over to the chair. She grabbed the other pillow from the bed to soften the hard wooden back.

Pete decided to cut his losses, "I'm going for a walk," he announced, grabbing his coat and shoulder holster. "Why don't you bring Rishael up to speed on what we know and what we suspect." As the door was closing behind him, Pete yelled over his shoulder, "And I'll register him for his own room!"

*

When Pete returned Rishael was lying on their bed, sans suit coat and shoes. Asya was sitting in a chair she had pulled up to the edge of the bed. They were deep in conversation. Pete drank a glass of water from the bathroom tap and stood near the other chair. He had reached an accommodation with his pain, but he intended to minimize his ups and downs for the next few days.

At the first apparent break in the conversation he inserted himself, "Anything I can help fill in or has Anastasia covered everything?"

Rishael asked, "What was your take on Boris?"

"He definitely intended to rape Asya." Pete paused but saw no reaction from Rishael, so perhaps the two of them had already covered this ground, "I got the distinct impression he wanted to punish her because she was talking trash about Russia. He was not drunk, although his associates were."

He at least had Rishael's compete attention, "Part of Boris' bad behavior may have been a challenge to me. He knew I had been a SEAL, maybe from my Internet bio or perhaps from something your father said. He was smart enough to know he would have to kill me to get to Asya, which seemed fine with him." Pete tilted his head, "So, all in all, I would say that I was not too favorably impressed with the man your father sent to 'protect' us…and, as Asya and I have discussed, if I can't trust your father's judgment in people, how can I trust him?" He looked directly at Rishael, "So what is the deal with his son who turns up so conveniently?"

Rishael swung his feet off the bed. Although it was obvious he was dizzy, the younger man began to struggle to his feet. "Peter! Rishael!" Anastasia's tone was apprehensive.

Pete had already walked out most of his anger in the Aqtobe streets. He put a hand in the middle of Rishael's chest to keep him seated, "We are both involved in a game which has very high stakes. For the moment, I am willing to follow Asya's lead and it's very obvious she trusts you."

Rishael's face was red, but, after glancing at Asya, he stayed seated on the bed. He swallowed and then raised the most immediate question in Pete's mind, "What did you think about the telephone number in Boris' book?"

"Asya had just discovered it when you knocked on *our* door." Pete made sure that Rishael heard the possessive. It's still too early back in the States. My contact at the CIA is not at work yet. Do you have any sources?"

"We do, and I already activated them while you were out walking. But all they can tell us is that it is a number from one of your State Department buildings. Boris placed nearly all my father's calls and he may have retained the number from one of those occasions."

"Well," Pete stood, crossed to the bureau and began rummaging through the drawers for the tie he had earlier left behind. "Maybe we should just mosey downstairs and ask Asya's Georgetown friends."

Asya's head snapped back to Pete. "What?" She said.

"When I came in from my walk," Pete watched Asya in the mirror as he flipped his tie around once, then under and grimaced as he pulled it into a loose knot, "imagine my surprise when your friends Winsor Asher and Alex Yates walked in our hotel immediately ahead of me. Apparently, they are dining in our fine restaurant. I thought we might wish to join them."

CHAPTER THIRTY

As the maître d' ed them between the tables, Asya carefully linked her arm with Rishael. She didn't believe he was as steady on his feet as he professed. Pete was in obvious pain, but he was a big boy.

Pete reached the American table first and immediately introduced himself. "Secretaries Asher and Yates, I'm Pete O'Brien. We've briefly met before, but you probably don't remember me." He moved aside to permit Asya and Rishael to step forward. "This gentleman is Rishael Parzarev, the son of the President of Kazakhstan." Rishael inclined his head to the two seated couples. "And, of course, you know Anastasia Conner." She gave the four people at the table a tight smile. For a few brief seconds, she had actually considered staying in the hotel room.

What were the chances this meeting was going to be pleasant? Peter was already unhappy about Rishael. Rishael had never met Alex or Winsor and she would have been just as happy if he never did. She resisted reaching down and running her fingertips over her thigh and along the comforting bump of the leather straps of her sheath. She was reminded of an old movie she had seen on late-night TV in Chicago. In this case, Anastasia was coming. Not for dinner, only for drinks. But she suspected the occasion would prove memorable – just not good.

The men at the table stood. Winsor, the closest, immediately shook Rishael's hand, while Alex made his way around the far end of the table to do the same. He remained there, taking Asya's hand in his. "We've just finished dinner, but won't you and your friends join us for dessert?"

Still holding her hand, Alex turned to introduce his companion: "This is Charlotte. She represents our Embassy here in Astana."

No surprise – Charlotte was a beautiful woman. She was in her early 20s, with large brown eyes and long auburn hair that fell straight to her shoulders. This was probably her first posting out of the United States. She was wearing a form-fitting black knit dress with a deep scoop neck. Did she even speak the language? Asya suddenly realized Alex had intertwined his fingers with hers as he continued speaking in the deprecating manner she had once found charming, "They have provided her as my escort to ensure I don't say anything foolish on my first official trip." Guess she does. Bet he will anyway.

Alex next nodded to the woman sitting next to Winsor, also a very attractive individual, and a person Asya seemed to recall she had previously met. "Mary is the Embassy Protocol Officer. Since this is Winsor's last official State Department visit, they are intent on rendering him full honors. Let's get some chairs. We can all fit around our table." He motioned to a waiter, pulling Asya to sit at his side.

She didn't even bother to look back at Pete. It was time for the Designated Personal Assistant to rise up and save the day. During their silent trip down in the elevator, besides considering if she should immediately take the return elevator back up, she had decided that the tension with Rishael had been largely her fault. She had been first concerned that

Rishael had been injured, and then it had been so many years since she had seen him. She had needlessly pushed Pete past – well, there was probably some fancy psychological term for his emotional point of no return.

Whatever the word, why had she done it, when she already knew she could send him over that particular cliff? It was like teasing a lemming to jump. What was the point? Pete might actually have ruined Rishael's lovely nose – or worse. Asya unwound her fingers from Alex's grasp and stepped away, motioning to the waiter to seat her between Rishael and Pete. Effective Personal Assistants kept their bosses from punching people, especially those few the Congress had voted to confirm – and in public places where pictures might be snapped.

Alex frowned, but finally eased down on the velvet bench next to his assigned Embassy guide. Despite Charlotte's fingers making an obvious move toward his thigh, he continued his bid for Asya's attention, "How in the world did you end up in Kazakhstan? I haven't heard from you since you asked me to feed your cat."

Oh nice, Alex. She could feel a migraine begin to throb behind her left eye, and she hadn't had one since the day before they left Washington.

"Actually," Winsor interceded, raising a hand to gain the attention of the wine steward, "she asked *me* to feed her cat. You were only responsible for watering her plants. And here we sit, both dismal failures. What does everyone want to drink? I think I'll have scotch."

"A Macallan for me – any year," said Alex.

"Ladies" – Asya was going to do her best to change the subject – "do you want to share a bottle of Chardonnay?"

"I'll take a Perrier," Pete said.

"As will I," Rishael added.

Winsor continued, "I was forced to board your precious Pitti-Sing, Anastasia. I hope she's no worse for wear when you return."

He took a breath and she looked at him. Where was he going next? Was Winsor planning to sail past the edge of decency? His eyes had narrowed. Yes. The son of a bitch. He was speaking to her while looking at Pete.

"I left the vet's address on your kitchen counter, underneath that crystal vase you like so much."

Asya caught a quick glimpse of womanly empathy flash across Mary's face before dying behind her diplomatic face.

The steward poured her wine and Asya swirled it. A few seconds respite. A short moment in which she only had to peer into her goblet. Maybe half a minute that she didn't have to look at anyone at the table. Almost 30 seconds until even that bitch Charlotte realized that half the men at this table had keys to her apartment and knew what possessions she valued. And, while Charlotte would not know this, Asya had finally decided she was not interested in any of them.

Thirty seconds to make a decision. One that – drat! – couldn't be solved by a sharp knife. She gave the wine another swirl. Fortunately, dinner conversation waits for no man or woman and it resumed around her. That's life. It is impossible to anticipate life's pivotal events. She dipped her head and let the wine vapors flow up into her soul. A boy had once taken her to watch spring come to a frozen river near their hometown. They were watching the rising waters push and pull. Stumps of trees swirled by, even a dead pig, but nothing extraordinary happened until, suddenly, dirty blocks of winter ice heaved up into the air with a loud crack and, minutes later, a new river channel had been carved from the bank, nearly sweeping her and the boy away.

She curled her tongue into the wine, tasted it, let the alcohol run back into her throat and nodded for the steward to refill her glass. She pushed her hair back as she, like that river's waters, silently chose her new path. She glanced around the table. I hope you got a real good look at my vase, Winsor. Perhaps you even rifled through my underwear. You have seen both for the last time. She took a drink of her wine before glancing down the table at his fraternity brother. Alex, you had better not piss Charlotte off, for you are going to need a new friend in Kazakhstan.

She shook her head, letting her hair fall free, and sat up straight in her chair. Winsor was now speaking to Peter, "…should avoid sailing under any false flags. I'm no longer 'Secretary Asher.' Senator Jones from Utah asked me to be his Chief of Staff and I felt my career could use some Hill seasoning."

Asya leaned forward as if she were listening. She edged closer to Pete, but he did not notice. He was frozen in place. His jaw rigid, lips nearly white. She knew this man. His mind was probably still jammed full of Winsor's jabbering about his past familiarity with her. It was possible his brain was accepting no new information. Time to alter his course. She placed her hand firmly on Pete's forearm.

"Although I truly loved my job at State, I accepted this new Senate role last Friday." Asher chuckled, "I think you've all caught me on my very first Congressional junket."

"Kazakhstan doesn't seem like the normal place for a junket," Asya commented, "I would have thought you'd be in the Caribbean"

Winsor leaned into the deep-cushioned back and put his arm on the top of the loveseat, his forearm just touching Mary's bare shoulders. "I'm just a cog in the wheel." He ignored Asya and focused on burrowing under Pete's skin, saying with what appeared a sense of humility, "It's Pete, isn't it?"

Pete nodded.

"Well, Pete, the Senator has heard some rumors about Kazakhstan instability."

To her left, Asya felt Rishael stiffen as Winsor continued: "And the Senator thinks it would be dangerous to the entire Caucasus region if there were anything going on that might disturb the United States' wonderful friends in Moscow. The Senator couldn't leave Washington right now, since they still haven't gotten the Defense Bill out, so he sent me over to nose around. I thought I would accompany Alex and we would visit Grozny and then travel up to see President Vostrov in Moscow. But while I was in the area, I didn't want to miss calling on my good friends in Kazakhstan. I stopped by the Embassy in Astana and, fortunately, Mary and Charlotte volunteered to be our escorts." Winsor slid his arm down Mary's arm and pulled her closer. His eyes were sparkling.

Alex decided to contribute, "Pete, I sincerely hope the Defense

Department isn't behind the volatility buzz we are hearing about. I can't even imagine what a naval officer is doing here in Aqtobe." He chuckled. "You are certainly a long way from water!"

Charlotte laughed as Winsor added, "Given Asya's facility with languages and the fact that we are old friends, perhaps the best thing would be for her to join our little group. I'm sure the other girls wouldn't mind."

Peter sat his water glass down and placed both his hands flat on the table. His gaze swung slowly back and forth between Alex to Winsor. It was clearly time for the Super Personal Assistant to again don her cloak. It had been a tough 24 hours for the poor man – first the awful roll off the train, then meeting Rishael. She hoped he hadn't bruised his left foot yesterday. Asya lifted her knee and drove her heel directly into Peter's instep. He took in a surprised breath and looked down at her in shock.

She held his eyes for a second, then pursed her lips in a small kiss and slipped her right hand from his forearm down inside his knee. She leaned up and whispered in his ear, "Remind me as soon as we leave to send an email to my landlord. I need to change all the locks on my apartment."

She looked across the table to the fraternity brothers, "Winsor, Alex, do either of you know Boris Valikhonov?"

Alex immediately shook his head no, and Winsor distractedly answered, "No, I don't think so. Should I?"

Asya raised her hand and placed it possessively on Pete's arm. "Peter and Boris got into a fight yesterday and Peter roughed him up rather badly. When he was asking Peter to stop, I thought I heard him cry out Winsor's name."

Pete should not look so surprised. Spies were taught to lie, and she had been an ace student. Not everyone was an officer in the US Navy.

Alex's gaze was focused on Pete, "Did you kill him?"

Pete remained silent. A good choice, since he had no idea where she was going with this. Actually, she was having second thoughts on sharing with Pete every little bit of training she had received; he might not approve.

"No, Peter only knocked him silly. I told the police to hold Boris on assault charges until Rafi can decide what to do with him."

"Rafi?" Alex seemed unfamiliar with the name.

Asya began playing with the black hairs on the back of Peter's hand as she replied, "Kazakhstan President Rafi Parzarev, Rishael's father. Boris was an assistant to Rafi and originally assigned to be our guide."

Alex changed the direction of the conversation away from her question, which, as one of her spycraft instructors had often pointed out, was in itself interesting, "What are you doing that is so important President Parzarev would provide – Boris, was it? – and now his own son as your guide?"

"President Rafi specifically asked for Pete to do an inspection of Kazakhstan's military facilities," Asya replied, as she linked the fingers of her right hand with those of Peter's left. "We are headed for the 36th Air Assault Battalion in Rudnyy."

Rishael gently corrected: "Actually, we moved them another city northward last year. The Battalion is now deployed in Kokshetau."

Alex's scotch was sitting forgotten on the table, the ice nearly melted. He was quizzically looking at Pete. "Why you?"

This question was in Pete's wheelhouse. "It's a joint world, Mr Secretary. One military facility is pretty much like any other."

"Well" – Alex had turned to Charlotte – "How convenient. Kokshetau was one of the places we were planning to stop by on our way to Chechnya." Alex raised his eyes to Pete. "The Embassy can dig up another car and then we'll be able to drive there together. I'll look forward to a pleasant and instructive day."

Peter shook his head, gaining his voice. "No."

"No, Captain?"

"No, Mr Secretary. I am on a mission for the Secretary of Defense, and since you have a representative of a key member of Congress in your party, we essentially represent two different branches of the government. I believe it would be best to keep our visits just as separate. If you let me have your schedule, I will endeavor to keep out of your way."

Apparently, her Peter thought very clearly when she was holding his hand.

"Captain" – Winsor's eyes had gone darker and his voice harder –

"Senator Jones is right now poring over your Secretary's budget. I don't think the Senator would be too pleased if he knew you were ignoring my simple suggestion. You know I speak for him."

Asya squeezed Peter's hand to cause him to pause while she kicked Rishael in the shin. It was time for reinforcements. Grozny, for God's sake!

Rishael finally joined the conversation. "Actually, I must protest your planned travel schedule. I do not believe my father had any idea you intended to travel from Kazakhstan to Chechnya to Russia, and I think this travel pattern might well be viewed as provocative by one or more parties."

"What do you mean?" Alex exclaimed.

"My father and I don't encourage Americans to perform official travel between these countries. That route offers the opportunity to attract unwanted attention."

Winsor exploded: "That is unacceptable!"

Rishael stood. "We are sorry you think so." He inclined his head and stood. "I appreciate your hospitality, but I need to call my father and report. We also have an early-morning departure. I recommend you check with your embassy before you depart for Grozny. Even if has been previously approved, I must officially notify you that it is both dangerous and ill-advised."

As they stood and moved away, Asya held tightly on to Pete's hand, ignoring any handshakes and moving him steadily toward the elevator. Rishael could find his room on his own. She was determined to get Pete out of the restaurant without incident. This Personal Assistant stuff was not easy. She might need to ask for a raise.

CHAPTER THIRTY-ONE

Rishael, Asya and Pete were underway well before dawn the next morning, headed northeast in a pair of Kazakh army jeeps. The drivers were members of Rishael's personal security detail. Four armed soldiers were crowded into the lead jeep, leaving the other vehicle for the three civilians. Asya directed Rishael into the front seat, and spread a thick blanket over her own and Pete's laps in the back. Rishael and Asya catnapped while the city disappeared behind them.

They stopped for coffee and gas at Qarabutaq. Rishael described what he expected while they stretched their legs: "We will stop for lunch in another three hours, then it will be about another 400 klicks to the missiles – quite a deserted area – nothing else between here and there. It's forecast to start snowing heavily sometime today. I want to get as far as we can before it does.

Pete leaned forward. "Who's guarding them?"

"We only learnt of the site's existence a few months ago. Apparently, the Soviets just sealed it off and left. The camp is now secured by a platoon of Kazakhs drawn from the 38th Air Assault Unit." He saw the silent criticism in Pete's eyes. "I know. But we don't have sufficient resources. And there is no indication anyone knows about them. There was no evidence the site had ever been disturbed. Probably because it is such a desolate area. There has never even been a whisper about the missiles. We had no idea they even existed until a former Russian soldier was arrested for armed robbery in Astana last year. He shot a policeman and was looking to..." Rishael looked at Asya for help.

"Plea bargain," she said.

Pete couldn't accept that nuclear weapons had been lying unguarded for decades! Didn't people recognize the danger? Didn't they realize they were dealing with plutonium and... He felt Asya's fingers on his arm. She had removed her glove and her fingers were slowly running up and down his scar. She was slightly shaking her head. Her eyes were looking at Rishael, but Pete knew her non-verbal message was intended for the man beneath her fingers. She was right – there was no real purpose in getting upset about something that was beyond Rishael's control. Pete took a deep breath and started back toward the jeep. Outside, the world was running just fine. The sun was bright. The skies were clear. People were enjoying their lives. As only one example, amateur pilots of several small planes over Qarabutaq were taking the opportunity to enjoy the break in the weather. He took another deep breath. In fact, it was all good. No more sitting around, no more planes or trains. No more feints. No more delays. They should be at the cave shortly after nightfall. It was a pace more to his liking.

He started to ask another question about security at the cave, but Asya's fingers closed around his wrist and she leaned her head against his arm. Another thing she was right about. A wise soldier never turned down the opportunity to sleep with a beautiful girl in his arms. He got back in the car.

When they stopped for lunch, Rishael asked to sit in the back corner of the restaurant and the soldiers took tables near the front. The men not only brought their Kalashnikovs into the café, but only three ate at any one time. The other two watched the front door, kitchen, windows and other patrons, eyes constantly moving, rifles lying at the ready across their laps.

Pete was impressed with their professionalism. "Rishael, those guys are on fairly high alert. Do you expect Boris to be around here somewhere?"

"No, Boris may be a threat, but Father has always worried more about Chechens. The Caucasus is only a couple of hundred klicks away. It is an unsettled area. Just like the Kurds when the British split up the Middle East, the Chechens feel they were…" he paused, his brow furrowed, and he looked at Anastasia "…what's the phrase? *Trakhat…*"

"Screwed," Asya provided.

"Right. They anticipated receiving their own homeland when the Soviet Union broke up. When they didn't, all hell broke loose. All the Caucasus – Armenia, Georgia, Azerbaijan, Dagestan, North and South Ossetia, even Iran – is a hotbed of unrest, but Father believes the Chechens are the wild card in our region."

Rishael took a deep drink of the dark tea he had been served. "We have no reason to believe they know about our" – he looked around the room – "things, much less the location, but he doesn't want to take any chances. The men with us today are part of the team that normally serves as Father's bodyguards."

The comment "Like Boris?" was on the tip of Pete's tongue, but he swallowed the words.

Rishael cut and ate a small piece of melon. "Now that Father has the necessary political support lined up, we need to move quickly before opposition reforms. If a random group approaches us, these are six of our best soldiers, and we should be able to successfully resist any chance raid." He sliced and ate another forkful of melon. "However, if we get hit with a company-sized attack, since I'm the only one who knows exactly where we're headed, those men will ensure I die first."

Rishael used his knife to cut yet another small piece and slowly chewed it. "Our dangerous neighbors are one of the reasons Father tried to give away all our nuclear weapons to President Clinton as soon as we were independent." The edges of his mouth twisted up. "Now we find we inadvertently missed more than a few."

Rishael motioned toward the jeeps. "We had better drive before the weather closes in. We'll get another break in an hour or two, when we have to put chains on the tires, but I recommend we skip dinner and push on while we still have daylight. The area we're headed for is only plowed once or twice a month and if we're late, we could easily get snowed out."

It was too noisy to easily talk in the jeep. Pete consequently had a couple of hours to mentally review recent events. Anastasia was also quiet, and he wondered if she were regretting publicly dumping both Alex and Winsor. He was comforted when she snuggled under his arm, tucking her feet under her in the seat. She reached for his hand and slipped it between the buttons on her coat and held his palm flat against her warm stomach just below her breasts.

Pete looked out of the window as the sun marched west. After a while, he realized he was mindlessly looking at the shadow patterns from the setting sun, of the jeep with their luggage on the roof, and the hummocks of drifted snow. Somewhere in the sky, a small plane droned its way among the clouds, its darker shadow intermittently intersecting with the grays in the swales of snow. It was a picture he knew he would always take home with him of the Steppes of Kazakhstan.

They changed drivers every hour, stopped to refuel again and forged onward. About dusk, the road shifted from concrete to groomed snow, which reduced the rumble from the road. Pete fell asleep, waking once only to hear Anastasia and Rishael quietly conversing in Kazakh. He kept his eyes closed. He didn't understand what she was saying but she sounded comfortable. That was not the best news. The longer she was here, the more he feared she was tempted to return to her native Kazakhstan. Damn, damn, damn!

"Dear Peter, are you all right? You are flushed." He felt her wrist against his forehead, "I think you are running a fever."

Anyone would be sick. Life around Asya was enough to wear a man down.

"How are your ribs?" She ran her hand down the bristle on his right cheek.

Not well, that's for sure. "Fine."

She leaned away from him and pulled at the tail of his coat, "Remove your coat and lie down in my lap. I will spread it over the top of the blanket and you. How long until we reach the cave, Rishael?"

"Several more hours. But now that he is awake, I should explain to Pete how the Soviets successfully hid the SS-9 missiles. It was an impressive engineering feat. They had to transport each one more than a hundred klicks from the Derzhavinsk missile field to the cave."

"You can tell me and I will make sure Peter hears about it later." Asya was unbuttoning her coat and spreading it out in order to fit Pete's head on her lap. "He is still healing. He needs sleep."

He let her position his head so his cheek lay on one pleasantly warm thigh. Might as well go with the flow.

The next time Pete awoke, it was dark. The two jeeps had turned off the highway, geared down and begun grinding through six inches of snow. He sat up. Ahead, he could see a crease between two of the foothills. High above them moonlight glinted off snow-covered slopes.

As they drove into the cleft, the road narrowed and the walls quickly rose on either side. Each few thousand yards of progress, the dark on the canyon floor deepened as less and less moonlight was reflected down the canyon sides. As the road narrowed over the next few miles, Pete thought he could occasionally glimpse light from somewhere up ahead. Finally, they crested a small rise, and a security post came into view, along with its barbed-wire gate. A single bare light bulb hung on the post anchoring the gate.

Pete tapped Rishael on the shoulder, "Is this it?"

Rishael nodded.

"Isn't it a hell of a bad location?"

"It's where the missiles are."

"Yeah, I understand that, but is there another way out?"

"No. We passed an aircraft runway a couple of miles before we reached the mouth of the canyon. I think you were asleep. It's not normally maintained, but I'm sure Father could have someone land there if the snow were sufficiently cleared. Plows and diesel fuel are stored nearby to work that runway and also to clear the canyons after avalanches."

Interesting, but not precisely what Pete had asked and also not terribly comforting. They were several miles into a dead-end canyon. The only way out was apparently subject to the whims of avalanches. Not what one might term an optimal military outpost.

After the two gate guards took a relatively obligatory look at the identification and visit authorizations Rishael had in his briefcase, they raised the simple wooden barrier. A half-mile later, the road made a sweeping right-hand turn and abruptly ran up against a sheer granite face.

The jeeps stopped on a flat area short of the rock, near several Quonset huts. Standing in front of the huts, apparently alerted by the gate guards, several men and women were gathered in two ranks. As Rishael, Pete and Asya alighted, the senior officer, a relatively junior *Sharshiy Leitenant*, stepped forward. He introduced his small military security detachment. The unit, except for the Sergeant, were all in their teens or early 20s. As a visiting senior officer, Pete walked the two ranks, shaking hands with each of the nine troops. He was also introduced to the two scientists assigned to monitor the condition of the stored missiles. One of the engineers appeared to be in his late 60s, while the other was much younger.

Three of the security attachment offered to help with the visitors' luggage and showed them to their rooms. Pete merely dropped his gear on the bed, grabbed Rishael and went to find the Lieutenant. He was anxious to examine the site. Construction in the compound was sparse – a row of five concrete pads, each topped by its own metal Quonset hut. Between each pad, eight feet of elevated planking served as a walkway, linking the huts above the snow.

There were three sleeping huts, one of which was for the officers and

VIPs; a communal living and eating area, with an honor bar that held at least a dozen brands of vodka; and a fifth Quonset that contained the power plant. In the latter, two diesels were fed fuel through copper piping from large oil drums that rested on their own concrete pads outside in the snow. The low, steady diesel hum vibrated unpleasantly through the soles of Pete's shoes when he stood on the pads, but the noise was nearly unnoticeable in the sleeping huts.

After a quick perusal of the power plant, he returned outside, into the cold mountain air. Rishael followed and, after a moment's hesitation, so did the Lieutenant. Pete needed to get a feel for the compound, and perspective was always better acquired on foot.

Within 15 minutes, he knew more than he wanted to. Even a naval officer didn't have to walk very far here to get damn uncomfortable. For example, there were no concrete barriers. There was no concertina wire, no machine-gun emplacements, no fire lanes, no tank traps, no mines and no kill zones.

Essentially no protective measures in place.

At the face of the cave, the canyon became very narrow, with sides rising higher than he could see. Pete walked back down the road a couple of hundred yards until he had the guard gate in sight. Further up the road, there were no lights other than the one bare bulb at the guard shack. The Lieutenant was visibly anxious to go back inside, and Pete motioned him to do so. The snow had stopped. Starlight filtered out from behind the remaining clouds.

He frowned. Asya would probably think it was lovely. It was pretty all right – pretty awful! They had no idea where Boris was – the same Boris he should have shot when he had the chance – and they were in the middle of the desert with no one to call for assistance. Who knew how many nuclear weapons there were in the cave! And with only a dozen kid soldiers to call on if something went wrong!

It was almost like sticking a sign in the ground saying "Plutonium – Cheap – Come and Get It!"

No one could reasonably expect Winsor or Alex to sit on their butts in Kokshetau. Who knew what their real games were? The only thing he was sure of was that it was past time to get Asya the hell out of here and back to America. Pete turned to start back to the main Quonset hut and bumped into the silent Rishael, who had been standing behind him.

Speaking of guys with unknown agendas.

Another reason to get the hell out of Dodge.

CHAPTER THIRTY-TWO

Amazing products could be produced using satellite photography and Abdulbek was presently examining a couple. The beautiful secretary in the pencil skirt was gone from the room next to his office. In her place was a pair of oak tables and accompanying dioramas. One was alive in the bright colors indigenous to Hong Kong. Thousands of shoppers were frozen mid-step at the Ladies' Market. Such precise verisimilitude! The scene even included Nelson Street, Mong Kok MTR station and a slice of Victoria Harbour.

The second table was more soothing to Abdulbek's eye. He supposed it was because he had spent those years at Oxford. Blue, green and granite-gray caressed the eye as the low islands and hump-backed bridges of Russia's St Petersburg nudged themselves up out of the mist that was drifting to the floor.

Economic engines that would both soon grind to an absolute halt, throwing their countries into upheaval.

"You like?"

"Very impressive, Abdulbek. Surprisingly classy."

"The man not know shit as a warrior. But he look at pictures good." Abdulbek pulled out his knife from its sheaf and reflectively honed it on the leather strip that always hung from his belt. "My sister's son. A mouth that must be fed."

Abdulbek's guest stepped to the Hong Kong table and ran his finger along the papier-mâché path the Chechens would take after they entered Victoria Harbour, "Each missile has seven warheads. Each

195

warhead contains eight kilos of plutonium. What do you intend?"

"Only need one missile. I have a man who swears he can divide the plutonium."

If he can't, his guest thought, the world's Chechnya 'problem' might be settled in a rather unorthodox manner.

"One stroll through the Ladies Market and Hong Kong is finished." Abdulbek brought his knife down in the middle of Nelson Street.

His guest turned to look at the other diorama, watching as the shifting fog slowly exposed one building and hid another. "And in Russia?"

"In St Petersburg, women with handbags join tours through museum. Then dump purses in the underground tourist shops."

It was hard not to catch his host's excitement. The guest drummed his fingers on the edge of the St Petersburg table. "When tourists start dying, no one is going to want to trade with China or Russia for a long, long time!"

Abdulbek was sharpening his knife on the leather strip. "I already recruited the martyrs." Suddenly, his grin turned to a grimace. "But where is the plutonium? I paid half." He flipped his knife so it whipped by the shoulder of the guest and sunk, with an audible thud, in the doorjamb.

His guest's voice instantly turned cold. "Don't play games with me. We both expect your cousin to have the location before the day is out."

"Bor...?" Abdulbek clenched his teeth tight.

"Right, Abdulbek – your cousin, Boris. I know about Boris. I know lots of things. I know about the tap you have in my Georgetown living room. I know about the janitor in our apartment block. I know your Zurich account number at Credit Suisse." Abdulbek snapped his head back in surprise. "I even know about that Muslim girl you killed in Paris. You, on the other hand, should know that all $22m in your Credit Suisse account will be instantly missing if ever I am even five minutes late leaving a meeting with you."

He continued in a flat tone. "You may play with knives to your heart's content, but don't begin to think you can control me. The United States is not a banana republic and I am not a figurehead."

The guest let a few seconds of silence fill the room before he folded his hands together over his stomach and looked around again at the room displays. Working with psychopaths could be occasionally edgy, but oh-so-rewarding financially, and sometimes rocking good fun. He was fortunate to have a slight psycho-bent himself. "This is certainly a very nice diorama. Please give your sister my compliments for her son's work. Are you comfortable with our plan?"

"Fuck you!"

"Good. I'm off to see your friends in Russia. I will be sure to convey to them your good wishes. Have Boris call me."

Asya was pleased to see Pete finish whatever he had been doing outside and enter the main Quonset hut. She had some interesting things to show him. She scooted over on the bench to make room and began translating as soon he sat down.

"The Lieutenant says he is honored with your presence. They have not had a visitor since he arrived with his detachment. He wants to know if you would like the television on? They are very proud of climbing the mountain to put up an antenna that receives the signal re-broadcast out of Arqalyk."

"No. I would like to look in the cave and get back to Astana."

Certainly not the best way to open a walnut, as her mother used to say. Peter always used a smashing hammer and sometimes a walnut tasted immeasurably better if a person would stop to apply a cracker and a sharp pick. "Peter, where are your manners? We are their guests. They are anxious for us to share their plain soldiers' lives for an evening." She gave him a sweet smile and interlaced their fingers, "The Lieutenant is sorry we drove in at night. In the morning, he wishes to show you his beautiful valley. He assures us the engineering marvel of their cave is best seen by daylight."

"I'm going to regret this, but I'll give him 10 minutes – how *did* they build it without our satellites picking it up?"

She turned to the Lieutenant and quietly spoke to him. He nodded once and sprang from his seat to disappear in the direction of the sleeping hut.

The Lieutenant returned in a few minutes with several rolls of maps and blueprints, all of which he spread out on the table. He secured the curling corners with salt and pepper shakers, leaving a large-area map on top. He then began speaking rapidly, tracing a point in the mountains back down the road toward Derzhavinsk, the town where they had last stopped to fill the jeeps with gas.

Asya turned to Peter, "Saken was told, since he was not here, being merely a child at the time, that the Soviets constructed a road and hauled rock from their mountain excavation to line the bank of the Ishim river at Derzhavinsk. The rubble was used to prevent flood and erosion damage in the bend where the river turns east toward Astana."

Asya waved in the general direction of the northeast, "The large engineering project was merely a ploy. The real purpose was to provide an explanation for your photo interpreters if they ever questioned a new road from the missile field at Derzhavinsk out to the mountains."

"You should let Saken know you are old enough to be his mother."

Anastasia let her eyes roll, but she continued, "Perhaps a slightly older sister, Peter, but certainly not his mother." She turned back to the Lieutenant and asked a question. Saken nodded, carefully rerolled the map and addressed the blueprint on top.

"He says the cave is 180 meters deep, nearly 30 meters high and 70 meters wide. It was cut out of solid granite by rock-boring machines." She was beginning to better learn what made Peter's engine tick over. She just needed to remember to frequently initiate skin-to-skin contact... "Over the retractable entrance, which itself is 12 meters high and 15 meters wide, they left a large rock overhang." Learning 'Peter-talk' was a simple enough adjustment – certainly not as hard as doing a hundred stomach curls, and she had done that each and every morning for years... So, the entrance was concealed from American satellites."

She could see Pete mentally making the conversion of meters to feet. It was easier for Europeans, who were more adapted to the awkward measuring system used by America. Math had always been one of her better subjects, so she had quickly done the same calculation earlier, while he was out in the snow tromping about without her. She even had a pencil sketch in her breast pocket, but it would be a cold day in hell before she would show it to the man who had invited Rishael to walk outside with him instead of her.

So far, the Lieutenant's description was consistent, especially with no railway in the vicinity. The dimensions he had quoted were about right. The cave would have to be large enough for flatbed trucks to drive the missiles into place. Now all Peter had to do was confirm there actually were SS-9s in the cave. It was nearly time to get the Secretary of Defense on the telephone. She had even looked up the number. It was at the bottom of the same piece of paper. In her pocket. For when Peter asked for her help.

Pete interrupted Saken, "Ten minutes are up, Lieutenant. Time to open the cave."

Asya frowned, "Peter!" The man wouldn't recognize honey if it came complete with bees and a picture.

"I know it is impolite, but figure out some way to say it nicely. I'm uncomfortable being at the end of a dead-end canyon." Pete ticked off additional reasons by tapping her on the end of her nose: "Two, if there are missiles in that cave, I think it is vital to get our Presidents talking as soon as possible, and three, the security here is atrocious. Kazakhstan is sitting squarely atop a nuclear powder keg and wouldn't know how to guard apple butter from a hoard of marauding Mennonites."

Asya didn't know whether to break his finger or kiss him, and he could be a little more gracious, with Rishael sitting right here, but the latter didn't seem to be taking offense, so she decided simply to stand, pausing just a bit to let Peter know he was not completely in charge and, of course, he then had to push just a bit too far. "Let's move! Tonight, Anastasia! Kiss your little soldier-boy goodbye and let's get this show on the road."

That was certainly uncalled for. She hadn't seen him doing any crash course in Kazakh interpretation lately. If he thought Rishael was going to help him, he had another surprise coming!

She spoke to Saken, and, as the latter rose from the table, she stood with him, kissing him softly on the cheek as she did. The Lieutenant turned and hurried from the hut, his face noticeably flushed.

Asya deliberately widened her eyes as she turned to Peter. "We'd better get our coats – Saken says it's cold in the cave. He has gone to have his people open the door and turn on the lights."

As Peter and Asya passed between the huts on the way to their rooms, he put his hand on her waist. "You didn't have to actually kiss him."

"Learn to be a little more sensitive and I won't."

CHAPTER THIRTY-THREE

"What's your situation, Boris?"

He began to smile as Boris relayed the details. This was one Chechen who could control his emotions.

Of course, he had paid him enough. And the man could organize, which was another very un-Chechen characteristic! Certainly, the detachment of troops he had put together today was impressive. Thankfully, there had been some Russians at Derzhavinsk who knew the value of money. That communism thing had certainly worn off quickly enough! Boris said they were less than an hour from the canyon. This phase of the plan should be completed well before sunrise.

He fed the man the praise he lived for and then cut the rest of the conversation short. He had another call to make. It was hell being the principal organizer, but the fewer people involved, the bigger the pie, and a man had to make a living.

"Abdulbek. Did you give your sister my message about her son's good work?" He held the phone out away from his ear for the reply.

"Good. Are you prepared to transfer the money to my Credit Suisse account?"

He listened for several seconds before losing his patience, "Now or never. You are either real or a pretender. I know you have the money. I get mine within the next hour or you kiss the plutonium goodbye. But," he paused, "if my account rings, you will become famous. Both Russia and China will quake like aspens."

The right-hand side of his mouth turned down as he listened to the reply, "It is an American expression, like *konakhalla* is a Chechen one. It means you will get what you want if I receive what I need." He looked at his phone in exasperation. Chechens took guidance no better than teenage boys. He reluctantly held the phone near his ear. "Call me back when the money has left your account."

Abdulbek had been an ass recently. Perhaps he should move a couple of million out of the man's Swiss account simply for that knife-throwing trick. That would send a message.

*

When Pete and Asya arrived, the lights in the cave were on and the heavy steel door to the cave entrance had already been raised eight or nine feet. The temperature inside was well below zero. Beneath their feet, the swirling wind was constructing lacy designs of snow crystals on the rock floor near the door.

As soon as Rishael joined them, Pete requested he have the jeeps reloaded with everyone's luggage while the other soldiers adopted defensive posts near the door. "If you and I inspect the missiles together, I can't see the task requiring much more than an hour." He paused and thought for a second, this time including Asya in his query. "Once we are on the road, how long before we are back in Aqtobe? I don't know when our hourglass turned, but I'm sure the sand is running fast. The longer we're here, the more I want to be somewhere else." She nodded her agreement.

Rishael ventured a rare grin, "I have good news. I just called Father. He plans to helo in a heavy-construction team as soon as day breaks. They will run a snowplow up and down the landing strip outside the canyon mouth. As soon as one runway is clear, he will dispatch an airplane. With decent weather, we should be in Astana tomorrow. He is arranging for you to be taken back to America on the night courier plane."

If it were true, that was good, but Pete was surprised communications were even possible here in the mountains. His own cell phone hadn't had a single signal bar since early yesterday. "You can't possibly have phone service out here in the middle of nowhere." He had also noticed Rishael had not been entirely specific about who was flying back.

"We use satellites instead of towers. It's expensive," he held up a telephone several times larger than Pete's cell phone, "and much bulkier. They don't work 24/7, but they work everywhere sometime, even in these mountains."

Pete turned to Asya, "How about you remain with the Lieutenant and try to keep him occupied – without kissing him." In reaction, he got a quick lift at the corners of her mouth. "Meanwhile, Rishael and

I will climb up the scaffolding and get the serial numbers of those missiles." Her mouth curled down again at being left out of the physical part of the job.

Pete knew what was bothering her, but somebody had to watch Saken. In addition, the missiles were large and Rishael was at least a foot taller. Besides, who knew what they would find. Nope – Pete was not taking the chance of her being hurt.

She asked, "Wouldn't pictures be even better?"

"A great idea – you and Saken take photos of the numbers which can be seen from the floor of the cave while Rishael and I get some exercise locating the numbers which can only be seen from above."

Pete handed one of Saken's clipboards to Rishael. "We have to cover an area about the size of a soccer field. Let's walk the cave together and make sure we understand what's here. First, I want to look at the motors. The stability of those things deteriorates with age and we may well need to request an explosive ordnance-disposal team."

They began at the far end of the cave and Pete was immediately surprised, "Rishael! Some of the firing squibs are still in place!"

The President's son had only a mildly interested look on his face.

Pete frowned. "Sorry, I know this is technical stuff. But these motors are filled with something more powerful than dynamite. The only different is this explodes more slowly – or 'burns', in rocket terminology – in order to start these big rockets moving upward."

The word 'dynamite' at least got Rishael's attention.

Pete continued explaining. "After the rocket is safely off the ground, the liquid-propellant lights off to get the missile up to supersonic speeds. The 'squibs' are the electrical firing fuses for the dynamite. They never ever should be left even in the vicinity of a motor. An ignited rocket motor would burn everything in this cave to a crisp! Once lit, there is no way to turn a rocket off! Whoever dumped these missiles was in a hell of a hurry!"

The squib discovery raised the hair on the back on Pete's neck. This whole cave was worse than a firetrap!

However, as soon as they had looked at the first missile, Pete realized he had seriously underestimated just how long it was going to take to acquire the serial numbers. There was wooden inspection scaffolding over each missile, but it was still a 30-foot climb up followed by an 80-foot balanced walk, without handrails, atop a round missile body, just to be able to see the engine serial numbers.

He was in good shape, but he was wearing leather shoes. Not the best outfit for this high-wire stunt. He was halfway down the body of his second missile when he suddenly stopped. He had been about to step on a suspiciously discolored section! He called over to the adjacent missile.

"Rishael. Stop where you are!"

Missiles had lots of unique smells. If whoever had hidden these had done their stowage jobs correctly, they would have drained the unstable chemicals that powered the rockets through space. But Pete's nose had been assaulted by the acrid smells of deteriorating complex chemicals as soon as he had stepped into the cave.

He had expected some residuals in a confined environment, but now, 50 feet in the air, he realized the odor was extremely strong. It wasn't because the cave wasn't ventilated. Somewhere up in the dark, there was a large overhead exit to the outside. In fact, snow crystals occasionally flew by him that were coming all the way from the door of the cave.

With that much air flow, this strong an ammonia odor indicated a great deal of hypergolic liquid was still around – after decades of storage! Pete knelt down and ran his index finger along the metal toward the discolored area. It felt like normal titanium for less than an inch and then his finger glided into something slippery and the pad began to burn.

He immediately called across the cave, "Rishael, back up. Let's get down. This is too dangerous. We'll do it with pictures."

Pete removed his shirt, spat in it and began trying to scrub the hypergolic fluid from his finger while he watched Rishael carefully turn around to start back. He should have asked Asya to help; she was the gymnast, for Christ's sake. No, not a problem, Rishael was going to make it. He was already within 30 feet of the scaffolding. But Pete could see the continual balancing during the last half-hour had tired him. He probably did a desk job for his father. But he was almost safe. Asya would never know Pete had made another judgment mistake. She was busy with the Lieutenant, who was probably still trying to make an impression on her. Even while he was climbing missiles, Pete had been watching the two of them. She certainly had that little "hand on a man's arm" trick down pat. Some men's arms must be wired straight to their groins. The Lieutenant had been moving the massive front door slowly up and down and demonstrating how the huge traveling cranes ran the missiles back and forth across the rough rock ceiling.

Just as Rishael was nearly within the safety of the scaffolding frame, the crane over his missile jerked alive. He startled, his hand reaching out for and missing the wooden structure. His tall frame tipped and, in slow motion, overbalanced his body, which slid from the missile, gathering speed as his hip caromed off the side. He managed to grab a four by six joist about midway down, where he swung back and forth once, vainly trying to thrust his leg up on the scaffolding before he slowly, painfully, lost his grip and fell heavily to the floor.

Pete heard him yell, "Asya! Help!"

Rishael was only unconscious for a few seconds, but he had suffered at least a fracture of his left leg. This decided it for Pete. Getting all the missiles verified was no longer necessary. It was time to leave. He wanted out of the canyon. The night was still relatively clear, but heavy clouds, which blocked out starlight in the western sky, foretold the coming of another blanket of snow. His priority was to get Rishael to the nearest town and proper medical attention.

Within a half-hour, Rishael's leg had been splinted and he had been situated sitting up in the back seat of one of the jeeps. Saken had assembled his people by the cave entrance and they were filing by the jeep to shake Rishael's hand. When Saken reached Asya, he expectantly leaned forward. With a mischievous sideways grin at Pete, she solemnly took the Lieutenant's hand and shook it vigorously.

Since he neither spoke nor understood Kazakh, Pete had moved a little apart from the group exchanging final pleasantries. Standing as he was, away from the conversations, he could hear the mountain night sounds more clearly. It was surprising how many owls were busily hunting before the new snow began to fall. As he listened, he could hear something totally unfamiliar. He raised his voice to get Asya's attention: "Listen!"

"What?"

"Have everyone be quiet for a moment!"

"*Teekheey! Slishat!*"

Within a few seconds, the last conversation died away and the drone of a small airplane, apparently flying high above the clouds, was now clear.

Saken murmured something quietly and Asya quickly translated: "He says there should be no aircraft here. This is a restricted area."

Pete had closed his eyes to enhance his senses. "There's also something else out there. Have them shut off the jeeps."

Asya reached into the nearest vehicle, twisting the ignition key counter-clockwise while giving a cutting motion to the driver of the second vehicle. As the engines abruptly stopped, Pete could discriminate between the low rumble of the Quonset generator diesel, the drone of the plane, a few high-pitched pings as the jeep engines quickly began to cool, and something he couldn't quite identify.

"Kamazs!" one of the soldiers exclaimed. The four not already in the jeeps immediately began running up the road toward the gate.

Whatever the undefined noise was, it was coming from the canyon road. Pete caught up with the soldiers in a few strides. As they reached the bend, the guard structure came in sight. Beyond it, a dozen troop trucks passed through a shaft of moonlight. They were barreling up the snowy road, lights out, nearly upon the post!

The gate guards had also seen the trucks. As Pete watched, a red warning light atop the shack came on and began slowly rotating and pulsing to mark the gate. One guard stepped out of the structure and fired his rifle twice into the air.

The truck caravan did not pause. Suddenly, the guard shack disintegrated under automatic heavy-weapon fire from the lead truck. Pete saw the guard outside the shack cut in half, while the body of the second one was flung, along with the shack's desk, through the back wall of the small building. The loud echoes of gunfire rolled up the canyon, over Pete and his small team, hit the cave face and reverberated back.

"Back! Cave!" Pete ordered and motioned them before him. The four soldiers ran. The trucks were less than a mile away. It was two hundred yards to the cave. The vehicles could probably do no more than 30 miles an hour in the snow. It was going to be close.

Pete stopped for a second, sliding in the several inches of snow. He filled his lungs and yelled at the group by the cave. "Anastasia!"

The smallest figure, which had begun running toward him, stopped.

"Cave. Everyone. Get Rishael in. Close door. Now!"

He saw her turn back and begin waving everyone inside. She grabbed a soldier and turned toward the jeep. As soon as she did, Pete put his effort into catching the four soldiers, who had opened up nearly a 50-yard lead while he stopped to yell the warning. His right knee began to burn with pain. It could not lock up now!

A hundred meters from the cave he had closed the gap in half. He saw Asya and a soldier lifting Rishael into the cave. For his sake, he hoped the Kazakh was still in shock. However, the door wasn't moving closed yet. Pete again slowed and yelled, "Now, Asya! Close! Now!"

Behind him, there was a loud metallic crash that could only be the first truck driving through the remains of the gate. He had lost ground when he slowed to shout his warning. He lurched into a run, his right thigh afire.

At 80 meters, Pete could see the door shudder once before slowly beginning to descend. His lungs were hurting from the cold and the high altitude. He wasn't sure he could run the last hundred in ten flat. Of course, I never could. Then, there's also the snow, but bullets are always an incentive.

Pete focused on the bottom of the door. Forty yards to go. Two of the soldiers ducked underneath. Now the other two were there safely.

The open space was down to six feet. The last one was crouched just inside the doorway urging him on. The door seemed to be gathering speed as it got lower. Pete was out of breath; his feet were slipping in the snow, his leg heavy. It was like the last hundred feet of the Ohio relays during his freshman year – that had been the slowest time he had ever run. He had not medaled then. Tonight looked like delivering similar returns but more serious results!

Behind him, the trucks were suddenly louder. They must be at the bend in the road. Twenty yards to go. The door was less than three feet off the concrete apron, maybe two. Pete closed his eyes for a second, leaned forward and forced his legs to churn faster. He could feel his damaged knee beginning to seize. At ten yards, he could still see light from the cave beneath the door. Pete took three more strides, threw himself at the bottom of the door. Maybe there would be some protection near the bottom –

A blow on his back pushed him through!

The door slammed against the cave floor with a dull metal thud as heavy bullets rang off the heavy steel. The noise was deafening. Nearly everyone was holding both hands over their ears. Asya was standing in the electrical control room by the door, wrapping a bandage around the Lieutenant's right hand.

She was safe! Pete let his eyes close.

CHAPTER THIRTY-FOUR

Asya had positioned herself on the floor between the blankets where the two injured men lay. It was very quiet in the cave while they waited for Pete to regain consciousness. Except for a few distorted echoes of lone conversations, it had been that way since Pete had rolled under the door. Rishael was resting easily, his broken leg slightly elevated by a wooden pallet, but Pete was in obvious pain. Only the pressure of the heel of her hand against his warm chest kept his body from continually twisting under the thin blanket they had found. The cave contained meager medical supplies. They didn't have bags of blood, antibiotics, or anyone with training. It was actually lucky Rishael had gotten hurt. That had caused them to retrieve the medical kit from the huts before they were attacked.

Pete suddenly regained consciousness and struggled to sit up, "Did you get everyone in?" he croaked. She used her palm to keep him down flat, "Yes, except for those two poor men on guard duty." His chest seemed warmer than she thought it should. Why hadn't there been a thermometer in that medical bag?

"I'm thirsty." He shivered and she took her coat from her lap and spread it over his blanket.

She directed a few Kazakh words to a soldier, explaining to Pete, "Someone will find water."

She watched his eyelids drift closed. She bent over and leaned her forehead against his. His forehead felt hot.

An hour later, he began to waken again and Asya slipped a hand behind his head to tilt it slightly forward, pushing three aspirin between his lips and bringing a beaker of water to his mouth.

"I'll sit up. My arm…" She held him while he realized his left arm was tightly bound to his chest by strips of adhesive.

"Don't move!" she whispered sharply. "You took a bullet as you rolled under the door."

Luckily, it had gone all the way through. She did not know what she would have done if she had had to cut a bullet out. It was bad enough that the bandages in the medical kit had been saturated with oil.

"You now have my silk panties in your shoulder, Peter." He swallowed a mouthful of water and she eased his head back down. She made her voice progressively more soothing. "I don't want you to start bleeding again." As he worked his mouth, she said, "Let me help you." She slipped her hand behind his neck to tip his head forward, "Drink some more."

Peter took a sip, and then another. Some water trickled down the side of his cheek and neck, but this time he did not stop swallowing until the beaker was dry. Asya eased his head back down on the coat.

His voice was weak, "We need to plan now, Anastasia."

She merely nodded. "I will have the Lieutenant gather his men."

No sooner was everyone in a semi-circle around Peter and Rishael than there was a startling 'boom' as a vehicle banged against the door.

A megaphone voice yelled for several minutes. When it ceased, the people in the cave began to whisper excitedly to one another.

Asya stretched her legs and rearranged her coat so it lay partially across Peter's chest and also draped across her lap. As she did, Rishael elevated himself up on one elbow and spoke for the first time since Peter had regained consciousness. "You need not prepare to go to war, Anastasia. These men and women are loyal."

"It takes only one," she said grimly, "and Peter is already wounded."

"What's going on?" Pete asked.

"Well," Rishael volunteered, "your friend Boris is on the other side of the door. He says that he has more than a hundred armed men, men loyal only to Russia, Chechnya or him. He was a little unclear on the faithful aspect. Then he rambled on for a bit about history and ugly Americans, nothing I'm sure you haven't heard before, and then he made a big deal of pointing out that we have no way of getting out of this cave alive. He was pretty definite on the last point."

"Is he still angry because Asya struck him in the head?"

Rishael flashed a brief grin. "He seems to have forgiven her. On the other hand, he appears to have quite a fixation on you. He offered to permit the rest of us to leave if we hand you over."

Asya's voice floated over Peter's head. "You forgot about the missiles."

"Oh yes," Rishael said easily, "he knows I am here and requests I remain as his 'guest' until Father returns the missiles to their rightful owners."

"He forgot to specify who those particular people were." Asya spat the words out.

Rishael only shrugged his shoulders and rearranged his blanket, "We both know he is lying, Asya. He intends to kill us all. By the way, I think the answer to the question you asked me earlier is somewhere near Groznyy. Maybe in the district west of the bridge. I don't know how I missed the accent during the time he was working for Father."

Pete offered, "Sooner or later, one of the people in this cave will decide that believing is better than certain death."

Asya answered by raising her Glock from under her coat and racking the slide back to ensure a round was chambered.

Pete shook his head, grimacing slightly at the pain. "No, threats won't hold them. Someone will break, and then we will be killing each other. What we have to do is provide hope. Gather them around."

The two scientists and Saken were the first to assume places around the two prone men. Saken had a white bandage wrapped around his hand. Pete looked at his hand and then at Saken inquiringly, but Saken looked away. "What happened to the Lieutenant's hand, Anastasia? A stray bullet?"

She ignored him, her hands busy carefully lining up two extra clips alongside her pistol atop her coat.

Rishael answered for her, "The Lieutenant was busy following your orders to close the door and Asya thought he should operate at a more deliberate pace. Saken explained to her he was simply saving the rest of us. Fortunately for you, his hand slipped and the door paused until you were under."

Pete frowned as he remembered. "As I was running the last few feet, it looked like the door had a mechanical problem, but I thought I was imagining it. But how did Saken injure his hand?'

"Asya drove her knife through it." Rishael sat up and shoved his gun barrel under his splint, using it to scratch his upper thigh. "I suspect while you were racing for the cave, Saken may have harbored the hope that competition for Asya was going to open up. I am not sure he fully realized the danger of dating a woman who carries her own pedicure implement strapped to her thigh."

Asya gave an audible huff. Rishael was simply enjoying this conversation too much. Talk about TMI! "You two gossip like 90-year-old ladies. Do you want me to have the cave searched for some yarn and needles? If you are going to natter, you might as well be making doilies so my knife doesn't mar any more tables." As she spoke she scanned the gathering crowd. She was counting. She was not interested in having anyone behind her.

When everyone was present, she removed her Glock and the clips from her coat, bundling the wool to slip under Peter's head. She would have given him another shot, but only three morphine ampoules remained and she was going to make him ask her for them. At the moment, his face was streaky white, but his voice was steady enough. She leaned down and he whispered to her, "Begin by saying that the Lieutenant and I are going to need all of them in order to make a good plan."

She raised her pistol. "OK, but first I establish the ground rules." She glanced to her right and triggered a round. Everyone jumped at the thunderclap inside the cave and two of Rishael's soldiers instinctively jerked their rifles to the ready, slowly lowering them as Asya trained the Glock muzzle first on them and then, after they lowered their weapons, progressively around the group.

When the reverberations had died, Asya lowered the gun to her lap and spoke in Kazakh for 30 seconds. When she finished, Rishael and his six soldiers said, "*Ya.*" A split second later, so did Saken, followed by a ragged "*ya*" chorus from his security detachment.

Pete looked enquiringly at Rishael.

"She told everyone, leaving out a couple of very unladylike Kazakh phrases that she should have been too embarrassed to use, that she would kill anyone who looked cross-eyed at you, and the rest of us said that goes for us, too. You may have noticed that some spoke up with more alacrity than others."

Rishael allowed a smile to touch his lips. "She also put a hole right in the middle of one of my Father's irreplaceable missiles, and promised that neither the Chechens nor Russians would get them before hell and Moscow both froze over.

"I recommend you begin – they all seem attentive."

Asya half-listened to the conversation, letting Rishael do the translation, while watching faces to see if any weaklings exposed themselves. Pete established there was water in the cave, available from the decontamination station near the warheads, but no food. While there was no heating system, they did have lights and power, fed from the cave's own diesel generator. That exhaust was vented somewhere outside the cave, and sufficient diesel oil remained for something less than two continuous days of operation.

There was no other entrance to the cave besides the massive steel door. In addition to the diesel exhaust pipe, which was about six inches around, there was an air vent, nearly four feet in diameter, drilled out through 40 feet of solid rock. The latter was designed to dissipate the decomposing noxious missile gases. It was an obvious escape route, but the vent exited 70 feet above the cave door, over the precise spot where Boris' troops would be expected to congregate. A large iron grate hammered into the rock face also blocked egress.

So, they had air, water and power, but no food. Rishael still had his father's special satellite telephone, but it couldn't be expected to operate under the tons of rock. They also were on the short end of the firepower spectrum. Their total weapons consisted of the six rifles Rishael's soldiers had been carrying, four Glocks and five knives. Of course, if they so chose, they could use the cave welding machines to alter the knives into spears. As different members of the group made contributions, it became clear that the thick steel door was the only thing between them and certain annihilation.

Finally, Pete asked, "Did Boris give some sort of time ultimatum?"

Rishael looked at Asya inquiringly and she replayed the megaphone demands in her mind before shaking her head.

"He soon will. He won't wait to starve us out. He doesn't have the patience."

Pete's face was now completely white. Asya knew he had to be in pain. But he was thinking clearly and his voice was steady. Maybe he wouldn't ever get the highest grades for sensitivity, but under stress...

"Boris is thinking about the same considerations we are, and he has several advantages – including unlimited communications, that plane we heard..." Peter broke off his musings and looked questioningly at Rishael. "Where could Boris get his hands on a tank or something like a handheld anti-tank missile? Either would go through that door like a hot knife through butter. Of course, so would acetylene... How far are we from the nearest military base?"

"The 36th Air Assault Brigade is at Kokshetau and there is a Republic Guard unit at Derzhavinsk. The first is about 400 klicks away and the other somewhat less."

"How long was I unconscious?"

Rishael looked at his watch. "Two to three hours. You rolled under the door just before 4am."

Droplets of sweat were beginning to form on Pete's brow. Asya mopped them up with a strip of his old shirt. He didn't seem to notice. "By now, Boris is through being pissed he didn't capture us in his first strike and has reported back to someone." She could see him doing a mental time and distance calculation "Within six hours, there will be a couple more trucks containing troops pulling into the canyon. Behind them will be two or three tanks, at least one equipped with a flamethrower. My best guess is the tanks should show up in eight to ten hours."

Even with Rishael pausing to translate the back and forth for their audience, and Pete pausing for interjections, no one in the little group had commented. The Kazakhs were all standing quietly. Finally, Saken raised his hand and tentatively stepped forward, speaking to the scientists. In reaction to their incredulity, he quickly lowered his hand and sheepishly stepped back.

Asya had decided there was no obvious weak link in the group and it was past time to give Rishael a hand. Continuous translation responsibility was exhausting. She took up the role, "Saken suggests we somehow alter the nuclear weapons in the cave, raise the door and bowl one out."

Even she knew this was not the best idea that had ever been suggested. It was equivalent to recommending nuclear hand grenades. The younger of the two scientists wasn't even trying to hide his shock.

To her shock, Pete smiled approvingly, "Anastasia, please tell Saken I think that's a great idea. In his honor, we are going to name our plan after him." Saken straightened his shoulders as Peter continued. "I think we have to take advantage of the assets we do have – and the only ones I see are these missiles and rockets. Now I don't know if you have ever seen one of these ignite, but I have, at Cape Canaveral, and the ground trembles for 50 miles around!"

She glanced at Rishael, who raised an eyebrow. Their American was interested in saving Saken's face? Maybe Pete was swimming upward on the sensitivity scale. Or was his pain so bad it was driving him out of his mind?

Asya reached in her bra for one of the three remaining morphine ampoules.

CHAPTER THIRTY-FIVE

As Asya finished translating, Pete saw the two scientists furtively glance at one another. The younger one actually blanched. He probably thought Pete understood nuclear physics no better than Saken.

It couldn't be helped. There was no time for discussion. The scientists would have to be converted on the fly. "OK, if no one has a better idea, then 'Saken's Plan' starts now and we'll all need to work together." From his nearly prone position, Pete assessed the group as best he could while Asya gave the preliminary instructions, and then he added, "First we need to get a message to Rafi – both for assistance and so he is not surprised." Hopefully, the National Security Agency would also copy to ensure the US President was not surprised.

Pete mentally replayed what he had observed in his walk around the camp after their arrival. Before it ended at the mountain face, the canyon was about 200 feet wide and the cliffs easily rose more than five times that high. He made a rough computation of what he knew about satellite low earth orbits and geometry.

"Rishael, if two of the soldiers can get you up to the opening of the ventilation shaft, there should be about five to eight minutes every couple of hours when you will have contact with a satellite. It is hard to predict satellite revisit time periods, so once you get through, you need to remain at the opening in case your father calls back." Rishael nodded and motioned for a soldier to help him struggle to his feet as Pete continued: "Tell him what's happening and ask him for help. Maybe those men who are helping in to clear off the airfield might be of use. Also tell him that if help doesn't arrive in time, he needs to bomb this cave and destroy the weapons.

"Saken, you and your people use the electric hoists to first raise Rishael and his team to the ventilation shaft opening, then rearrange the missiles. Asya will provide you a sketch of how we need the one motor positioned. We will need a rocket booster with an intact firing squib brought front and center as soon as you get Rishael in the shaft."

Within a few minutes, Anastasia had made certain everyone understood their roles. She and Pete waited while one of the soldiers found her some blank pages for sketching. Pete was talking to himself, his voice low, his lips barely moving. "The problem is that I have no idea how much of the heat from the motor will blow back."

"Peter, I know you are hurting. I think…"

Pete ignored her. His eyes were closed and he could feel her breath against his cheek as she leaned close to him to hear. "The motor is built to push the flow away from the base so the missile doesn't melt, but normally the missile is moving away from the firing point. If we get the timing right and the cave door completely open, I assume most of the gases will follow the path of least resistance, but I am only guess…"

"Peter, we have a few ampoules left. I think we can spare one if it will help you think…"

He answered what he assumed was her unspoken question: "Someone needs to ensure the squib fires. No time to test a remote electrical firing circuit. I will be the Squib Firing Officer." He opened the eye furthest from the light and squinted up at her. "You supervise Saken raising the door." He took a deep breath, forcing himself to speak slowly and distinctly. "You should be safe if you remain in the operating cage. Just don't touch metal after the missile ignites. That frame will heat up fast."

He fought to keep his eyes open. "And your blouse will need to be buttoned all the way up."

"Are you OK, Peter?"

"Fine." Pete closed his eyes for a second, but still the heat calculations were simply too complex. He could feel his voice trailing off. "Stack...cradles...high..."

Pete was awakened by the crash of metal striking the cave door. Heavy wheels spun outside in the snow and an engine revved. A moment later, a bullhorn began screaming. Than the engine died away and it was again quiet.

Asya summarized. "Boris says we have two hours left to roll your body under the door. He has tanks on the way and does not want to have to kill us all."

Pete shook his head, wincing as he did. "I would have bet this month's paycheck he would go for the tanks." He forced a smile. The sleep had refreshed him. "He's into brute force. He's also probably afraid torches might ignite something inside the cave. This is all good – it's a gift of another couple of hours. We need the time." Pete looked up at Anastasia. There were shadows in her cheeks from the hours of strain. She was continually scanning, checking the cave for someone in their midst who might be thinking of accepting Boris's offer.

The next time she glanced down, Pete winked. "Don't kill anyone yet. Everyone is too busy at the moment to be a traitor. The danger will be in a couple of hours. Ask our scientists to come over. I need to know everything they know about squibs and motors. They likely have a lot of information right in their heads."

Three hours later, the air in the cave was acrid with smoke from the welding, but they were as ready as they ever would be. Unfortunately, Rishael had not yet been able to contact Rafi, so there was no possible relief on their way. Pete had Asya quietly inject him with one of the morphine ampoules. Life was about to get more difficult.

If he wanted to consider all the catastrophic possibilities, there was a chance that either Russian or United States space sensors would see the bloom of a missile motor light off. Worse case: an overeager Russian or American watchstander would target the source of that fiery signature for counter-fire. This would place the cave right at the center of a nuclear burst.

It would certainly screw Boris, but it also didn't seem like the very best outcome for the good guys. Wasn't much he could do about that eventuality. It would or wouldn't happen. Pete was used to ignoring events he couldn't control. As his first Commanding Officer had so often told him, "Work only with what you have."

With Asya's assistance, Pete painfully repositioned himself. He was now lying immediately behind one of the massive steel cradles, the oak pads of which had previously cushioned the stored missiles. Saken had pulled 16 missiles out of their cradles and dumped them unceremoniously on the cave floor. From the growing smell of hypergolic liquid overlaying the acrid welding fumes, Pete suspected that, in the haste, some more missile bodies had been damaged. He mentally shrugged. Greenpeace would never approve, but no one in this cave was worried about dying from air pollution.

The empty missile cradles had been stacked two high and perpendicular to the doorway. Each cradle reached up 12 feet, only a couple of feet below the cave ceiling and higher than the door opening, extending back 30 yards into the cave. Pete guessed they weighted at least five tons each.

In the exact center of the cave, a ninth cradle held the largest solid rocket-booster motor they had found. The firing end of the motor was pointed directly at the door. It was anchored in place by six stanchions. Cables from the stanchions were in turn welded to a girdle cinched around the motor. All the steel hoisting cable in the cave had been used. The girdle was makeshift, but fashioned from titanium, so Pete hoped it would hold. The rocket nozzles had been oriented until they were only three inches from the steel door. Ignition had to take place outside the cave!

With all the steel cabling in place, the rocket motor looked much like a hornet caught in a giant spider's web.

It was a simple plan. If they could only get the rocket motor to fire, there was certainly enough solid-grain explosive fuel to incinerate everything in the canyon.

Of course, there were a few potential drawbacks. The rocket might burn hellishly fast with no way to stop it or even throttle it back. The older scientist couldn't quite remember the design burn time and there were no technical manuals in the cave.

Even if the rocket fuel burned out before its heat killed them all, if the cradle happened to slide further into the cave, or even shifted a few degrees, the rocket flame could catch the side of the cave entrance. If it did, deadly gases would be reflected back into the cave. No one would survive that toxic atmosphere. Then there was the question of the age of the rocket motor itself… Pete had stopped making mental lists of things that might go wrong – too long a burn, slips, cracks – it was like stopping to shoot craps with a dozen strangers you stumbled across in a dark alley. It was possible the evening might produce a profit, but the odds weren't good.

One thing he did know for sure. He did not trust Boris with Asya's life.

Rishael was now positioned up in the ventilation shaft with two of his soldiers. With tons of cool rock to protect them, those three might well survive – if Rishael ever got through and his father's loyal commander subsequently moved heaven and earth to arrive.

The other soldiers were in the rear of the cave, ready to surrender if things went south – and if they survived 'Saken's Plan.'

Of course, if Boris's tanks ran into trouble on the road and Rishael got through to Rafi, then all of these preparations would be for naught. That was a cheering thought. Then they wouldn't have…

Pete's optimistic reverie reached an abrupt end with the unmistakable grind of metallic treads on the cement outside the cave. There was a loud screech as the bottom of the door bowed several inches inward.

Still more grinding as the tank reversed and millions of steel molecules strove to return to their previous alignment in the door. Most made it back. However, from where he stood, Pete could see stress deformation wrinkles at the top where the door disappeared up into the rock. The bullhorn started up again.

Asya cupped her hands around her mouth and yelled to Pete, "Boris is saying, 'Last chance. Open the door and surrender or you all die.'"

Grasping the cradle for support, Pete struggled to his feet. He had delayed this action as long as he could. By the time he was standing, he could feel a warm ooze from his shoulder begin to work its way over his chest down toward his belt. Maybe he would be losing less blood if Anastasia wore bigger panties. He would have to remember to mention… Pete gave her a thumbs-up. She extinguished all the lights in the cave and Pete heard the door start to move.

Now, it was all timing and the question of whether that goddamn tank had stressed the door too far. He hadn't anticipated them striking the door before they gave a last warning. He heard the motor labor as the first steel wrinkle disappeared into the door gearing section at the top. Keep opening…

The pitch of the motor increased as the torque wound up. At some point, the motor could stall or blow some circuit-breaker. If the door didn't open, 'Saken's Plan' was so much garbage. He felt the warm flow widen. He pressed the plunger on the second morphine ampoule he had kept for this moment.

The space beneath the door slowly expanded to six inches, then seven. While the motor whined even louder, the door continued to inch upward. He could see the undersides of two wide metal tank treads.

Suddenly, with an audible bump, the door operating sprocket passed over the deformed section and the door started to move upward faster. Showtime in the Urals, Pete thought.

He saw motion out of the corner of his eye. Anastasia had left the door control station and was racing down the metal steps to the rock floor. Where the hell was she going? She ran toward him and slid around the cradle, shoving her arm tightly around his waist. No time to tell her any differently and he could use her help.

Now he could see the bottom of the turret. In a moment, it was possible the tank crew might begin to see the business end of a rocket motor. But it was nearly noon outside. From the outside, the tank crew would be looking directly into darkness. Pete hoped the Russians would have trouble adapting their eyes to the dark and even more in understanding what they were seeing. Boris's troops were only human if they hesitated before entering a cave full of nukes. These next few seconds were vital – the door needed to be completely open so flames didn't reflect back.

To Pete's eyes, accustomed to the dim light of the cave, everything was crystal clear. He even recognized Boris behind the second tank. He wondered if he should try to shoot the son of a bitch and ensure the bastard accompanied them to hell. The door was now inching above the turret vision ports.

Pete seated his Glock in his holster, located the red-painted square on the side of the rocket motor and shoved the firing plug into the socket. Using both hands, he rotated the plug to engage the locking pin. For a second, nothing happened. He wiggled the plug and put all his weight into pushing the squib flush into the electrical connection. Despite the morphine, his ribs instantly reported they were giving more than their all. The door had cleared the tank turret. The turret gun was swiveling toward where Pete and Asya stood. Did the gunner see them?

Pete pushed Anastasia to the cement and fell atop her, peering through one of the holes cast in the cradle.

CHAPTER THIRTY-SIX

The rocket ignited with a roar. An immense yellow-orange flame leapt out from the cave. A pain instantly knifed through Asya's head. Waves of pressure shoved her body into the rock floor. She clamped her eyes tightly shut, turning her head away to avoid the eyeball-searing light. She looked back toward the cave entrance with her eyelids firmly shut and saw through them the fire engulf the tank, flowing over and around it – the 60-ton steel vehicle dancing in the superheated air. She covered her closed eyes with her hands. She still saw the flame, but now more darkly.

Her chest was compressed by another immense pressure wave as ammunition in the tank exploded, shoving Pete's body down on hers. The stack of cradles above them wavered and slid back several inches. She felt him curl protectively around her.

A few seconds later, still with her hands over her eyes, she forced her head up. The tank at the door was only a carcass, its turret completely gone. The second tank was rising leisurely up on its treads like a ballet dancer rising en pointe. As Asya watched, it tumbled inexorably backward, a metal tinker toy, melting like cheap plastic in the thrusting flame.

She partially unshielded her eyes to look up at the thick steel cables that held the burning rocket in place. Each vibrated with strain as the motor strove to fly deeper into the cave. The cables wouldn't hold much longer. As she watched, one slowly began elongating. Her eyes hurt so badly, she again covered them with both hands.

Asya suddenly realized she couldn't breathe. The missile flame was sucking oxygen out of the cave and what air that remained was too hot. She had never felt such scorching air. She forced herself to slowly take in air through her nostrils, letting her passages cool the blistering stuff a few degrees for her lungs. She coughed.

She squeezed her eyes into slits and peered around her cupped hands. The temperature was still rising. Her blouse was actually beginning to smolder. The scientists had estimated the rocket would burn out in 15 seconds. They had been wrong! She could feel her energy ebbing...

Above her, she felt a loss as Pete lurched to his knees. He leaned down and threw her over his injured left shoulder, staggering for a second. She felt him shift under her weight. She wanted to help. She should have insisted he take all the morphine. He got to one foot and then the other, and began to run toward the back of the cave.

She was bouncing like a ragdoll on Pete's shoulder as he took six quick strides and then two more faltering ones. She felt like her clothes were going to burst into flame. She was so weak… She felt him pull her from his shoulder into his arms and begin rolling them over and over, ever further away from the heat. He was holding her tightly against him, crushing out the flames with his body. She could still hear the rocket burning.

Asya woke with the roaring of the rocket still in her ears. How long had she been out? How was she still alive?

She lifted her head. The intense light was gone. She rolled to her knees. Peter lay immobile beneath her, his upper body drenched with blood.

As she stared down at him, another few red drops formed on his chest. She clapped her right hand to her ear, felt the slipperiness and saw the red on her fingertips. The overpressure must have blown her eardrums. The noise in her head was the memory her brain had of the roar. The orange light was gone. She could breathe. The missile had burned out!

Asya felt for the pulse in Pete's throat. She could feel a steady beat, and, as she watched, his chest rose and then fell. She looked back at the front of the cave. He carried me 30 or 40 feet on a wounded shoulder to ensure I did not catch on fire, she thought. I may sometimes overvalue sensitivity. I should check his bandage. He must be bleeding.

Sometime later, supporting each other, Pete and Asya limped to the cave entrance. The heavily falling snow was already beginning to whiten the canyon's edges. Thick flakes still hissed into steam whenever they lit on any rock within a few hundred feet of the cave. Only blackened concrete slabs indicated the former location of the four huts. The twisted steel remains of two diesel engines marked the fifth. Despite the sub-zero weather, water was freely running down the rocks on both sides of the canyon. As they watched, a large overhang of snow, its lower support melted away, broke free to slide to a steaming rest against the still-smoldering carcass of the second tank.

There was no evidence, except for the stench, that men had ever been here. Asya breathed through her mouth. While the intense flame had cremated the flesh and bones of the attacking force, the sickening sweet reek of burned flesh still clung to small piles of chalky white smears atop the rapidly refreezing mud.

At her side, Peter put his mouth close to her ear and suggested, "Let's move down to the Guard Building. Shock. Warmer there." Without waiting for a reply, he started slowly walking up the road, leaving her to organize the others.

She knew he was probably in shock and needed to keep moving, but there was no way Rishael was going to manage the deepening snow, so she sent the Lieutenant and four of the soldiers after Pete, keeping the rest with her and Rishael at the cave entrance. Rishael had managed to get through on his satellite phone, was eager to talk, and had quickly learnt he had to lean in to her ear to speak. "I got hold of Father. He has helicopter assault teams on the way."

With Peter walking down to the gate, it was an opportunity to ask a question that had been bothering her for the last day: "Rishael, we have known each other for a long time. What has been your real role?"

He blanched and looked around to ensure no one else could overhear them. "I'm sorry I haven't been completely honest. When Father discovered the rogue weapons, I wanted to keep them. The last years have been difficult with Russia and China. I don't think you realize how hard. You left. I wanted to keep the weapons to induce them to leave us alone. Father and I have argued about this for months."

She raised an eyebrow. "And what about Boris? Were you helping him?"

Rishael's quick look toward Pete's back foreshadowed his answer, "Not exactly." Then he leaned in even closer. "I knew Boris disagreed with bringing you to the cave. I suspected he might try to sabotage your mission, but nothing like this, I assure you."

Rishael suddenly straightened, looking down the canyon and cupping his hand to his ear. "Listen!"

CHAPTER THIRTY-SEVEN

Pete couldn't see. He couldn't move. His head was pounding. It had been several years since this had last happened, but he remembered what to do. It was a process. Whoever had gotten him in the bed obviously didn't understand. It was a simple five-step process. The first involved getting to the floor. Then you got to your knees. You reach up for something to hold on to – like a bed rail. Steady your body while your knees remember their job. Open eyes. Voila! No longer drunk! The difficulty was always the initial drop. Some floors were damn hard. But it had to be done. Pete leaned right to begin the roll. Damn! He was paralyzed. That made the next steps harder. What had he been drinking?

Not ouzo. He could still blink his eyelids and he hadn't been in Greece for years. Have to bypass steps one through four and improvise. He opened his eyes, trying to focus on the only splash of color in the room. That was probably the jerk that had put him in this bed and made the problem. It was always easier to start from the floor. He must have really tied one on.

The next time his eyes opened, it was dark. His brain was still disengaged and his body was just lying there. This had gone on long enough. The alcohol should be long gone. Pete decided to simply sit up. He felt a prick in his right shoulder and a hand push against his chest. His eyelids again slammed shut.

It was dark. Still? Again? He had no idea. But he did know he wasn't drunk. "Asya, are you there?" He could hear his words in his head, but unclearly, as if he had a severe head cold. He wasn't sure he was speaking.

"Yes, Peter."

He was exhausted. It was much easier to leave his eyes closed. He put his energy into moving his lips. "Are you OK?"

"I'm fine. I have one cracked rib. The doctor thinks some brute fell on me. But my hearing has returned. My eardrums are nearly back to normal."

"I…"

"Sleep, Peter. You lost much blood. We are safe in Astana. We will talk tomorrow."

He heard her speaking with someone else in the room, "No! Wait! Asya, I must call the Secretary of Defense."

"I did so, Peter." She had stood up. Her voice now sounded like an echo in his head. "I reported what happened. I also told him you had tried to take advantage of me. Your administrative assistant said that was just like you, but they still wish that you get well soon."

"But…" He again felt a sharp needle sliding into his arm. He tasted the metal tang of morphine in his mouth and felt the warmth begin the race down his arm. He felt his mind began to slide back to sleep.

"Tomorrow, Peter. We will talk tomorrow." Asya had moved back to the bed. She was now behind his head. Her palms were on his cheeks. Her cool fingertips smoothed the wrinkles on his brow and then slid down, firmly closing his eyelids. He took a deep breath and then, nothing…

Pete awoke to light streaming in the windows. Around him were the sounds of a hospital. Across the hall, someone clanged a metal bedpan against a plaster wall, a door hissed closed and a woman in heels clicked down the hall.

A nurse was leaning over him, replacing the IV bag on the hooked metal stand. She saw his eyes open and reached down for his wrist. He tried to lift his arm to assist her, but she shook her head with the full authority of her bobby-pinned white cap and silently counted his pulse while looking off into the distance.

When she had finished, she crossed to the other bed and murmured something before departing. Left alone, Pete decided to see how much he had broken. He tightened his stomach muscles to lift his legs. Sweat broke out on his brow but nothing moved.

"Peter, are you in pain?"

Anastasia stood over him, her hair mussed, sleep still in her eyes. He could see the swell of one breast between the buttons in her sleeping gown.

"I can't move."

"You can't move because you are strapped to the bed. You were thrashing around when we got you here." She scrubbed the sleep from her eyes and pushed her hair back with both hands. She followed Pete's gaze. She laughed as she brought a hand down and straightened the V-neck of her gown. "Peter! You must be better! Good. Rafi and Rishael have been waiting impatiently for you to awake. They need to talk."

Fifteen minutes later, Pete had been unstrapped and the bed was folded up into a sitting position when the Kazakh President and Rishael, the latter on crutches, came into the room. Pete fired an immediate question at Rafi: "Did you get through to my President?"

The nurse wheeled a tea cart into the room. Asya motioned for the woman to leave and began serving tea herself.

Rafi took the first cup Asya offered and pressed it into Pete's hands. He sat back and quietly looked at Pete with tired eyes. At last, he leaned forward and softly spoke, "Yes, I did." Rafi paused. "But before we talk about other things, I want to sincerely apologize for Boris and his comrades. I thought he was loyal to Kazakhstan and to his President."

Rafi took a deep breath and glanced at both Asya and Rishael before patting the latter's knee, "I also want to thank you for saving my son's life. Now, with respect to the telephone call, your President wanted me to tell you the warning was just in time. Does that mean what I think it does?"

"The United States has a system of satellites to warn them of missile launches. I was afraid someone in our Colorado 'Iron Mountain' command center might think they were seeing valid indications of an unexpected ballistic missile launch from the old Derzhavinsk site."

"Would the United States have done anything as a result of that one signal?" Rishael looked incredulously at Pete.

"Nuclear weapons scare people, Rishael. People behave rashly when they are scared. That's why your call was so important." He shifted his attention to his father. "What else did you and my President discuss?"

"We both agreed time was of the essence to destroy the missiles. However, I am concerned about the Russian military. If Boris didn't alert them before he died, that rocket motor certainly did, because I know Russia has a similar alerting system. When I spoke to President Vostrov in Moscow, he implied he was anxious to meet, but believed it would be best to do so some distance from the Russian capitol. I think he has some information about what went on last week, but no details, and he may have the same problems I have with our respective right wings."

Rafi rubbed his brow. "He definitely knows something we don't. In the meantime, your President is sending instructions to the American Ambassador in Moscow and that gentleman is arranging for a meeting. If your health permits, your President wishes you to attend, and, in any case, Asya will accompany me."

Pete nearly spat out his tea. "We can't take her where she is still wanted for spying!"

"Vostrov has guaranteed her safety."

Pete was surprised by Rafi's quiet assurance. Before he could object, Anastasia pressed a fresh cup of tea into his hands and whispered in his ear: "Rafi is correct. Besides, if I am not there, who will change your bandage?"

He was too tired to resist further. In fact, he was just tired. She clicked on an iPod on his night table. Soft music began and the other three shifted to Kazakh for their discussion. Pete began composing his own mental checklist. He needed to get his Glock back. He also needed to call the American Ambassador in Moscow to see what measures were available to protect Asya.

He did appreciate her choices in music. He wondered if she knew she had keyed in Nat King Cole.

An option might be to have a Navy ship with a helicopter detachment standing by in the Gulf of Finland. Damn, he was weary. He wondered if anyone in the room would notice if he closed his eyes for a...

The American visitor was doodling on the pad of paper the Grand Hotel Europe had provided. So far, the paper was nearly filled with black swords and euro signs marching across the page. It was a lovely piece. He cocked his head and admired his creation. Nearly Salvador Dalí in concept. Perhaps he should save it.

Son of a bitch! He drew a heavy X over the page, ripped it from the pad, balled it up and threw it into the wastebasket!

The best-laid plans of mice and men be goddamned, and while you are at it, also damn the black soul of that incompetent Boris Valikhonov! This was not going to be a pleasant phone call. Simple arrangements had become very complicated. Unfortunately, $7M was a great deal of money and Chechens were not the very best people in the world to leave with the impression they had been double-crossed.

On the bright side, he was the man when it came to complicated arrangements, and trouble meant more earning opportunity. He pressed down hard on his vibrating pinky finger for 15 seconds before pushing a saved number on his cell phone.

"Abdulbek! We need to talk."

He listened to the tirade for a few seconds before imperiously cutting his partner short. Staying on the offensive was critical, whatever the facts. "Abdulbek, I am sorry about your cousin but, in the larger scheme of things, this is a very minor setback. In fact, only a few people can turn around what your cousin managed to screw up and, this time, I will personally lead the effort." He paused for that to sink in. "The time is now. What kind of muscle can you arrange to meet me in Semey?"

He frowned at the answer. "That isn't sufficient. Do you think you could cut a deal with your friend Vostrov?"

He held the telephone away from his ear for a moment while Abdulbek loudly cursed.

"If you're not talking to him, who is? I am going to need some armor and preferably air cover."

He listened for a while, staring into the distance, while he fingered a strand of his hair that tended to get loose now and then. His mother had wanted him to adopt a shorter cut, but he had seen Redford in *The Sting* and… "It will cost you another three million. Euros this time, not dollars." *Audentes fortuna iuvat.* Especially when asking for money. He learnt more about politics every day.

"I'll book a flight when and if the balance in my Swiss account changes. If you decide you want me to recover what your cousin fucked up, line up whomever you can find in Semey and text me their contact numbers."

CHAPTER THIRTY-EIGHT

As Rafi's airplane descended below the clouds, Asya borrowed a cloth napkin from the steward to wipe away the window condensation before putting her arm around Peter's shoulder and carefully turning him to better see the islands below, "Pretty, isn't it? The city is built on more than forty of them in the River Neva delta. It is almost like Venice or Bangkok."

She continued her travel dialogue as he looked through the window. "Sweden and Russia fought over this land for 500 years. Not only did these islands serve as a land bridge between the two countries, but a curl of the Gulf Stream also brings enough warm water up to keep the area ice-free, so before air travel, this isthmus was key to the control of the entire region."

She was still emotionally processing what had happened in the cave and she found it comforting to keep him within reach. She was trying to break herself of that bad habit, but it was proving difficult, "When Peter the Great pushed the Swedes out in the early 1700s, he established St Petersburg as the capital of Russia and home of the Tsars. After he died, the capitol was moved back to Moscow."

Asya took a deep breath. "Everyone says St Petersburg is much different from Moscow. Freer. You feel it when you walk in the streets here. St Petersburg is good for Russia. Freedom produces ideas. Lenin lived here, as did Pushkin and Dostoevsky. Petersburg is where the Great Revolution began. There is always something stirring in the atmosphere here."

She turned away from the window and, remembering all his injuries, carefully unwrapped her arm from around him, "It's a very un-Russian city. Do you dream in color, Peter?"

The man she was speaking to had silently settled back into his seat. He must learn to be more articulate, she thought. Sometimes it was like talking to a wall.

"You should. The world is more interesting in color. I think of St Petersburg as blue – brilliant blue like a Fabergé egg. On the other hand, Moscow is gray. Gray like your Pittsburgh."

The co-pilot walked back and spoke to Rafi, who turned to Asya to see if she had heard. She nodded once before continuing her conversation with Peter. "And do *not* tell me how much you like the Three Rivers Stadium. It is an exception. The pilot would like us to prepare for landing. We will be over the airport in 15 minutes." Pete had been wearing a sling on his arm since the hospital.

"Do you need me to help with your seatbelt?"

Across the aisle, Rishael read from some papers he had extracted from a folder: "Our reservations have been confirmed at the Grand Hotel Europe. We will all have rooms on the fourth floor, and President Vostrov and his people will occupy the third floor."

Did Peter realize she was a little nervous about returning? She trusted Rafi, but the Russians had condemned her to death! She might be talking a little more than usual, but she had her emotions under control. She was not afraid. Peter was here. Rafi said it was good. She had escaped before. She smoothed her skirt and let her fingers run across the leather sheath wrapped around her thigh. Who was she kidding? Vostrov scared her to...

Rishael was still reading: "Your Ambassador will meet us in the lobby in an hour, so we will immediately begin our first session with Vostrov."

Asya and Pete met with Ambassador Wright shortly before five just outside the hotel entrance. Peter wanted to introduce himself before the meeting started, as well as to determine what the Ambassador understood regarding the President's desired outcomes. Also, which she particularly appreciated, he wanted to specifically introduce Asya as his teammate. They conferred in his car for a few minutes.

The Honorable Daniel Wright was a short, round man with an easy smile, dressed in an expensive suit cut to minimize his weight. He immediately launched into a well-honed effort to make them his new best friends: "I called Secretary Johnson this morning. He and I campaigned in Ohio for the President. Bill said he has full confidence in you, Captain, and I should follow your lead."

The Ambassador paused before adding, "The Secretary also added that he counted on me to use my good political judgment if I felt you took a wrong turn. Other than that, I am only present to assist you and Ms Conner in making history."

Asya could sense Peter's relief. She knew he had feared Wright might wish to personally run the negotiations.

Peter's reply was carefully bland: "We may have to zig and zag a little, Ambassador. I spoke to the Secretary of Defense last night. He suspects Vostrov has to receive something to satisfy his right wing, but we need to insist on American control of the plutonium. We want to ensure that stuff is destroyed."

"Not a problem, Pete. I've cleared my schedule for the next few days. The only possible side issue I have is that if we get the chance while we're in town, my wife has always wanted to visit the Hermitage. By the way, the President said the *USS Antietam* will be positioned where you requested. The ship will be in constant communications with my office, and my office with me."

Pete grasped her arm. They had used an encrypted telephone from Rafi's airplane to contact the SEAL team aboard the *Antietam* less than an hour ago. Pete seemed to think the plan was solid, which assured Asya. "OK, sir. I hope we won't need them." He paused. "Have you met Rafi before?"

"No, I haven't had the pleasure."

"I think you'll be impressed. He and his son should be waiting for us in the lobby."

"Let's go."

After introductions, the combined American and Kazakh party took the same elevator to the third floor. As they exited, Vostrov met them, accompanied by his interpreter and his own special assistant, the latter an Army Lieutenant Colonel burdened by two metal briefcases.

Once they met, Anastasia found herself unable to take her eyes off Vostrov. He appeared just like in all of his photos. A short man, barely five-seven, somewhere in his early fifties, with shoulders nearly as broad as Peter, and a very thick neck. His eyebrows were coal black. She had always thought they were touched up in photos – maybe he colored them. They were bushy and grown together across the bridge of his nose – so Georgian. His thick hair was swept smoothly back along the sides. A full black mustache completely covered his upper lip. A shiver ran through her. She needed to control herself. Peter might not be very sensitive, but he had proven susceptible to her emotions. She wondered if from his height advantage Pete could see the balding area rumored to be on the very top of the Russian leader's head. It had never been shown on Russian television.

While Vostrov shook Pete's hand, he motioned at the sling and spoke. The Russian translator had a British accent but seemed accurate, and Asya let him work without comment. "An accident? The President hopes it was nothing serious."

"Just a sprain," Peter replied.

Vostrov stared at him, his eyes seemingly amused. "Good," he said, still holding Pete's right hand. He spoke again, his hand still tightly gripping Pete's.

"The President wouldn't want you to get tired in the middle of a tough Russian negotiation."

As Pete focused on listening to the translation, Vostrov reached over with his left fist and, apparently playfully, hit his shoulder directly on top of the bullet wound.

Anastasia flinched but Pete kept his party smile firmly in place. She had warned him to suspect something physical in the first five minutes. Russians lived for opportunities for physical intimidation. Obviously,

Vostrov also wanted to make a point about how well he tracked what was going on in Kazakhstan. Of course, he had not seen Pete fight Boris. She had. Vostrov's loss.

Getting not even a grimace, Vostrov looked away from Pete and spoke in turn to the Ambassador and finally to Asya. He raised his eyebrows as he welcomed Asya in Russian. Both Rafi and Rishael flushed at his words and Pete looked at her questioningly. She was not about to interpret his words for Pete. She raised her chin a bit for the benefit of the two Kazakhs in the room and kept her face carefully expressionless – Vostrov was exactly the pig she had heard. It was so good that Pete did not speak Russian!

When she refused to react, Vostrov gave a little smile and turned on his heel, leading them into the living room of his suite. In accordance with the Grand Europe's standards, the room had 16-foot ceilings, and was 30 feet on each side. The walls were draped with heavy red velvet wherever an arch or window offered an excuse. Below their feet, the thick nap of a golden carpet swallowed every step.

The four large windows at the far end of the room was fronted by a large 'partners' desk and looked out onto a nearly deserted street. Asya remembered that Grand Europe employees had been blocking off that very street when they were exiting the Ambassador's car.

A well-polished long heavy wood table was positioned in the exact middle of the room. Drawn up to the table were five leather chairs, each one padded and embossed to a fare-thee-well. Positioned precisely in front of each chair were black leather blotters, along with individual paper pads, pencils, glasses, delicate china cups, saucers and linen napkins. Individual bottles of water were grouped in silver bowls on each end of the table, white linen catching the condensation off the silver. At each end of the table were silver coffee and tea services, and white Imperial Porcelain vases containing miniature yellow chrysanthemums.

Vostrov sat down in the middle chair on one side, his interpreter at his left, the Army officer at his right. Rafi took the seat directly across from Vostrov, Rishael at this right and Ambassador Wright at his left. Peter took the end seat on the American side, placing Anastasia between him and the Ambassador, so she could interpret simultaneously for both of them.

Asya watched the Russian Army officer, who carefully placed his dual briefcases in the chair seat next to him. Peter had told her this officer would be present. He was the one assigned to carry the Russian nuclear-weapon release codes and a special radio for contacting their nuclear forces. She returned her attention to the American at her side. She wondered if the bandages she had carefully wound around his chest this morning were stemming the bleeding from Vostrov's jab.

CHAPTER THIRTY-NINE

"Mr President, I recently journeyed to the United States and met with their President and Secretary of Defense." Asya's simultaneous translation to Pete and the Ambassador easily kept pace with Rafi's very measured conversation with Vostrov. "I reported to him the unfortunate, perhaps inadvertent, Strategic Arms Limitation Treaty violations by our predecessors. Later, as I am sure you have heard, he and I discussed options for the old nuclear weapons that I recently uncovered in Kazakhstan."

Vostrov had his hands clasped before him in the center of his leather blotter. At Rafi's first pause, Vostrov looked across the table and impassively rolled out the initial lie. "Russia has never violated any treaty, much less one signed with our good friends in the United States."

Rafi pulled his porcelain cup and saucer toward him. In the silence, as Rishael poured his father some tea, Asya leaned toward Pete ("They use such lovely *Lomonosov*," she whispered). Rafi added two sugar cubes and stirred carefully for several seconds with an ornate silver spoon, staring into the light brown liquid.

After a few seconds, Pete realized the response delay was Rafi's silent signal to Vostrov that this was no basis for a conversation. Rafi's non-verbal approach emphasized the power difference between the two countries. Kazakhstan would have a multi-thousand-mile border with Vostrov and his successors for a very long time, and Russia would always be an Asian power.

Rafi looked up from his delicate cup, his face expressionless, to Vostrov. "I imagine you are as shocked as me."

Let's review, Pete thought. A few rogue soldiers apparently dug an immense cave out of solid rock and then snuck in some 10-story-long missiles – unnoticed – in a country with more security checkpoints than chickens. And bears don't defecate in the woods.

Vostrov was now mimicking Rafi's tea farce. In fact, he was building on it by carefully blowing on his tea and then sipping as if to test the temperature, before placing the cup back in its translucent saucer. Now he looked across at Rafi. "If you suspected such a violation, I am surprised you did not immediately bring it to my personal attention." Vostrov's black eyes were as dead as his voice.

Pete realized he was holding his breath. Vostrov undoubtedly suspected Rafi was using the hidden nuclear weapons to enhance his relationship with the United States, which would be a big no-no in Kremlin circles. Could Rafi provide Vostrov with a believable alternative?

Rafi was equally expressionless. "I chose not to do so only because of the great value I and all other Kazakhs place on the importance of your personal leadership to Russia."

Rafi stared into his tea and gave the contents a careful stir as if searching for the right words before continuing. "I was not sure you had been in power long enough to root out all the divisive elements you may have inherited from your predecessors." He carefully placed the silver spoon he had used on a napkin and lined both the spoon and the double-headed eagle on the napkin parallel with the edge of his blotter before spreading his hands wide, palms up. "I did not want to give my neighboring friend and fellow President a serious problem that might impede his progress."

Pete watched Vostrov as he evaluated Rafi's unstated question – do you really want a fight with the right wing in the Politburo and your Army over Russian national security? If you do, I think I have the ability to start your whole hive buzzing!

Vostrov's face suddenly darkened. "I control Russia completely!" He slammed his right fist on the table. A wave of tea slopped into his saucer. "You peasant from the Steppes! How dare you presume to judge my power?" Asya was softly whispering the translation, but Pete had no trouble understanding the thrust. He quickly wrote a few words on the paper pad in front of him.

Rafi was unruffled. "As you correctly noted, Kazakhstan is but a poor country of farmers and traders." Right, Pete mentally interjected – a poor country possessing all of the known gold mines in this part of Asia, as well as most of the oil and gas. "I am overwhelmed with the details of running our young country. You, of course, know everything about Kazakhstan. You have powerful agencies that monitor the world. My sole concern is we few Kazakhs."

Pete slid his pad in front of Asya. She read it, then took her own pencil and added a line before pushing the pad back to Pete. Rafi was soothingly continuing and she did not miss a sentence. "I do not closely follow Russian internal affairs. I was only doing my best to aid a powerful and respected neighbor leader. I beg your forgiveness if you think I erred."

Abruptly, Vostrov looked down at his cup and appeared to notice the spilled tea for the first time. His powerful left arm swept the offending cup and saucer from his blotter. The tea splattered the Army Lieutenant Colonel who didn't even flinch. Pete could see the look of anguish on Asya's face as the cup tumbled high in the air. It was only when the cup landed unharmed on the golden rug that she tore her gaze away, and then her eye followed the saucer as it skittered down the length of the table until it finally stopped, like a shuffleboard puck, teetering on the end of the table.

Vostrov's face was mottled with rage as he shoved his chair back and stood, pointing at Rafi. "You will not give Russian missiles to America! They – his hand swept to indicate Pete and the Ambassador – will not steal Mother Russia's secrets."

Pete whispered to Asya. "Translate everything I say." He tore off the top page from his pad and deliberately pushed his chair back from the table. "And, of course, we don't want your secrets either." He stood, folding the note and tucking it into his breast pocket. When his hand came back out, the tips of his fingers were tinged red. "Well, I'll be doggone. Apparently, my bruise has started to bleed."

He lifted his sling over his head and used it to wipe the blood off his fingers before dropping the cloth dismissively onto the table. "I must get cold water on this shirt before it's ruined." Pete looked around the table, "President Parzarev, we are about the same size. Could I borrow a shirt so I don't catch my death of cold?"

Rafi appeared startled, but quickly stood, smiling, "Certainly Captain. Why don't you come to my room?" He turned to their host and bowed slightly. "President Vostrov, please excuse me. Perhaps we should take our first 15-minute break a little early?"

Pete rose to walk out. As he passed the end of the table, he put his finger under the saucer and flipped it high above his head. Ignoring Asya's gasp of disapproval, as the rotating porcelain dropped he caught and cushioned it on the back of his right hand, flipping it again to catch it between two fingers. He handed it to the startled Army officer with a slight smile before turning to Asya. "I will need my personal assistant to clean the shirt. Miss Conners?"

None of them spoke until they reached Rafi's sitting room. Although large, it was only half the size of Vostrov's, with half a dozen overstuffed chairs grouped around a low coffee table in lieu of a formal conference table. After closing the door, Rafi offered everyone seats. "I assume you wanted to say something, Captain? You may talk freely – my security people have swept this room for listening devices and installed white-noise counter-surveillance machines."

"OK, I don't know how you can get past the guidance-technology issue. We all realize the facts. Our CIA *could* learn a great deal about Russian science and Russian missiles if our scientists ever got their hands on an entire missile and warhead. Even if it's very old stuff, it would be great intelligence to confirm where their development was at that time. I know you promised my President you would deliver the SS-9s to the United States, but I can't see how Vostrov can ever sell that to his allies in Moscow."

"So, I am in, what do you call it, a 'spot'?"

"Sir, I know my President wants these weapons off the street. He also doesn't want you embarrassed. On the other hand, Russia is a big dog, so my President will always be interested in maintaining a relationship with Vostrov."

"But your President is not in St Petersburg today. What do *you* think?"

Now was the crucial moment – "I think my President and Secretary of Defense would be willing for Russia to keep their outdated missiles and guidance systems *if* the United States were sure the plutonium in the warheads was destroyed. I think my President can only believe the plutonium is gone if Americans see it burned."

Rafi stood and paced thoughtfully across the large room, stopped at the windows, looked out, paused, turned and paced back, his hands clasped behind his back. "What does the US plan to do with the plutonium?"

"We will request our Canadian friends assist us. They have a special reactor that uses plutonium as fuel. This solution has several advantages. One is that the power generated will eventually reduce the cost of making automobiles in Ontario and Detroit. It won't produce more weapons or help make products that will compete with Russian or Kazakh exports."

Pete saw the weariness in Rafi's eyes. Pete understood the pressure he was under. The very existence of Kazakhstan was sometimes an irritation to both Russia and China. Rafi was betting the ranch on continued support from the United States.

"Captain, you've obviously given this a great deal of thought. Why should Vostrov agree?"

Pete retrieved the note from his breast pocket and read what he and Asya had together written. "There are several important reasons. To begin with, you personally are a known quantity. Secondly, because it is in Russia's interest that Kazakhstan exists – only hotheads would ever desire an even longer common border with the Chinese. Third, because Vostrov will never have to admit Russia deliberately violated one of the most sacrosanct treaties ever written. And, finally, which is a variant on the initial point, you have personally shown yourself to be a responsible President. You have not persecuted the Russians within your borders and you teach both Russian and Kazakh languages in your schools." Pete refolded their list. "I think when Vostrov and his allies consider all these, only one conclusion is possible.

"If Asya and I are correct, his counter-proposal will end up in the ballpark of what is acceptable to the United States. In fact, I will bet next week's paycheck we are in St Petersburg rather than Moscow because Vostrov realizes he is under a time constraint. He needs to cut a deal before the Politburo begins hearing rumors for which Vostrov does not have answers. He also needs to come to an agreement before someone like Boris makes a move." Pete raised his eyebrows. "What happens if you eat some bad fish and get a stomach ache?"

'I am a Kazakh," Rafi replied, and Pete watched his public persona slip back in place "I eat only meat."

"I wager Vostrov still worries."

Rafi nodded his agreement and stood. "Very well. Let's go back and see if someone has cleaned up Vostrov's tea stain."

Pete stood with him. Only Asya remained sitting.

"Peter, do you want me to wash out your stupid shirt?"

"No, sweetheart. I wanted Vostrov to worry a little. The trick with the saucer was to remind him the two of us killed a couple of assassins in Astana without a second thought. To make sure he knows I was twisting his tail, I will wear this same shirt back in." Pete held out his right hand to help her up. "But I do appreciate your asking."

She snatched her hand back. "Next time you want to play with something, don't do it with *Lomonosov* porcelain! There are enough jerks like Vostrov breaking our priceless things."

Rafi, Pete and Anastasia returned to the meeting room, greeted Rishael and the Ambassador and then waited quietly. Suspecting the room was bugged, no one spoke. It was another five minutes before Vostrov re-entered with his own party.

As Rafi and Vostrov cautiously re-engaged, the others only listened. Slowly, Rafi allowed himself to be talked into understanding exactly why Russia could not permit the United States to have the SS-9s and Vostrov acknowledged the difficult position in which Rafi found himself.

Pete knew Vostrov was dying to know exactly what the American had learned about Russian guidance and fusing systems during those few hours in the cave, but he had to give the leader credit – Vostrov did not ask this question. It was the elephant in the room, the one factor that might sink any arrangement, and everyone ignored it. When Pete realized Vostrov didn't want any answer or non-answer on the record, he knew a deal was possible.

Finally, Vostrov made a proposal of sorts: "Perhaps, Rafi, we two Presidents should discuss this situation in private."

Did Pete imagine it or had Vostrov glanced at his own assistant right before he proposed the executive meeting? Was the Army officer someone of Vostrov's own choosing? Was he loyal to Vostrov or the Army? Was he a Boris protégé?

President Vostrov continued to speak as he rose from his chair, "Maybe, between the two of us," Asya translated, "we can solve how to return our missiles to Russia this very evening."

As the others politely rose with Vostrov, Pete put his right hand lightly on Anastasia's shoulder and held her in her chair. When Vostrov finally noticed the two of them were still sitting, he turned to them with a frown. Pete smiled at Asya. "Tell him he can't have the plutonium back. My President's already sold it."

The second the words were translated, Vostrov wheeled to lean across the table and speak directly to Pete for the first time since they had shaken hands. "You sold Russia's plutonium?" he shouted.

Pete leaned back in his chair. "Americans have been making capitalism work for a long, long time. Time is money, a bird in the hand, and all that. No one wants to buy old missiles. But there is a market for plutonium. Canada will use it to fuel a reactor that powers Ontario. After President Parzarev offered, we cut a deal with our Canuck friends within a week. My President intends to use the money from Canada to build child-care centers in one of our swing-voting states. Those votes are important to his re-election."

Pete released Anastasia and used his right hand to push himself to his feet. "I am a simple naval officer, sir. The President ordered me not to leave Kazakhstan without the plutonium. I follow orders." Pete looked past Asya, "Mr Ambassador, may I buy you a drink?"

Since Pete's room had not been electronically swept, they again repaired to the Ambassador's.

Ambassador Wright went immediately to the bar, apologizing over his shoulder, "I'm sorry my wife is not here. The shops are open until ten tonight, and she is off with the staff wandering through the underground mall. Scotch?" He was holding up a single malt. Pete nodded, and the Ambassador continued as he poured without measuring. "I would like both of you to meet her. Her father was a rancher, so she appreciates bullshit. That stuff about the President selling the plutonium was just great."

Pete accepted the Ambassador's compliment along with the drink, while Anastasia poured herself a glass of water. Sitting next to Pete on the couch, she reconsidered and appropriated a sip of his scotch while he explained, "They have been Communists all their lives. That makes capitalism difficult for them to understand. That goes double for grassroots politics. I thought what I said might be in line with what Rafi and Vostrov believe from what they have read about American capitalists and politicians. I also hoped it might strengthen Rafi's hand for any private conversation he might have with Vostrov. Now we will just have to wait and see."

CHAPTER FORTY

By 10.30 the next morning, the checkpoint guards at the end of the hotel corridor had passed Peter and Asya through. The cafetière of coffee they were carrying had been deemed non-contraband, along with the hotel ceramic coffee cups on two of Peter's fingers.

About a dozen feet short of the door to yesterday's conference room, there was a floor lamp, a small table, two overstuffed chairs and a coat rack, along with a light green umbrella and a cable-knit scarf left behind by some previous patrons. Asya and Peter settled there to wait for the rest of the team and the 11 o'clock start to their scheduled meeting.

The Grand Europe carried American newspapers, and Peter was reading the sports section of the *Financial Times* as he drank his coffee. Asya had previously noted, for someone supposedly interested in world events, that Peter immediately gravitated to the sports section of the local English-language paper in every country they visited. At breakfast, he had actually questioned Rishael about the form of a particular Pakistan bowler! Both men had then spent several minutes discussing something to do with Australian Rules, something she suspected neither knew piss-off about. She was casually leafing through her mystery novel, searching for where she had last paused, imagining Peter doing a run-up to a wicket and falling flat on his face, when Vostrov's door suddenly swung open.

"Winsor!"

The Honorable Mr Asher's his mouth was twisted in anger. Behind him in the President's doorway, Asya could see Vostrov was personally escorting Winsor from the suite.

From the pulsing in his temple, she realized Winsor was struggling to control his temper and keep his mouth shut. "I know why I am here. I am required to do lots of things for Senator Jones." She had seen this happen before. If he were talking, he wasn't thinking. She involuntarily stepped forward before realizing that Winsor was no longer her problem. He was ignoring her anyway, looking through her, lashing out at Peter. "But what is one of America's tin-badge military heroes doing in Russia?"

The President of Russia was watching, and they were all Americans, so Asya made a half-hearted attempt to pour oil on the waters. "We are just sightseeing, Winsor. We heard we might catch a glimpse of famous people on this floor of the hotel." Behind the tableau, Vostrov still held his door part way open. His interpreter was whispering quietly near his ear. Her explanation did not deter Winsor's focus on Pete for even a second. He bore down on the two of them. "I see you hurt yourself."

"I had an accident in…"

Winsor's eyes were wide with anger. "There are other people who may run into accidents if they don't start showing a little more spine!" Asya reflectively slid her hand down to hitch up her skirt and remembered she had left her knife at the corridor screening station.

Pete got to his feet and Winsor stepped even closer, and, using the back of his hand, began repeatedly tapping Pete on the chest. "I have been meaning to tell you something: if you think you will ever get another good Navy assignment, you had better think again. Chairman Jones controls your inconsequential career, buddy, and don't you forget it."

His knuckle was getting closer to Peter's bullet wound.

"Your name is never going… Jesus, Asya, what the…"

Asya had taken the umbrella from the stand and hooked it between Winsor's legs. She was now pulling him away from Pete. As Winsor grabbed at the crook in his groin and tried to jerk the umbrella away from her, Pete brought his right hand down on top of Winsor's hands, immobilized him "Don't try to hurt the woman, Winsor. You need to get a little control of yourself." He leaned in very close and whispered something Asya barely caught: "If you ever touch her again, I will hunt you down and gut you like an Arkansas hog."

Pete then jerked his own hand up, pushing the crook of the umbrella sharply into Winsor's groin.

Winsor staggered but caught his balance. For a second, Asya thought Winsor was going to run at Pete then and there. Could Pete beat him one-handed? Would he even stay upright?

Winsor shoved the umbrella away so it clattered down on the floor, took a ragged deep breath, squared his shoulders and ran his hand back through the hair that had fallen over his face. The back of his neck was flushed. "You are correct." His voice was oddly calm. "I do need to get a little control."

To the side, Asya saw Vostrov quietly press his door closed. There was no audible click.

Winsor took another deep breath and looked up and down the corridor, his gaze finally settling on the watching guards. His hand went to the knot in his tie, apparently checking it was exactly centered. Quickly, his normal slight smile was back in place. He looked over at Anastasia. "When your boyfriend is sent back to his farm, you will still be welcome. You know my number."

When he started moving down the hall, Asya moved over to stand beside Peter, her hip resting lightly against his thigh, careful not to touch the parts she knew were still raw. As she suspected, the guard station was the right distance for Winsor's next volley, "Of course, I may not answer the phone. I am more particular than some about used goods."

Pete did not flinch. Instead, he simply turned to warm her cup of coffee from their thermos. As he did, Ambassador Wright, along with Rafi and Rishael, appeared at the guard station and were immediately passed through, and Vostrov, apparently notified of their arrival, threw open the corridor door and loudly invited them in.

The room was arranged precisely as it had been yesterday, except today the flowers on the table were red. When everyone was seated, Vostrov insisted on pouring tea and personally handing it across the table to each of his guests.

She would never know how she knew, but Asya sensed that Vostrov intended to use this courtesy to snub her. She therefore announced she was only drinking water this morning and had the satisfaction of watching a momentary frown flit across Vostrov's brow. How nice. He felt the same way about her that she felt about him – not a surprise – she had also always hated slopping the pigs at her uncle's farm.

She let a smile flit across her face, just to irritate the Russian President and then began gathering her papers. It was time to get down to business.

Vostrov offered Rafi milk and then expansively looked around the table. He must have gotten a good night's sleep. He was full of energy; his short body was almost bouncing in his chair. Finally, he began to address the Ambassador and she and the other interpreter went into action. "Rafi and I shared a bottle – no, two bottles – of good Russian vodka last night and we reached an agreement. He will return all missiles to Russia and we will build new silos for them on Russian soil. Agreed?"

Pete didn't waste a second interjecting: "I am sure that will be very disappointing to our President. I had heard that you and he consider yourselves to be friends. How will he ever explain to our Congress that a supposed friend is breaking the Treaty – again?"

Vostrov's head whipped from Rafi to Pete. "Those are our missiles, no matter what soil they currently sit upon. My Army will *never* accept losing them. The security of our State is at stake!"

Pete's voice was very deliberate, "If those obsolete missiles were so essential, I would think your generals would have brought up their existence 20 years ago."

Asya realized he was obviously hoping Vostrov would recognize Peter was about to provide an argument the Russian could himself subsequently use in Moscow. It might work. Pigs were among the smartest of nature's animals. It was difficult to tell if this particular one yet understood but Pete was soldiering on, "In fact, Mr President, there are several ways in which your generals have betrayed you." She got out a piece of paper and began making notes. It might help the other interpreter (and Vostrov) eventually realize this line of reasoning was important for them to record.

"First of all, during the Cold War someone broke the Strategic

Arms Limitation Treaty. I cannot even conceive what politics might have forced an American President to do if this treachery had come to light back then. Those men placed Mother Russia in serious danger!" Vostrov was listening, rather than automatically protesting, which was progress. He apparently hadn't noticed no one on his side was yet writing anything down.

Pete continued, "Secondly, Russia doesn't need any of the Kazakh weapons. Both the Politburo and your military have made arms agreements with the United States listing all the nuclear weapons necessary. Those lists do not include these missiles." Peter had let a tone of incredulity creep into his voice, leading Asya to think the man might well not be as ingenuous as he preferred everyone think.

"I can't imagine any Russian politician or general would have agreed to these treaties if he were not positive Russia had enough power to be safe." Vostrov finally nodded to his executive assistant, who began making notes. Asya tore off her last two pages and passed them across the table to him. Cribbing is permitted between special assistants.

Pete slowed his speaking pace even more, which eased both assistants' jobs. "Third, only a fool would recommend you waste Russia's precious defense rubles digging holes for old missiles that you no longer need. And, finally, any general who objects to destroying these weapons is a traitor..."

Vostrov was now not only listening, but also nodding approval.

Pete extended his right fist across the table toward the President and mimicked the manner in which the late Boris had counted. He stuck his pinky finger out – "A traitor because hiding the SS-9s was foolishly tempting a nuclear strike on Russian soil,"

Pete kept his arm level with the tabletop and stuck his ring finger out – "or, a traitor because he failed to alert you to the need for more missiles for your arsenal, or" –he closed his fist and slammed it against the top of the table and Asya winced as his heavy Naval Academy ring nicked the table's satin finish – "a traitor because he wants you to endanger the security of your country by throwing money away on unnecessary old-style nuclear grandstanding."

The fist slam teased a narrow smile from Vostrov, who spoke for five seconds. Asya quickly translated for Pete and the Ambassador: "He says Russia either keeps the plutonium or is transferred all the money the Canadians save on fuel for their power plant."

Pete pushed his chair back and stood up. "Nope, a deal is a deal, as my sainted grandfather used to say. You knew what was non-negotiable long before we arrived. Perhaps you should spend some more time discussing this with President Rafi – without the vodka."

He reached down to help Asya out of her chair as she completed translating these last words. "I would like to visit the Hermitage Museum before we leave tonight. Ambassador, do you and your wife want some company this afternoon?"

"You bet."

Pete turned to Rafi as if with an afterthought. "President Parzarev, will you please have the little landing strip near the cave cleared of snow? I asked my President to have one of our large military cargo planes land there in 72 hours. I thought we should go ahead and start accepting missile components as soon as possible. That plane should be large enough to carry all the warheads, and we can disassemble them at our convenience at Oak Ridge."

Peter took Anastasia by the arm and walked out of the room. She didn't look back. Pigs reportedly have excellent memories for faces.

CHAPTER FORTY-ONE

After paying the Hermitage admission fee, Asya and Pete, along with the Ambassador and his wife, joined the queue forming for a tour. Their guide was a small spritely woman, her graying hair covered by a bright red-and-blue silk scarf. When 20 people had assembled, she raised her hand for silence and began her spiel in unaccented American English, "The State Hermitage occupies six buildings centered around the Winter Palace of the Tsars. It demonstrates Mother Russia's early interest in the West…"

The Ambassador had been quiet during the ride from the hotel to the museum, but as soon as the tour group started moving, he pulled Pete and Asya aside. He was frowning.

"I'm not sure it was wise to call the President just yet."

"I agree, Mr Ambassador. I didn't. I thought I would leave the next telephone call to you after Vostrov agrees with my proposal."

The Ambassador's was puzzled. "You didn't?"

"Let's walk." As the crowd swept them along, Pete took the Ambassador's arm to keep him close, "No sir. I am afraid I lied to our Russian friend again. It will take the Air Force less than 36 hours to get a C-17 here once you do make that call. I would like to expedite action, but I can't believe Vostrov will agree to lose anything more than the plutonium – certainly not the warheads I asked for."

"You don't think we should be back at the table, talking?"

Pete pulled the Ambassador off to the side and waited for Anastasia to slip through the throng to join them. They were standing in front of an ancient Italian picture of a crucified Christ painted on a rough wood board. The humidity from the seawater surrounding the museum was inexorably pulling the piece apart along the age rings in the wood.

"Just what would we be talking about if we were back at that table, Mr Ambassador? You and I both know this opportunity fell into our President's lap. The only bargaining chips we have are in Russia's imagination. We have no military influence in this part of the world and damn little trade pressure to bring to bear." Pete grinned. "Mr Ambassador, all America can do out here is talk and reason. We're certainly not going to send Special Forces into Kazakhstan to move missiles or steal plutonium."

The Ambassador nodded and the three fell back in with the tour group, which was now proceeding down one of the long hallways of the Menshikov Palace. Soon they were standing before Vincent van Gogh's *White House at Night*. Asya had only glanced at the painting, but she and the Ambassador's wife seemed absorbed by the adjacent wall, where *Lilac Bush* was hanging.

Pete and the Ambassador lagged to the rear of the group. Pete could tell the Ambassador was still uneasy not to be in the thick of where he believed the action was taking place. "Mr Ambassador, I think the greatest thing we can do for America this afternoon is to soak up culture. Those two back at the hotel are busy worrying about how best they can stay in office. In the end, they are never going to do anything not in their best interests. At the same time, I am willing to bet – after Vostrov chews on this for a long time, he is going to decide – those interests are aligned."

When the crowd started to move on to the next gallery, Pete literally had to pull Asya away from *Lilac Bush*. As soon as she was safely in the Rembrandt Room, he picked up his conversation with the Ambassador. "Each of them has his own reasons for wanting to remain friends with your 'bud' back in Washington. I am willing to lay six to five that someone will come to find us before we complete this tour."

"If that happens, remind me to never play poker with you."

Anastasia interrupted them by grabbing Pete's hand and giving them both a scornful look. "Pardon me, Mr Ambassador, but Peter, shut up... You are in the most famous gallery in the world and this is its most glorious collection. You should be looking and listening, not talking." With her words, Pete and the Ambassador sheepishly turned their attention to the tour guide.

"...was sent by the Empress Catherine the Great to collect these pieces. Prince Golitsyn was responsible..."

Two galleries later, an excited Rishael caught up with their group and pulled Pete aside. Asya expressed her feelings with a look that would cleave marble.

"Vostrov wants to see you."

"OK, grab the Ambassador and Anastasia."

"No, he was very specific. Only you."

Pete made eye contact with the Ambassador and Asya and they both broke free from the tour, although Asya did not bother to pretend to appear pleased. They formed a small tight circle in one of the side galleries and Pete queried Rishael: "So, what happened?"

"Father agreed to give all the nuclear missiles back to Vostrov. In turn, Vostrov said he would not build new silos for the SS-9s as long as your President and Secretary of Defense do not personally visit Kazakhstan in the next 24 months, but do find a reason to call on him in Moscow. Father agreed as long as your Vice President visited Kazakhstan."

Pete turned enquiringly to the Ambassador, who nodded. "I can arrange that, but what about the plutonium?"

"This is the subject of the last two hours and involved raised voices. Finally, they sent everyone from the room. Father told me afterward that Vostrov is going to come down with the flu, be unable to travel, and have to remain in St Petersburg for three days. The United States can have the plutonium if it is out of Kazakhstan before he returns to Moscow."

Fair enough, Pete thought. He would need some specialists to disassemble the warheads, but that could be worked. He placed his right arm around Rishael's shoulder. "You and your father are doing the right thing for Kazakhstan." Pete was momentarily nonplussed when Asya reached up and pulled Rishael down in order to deliver a kiss on his cheek, but decided to ignore the byplay and turned to the Ambassador. "I think it is now time for your phone call to the President. I will parallel your call with a report to the Secretary of Defense."

Rishael interjected, "But Vostrov said he wants to meet immediately!"

Asya inserted herself into the conversation: "I will finish the tour with the Ambassador's wife and then join you both back at the hotel. The Ambassador can make his phone call while you are seeing Vostrov.

Rishael will escort you back and stand by if an interpreter is needed." She turned, took the Ambassador's wife's arm and they walked off in the direction of their group.

"Captain, thank you for seeing me," the translator repeated. The four of them were seated in leather-upholstered chairs that had magically replaced the long table. Vostrov waved at the interpreter and the Lieutenant Colonel with his aluminum cases. "We did not complete introductions before. I would like you to meet my brother" – the interpreter pointed to himself – "and my oldest son" – he gestured at the Lieutenant Colonel.

Vostrov paused, pulled a large white handkerchief from his pocket and blew his nose vigorously, mumbling as he did. His brother smiled as he interpreted, "He is asking you to please excuse him – he seems to be coming down with a cold."

As Vostrov carefully wiped his mustache, his brother added, "A 72-hour cold, no more."

"I fully understand, Mr President."

Vostrov carefully refolded and tucked the handkerchief away in his side coat pocket. Whatever else he wanted to say was obviously difficult for him. Throughout this conversation, he had been looking at his brother, rather than Pete, as he spoke.

"Captain, he wants to thank you for asking Rafi to warn him before you started that rocket motor."

Vostrov leaned back in his chair, speaking slowly as he interlocked his fingers over his chest. "Without that warning, I could have had much difficulty with our Generals when our own satellites detected a signal in the vicinity of our old missile field."

Pete could only guess at the excitement in the Politburo that night. Had the event, and the Russian President's foreknowledge that it was not a real missile firing, helped Vostrov cement his power? Probably hadn't hurt.

Vostrov finally looked at the American, "I assume you also warned your President?"

"Yes."

"Good. So I believed." Vostrov's face expressed relief before he again adopted the persona of the jolly Rotarian and pushed back his chair to stand. The audience was over. "You are leaving Russia?"

He had risen as Vostrov stood, "Yes, tonight."

The President put his hand in the middle of Pete's back and guided him toward the door. Pete took two steps before abruptly stopping. Out of the corner of his eye, he saw Vostrov's son quickly flip up the holster flap that lay over his sidearm.

"Mr President. I am glad the warning was useful to you. I would like a favor in return."

Vostrov smiled, "Of course. What?"

"I want to know which American betrayed Anastasia."

The smile immediately disappeared from Vostrov's lips and he stepped back, spitting his words.

The translation followed quickly, "My brother says you are lucky he let her live. Your cruiser in the Gulf would have been useless. She is a traitor. We only not kill her because of his promise to Rafi. If she ever returns to Russian soil, he will take her silly little knife and cut her throat with it."

As the angry words spilled over him, Pete stood mute and motionless, letting the President's hot words wash over him. When the emotion halted and the flush began to leave Vostrov's face, Pete softly asked, "I killed 100 men to give you that warning, Mr President. Was it worth it?"

Pete watched Vostrov think. His eyes made one calculation, then another. Finally, he reached a conclusion, looked back at his son and said a few short words. The son picked up his two metal cases, walked across the room and placed one on the partner's desk. Vostrov followed, motioning Pete to accompany him.

"These two cases are the best shield Mother Russia has against America."

Vostrov indicated the silver case on the floor, "This is the machine that would release our nuclear arsenal in retaliation if America ever attempts a sneak attack."

He moved to the case on the desk as his son stepped aside, catching Pete's eye as he slid his weapon slightly out and back within his leather holster. "This case is how I ensure America does not surprise Russia." Pete gave one slight nod to the son to indicate he had received the warning as Vostrov undid the top two buttons of his shirt, fishing out a long chain with two keys.

The father selected one of the keys and leaned over the case on the desk, carefully unlocking both latches. As he stood up, tucking the keys back inside his inner shirt, he commented, "These are the files on our most productive spies." He looked at Pete with some pride, "My son and I maintain these ourselves!"

A hell of a way to run a railroad, Pete thought to himself, but as long as the track's headed my way, who am I to comment? My only role is to keep a poker face.

Using his broad body to shield the contents of the case from Pete's view, Vostrov raised the lid. Pete glimpsed a thick pile of gray folders inside. The one he could see also had two diagonal red stripes imprinted across the cover and was stamped with heavy black Cyrillic printing.

Vostrov ran his thumb over the edges of the organizer sleeves while he obviously pondered. Then, without looking at Pete, he used the thick nail on his right thumb to fish out one of the folders so the cover was partially exposed. He pulled that one loose and took a cursory look inside before placing it on the table beside the case. Picking it up, he turned to Pete and tapped the file against his palm as his son carefully closed the case and re-engaged the latches. "Your warning was very helpful, very helpful." He repeated calmly, "Very helpful. Moreover, I think this particular spy's usefulness to Russia has run its course." Vostrov's eyes flicked to his brother, who gave an almost imperceptible nod.

Vostrov opened the file. Slowly and deliberately, he scanned each page. Twice he paused and tore a flimsy yellow-colored sheet of paper from the file, handing the removed piece of paper back to his son. Finally, he closed the folder and extended it to Pete as his brother translated. "I needed your call about the rocket and I believe this man has become dangerous. He is making very stupid choices!"

Pete closed his hand on the folder, but Vostrov still held on tightly as he spoke and his brother translated, "Tell your President how much I value his friendship."

"I will, sir."

Reluctantly, as if part of him were still undecided, Vostrov released his grip on the red-striped dossier.

CHAPTER FORTY-TWO

When Peter returned to the suite, they were all packed out, their coats and guns laid out on the bed. Anastasia was seated at a small table by the window where she could look out over the canal. She was intermittently glancing through a book she had purchased at the Hermitage gift shop and comparing the intensity of the photos with the colors produced by the sun glinting on the water.

"Asya, I just spoke with the Ambassador. A C-17 aircraft will arrive at the cave in 24 hours. Rafi and Rishael have already lifted off for Astana. The American Ambassador has agreed to let us join him on his plane, so we will be able to personally meet the C-17."

She closed the book, using her finger to mark her place and shut her eyes. She could tell Peter was upset. And he knew she was only interested in what had happened in his discussion with the pig – but instead he was talking travel arrangements. Ergo, something was wrong. She reopened her book and slowly leafed over another page, watching him through her lowered lashes.

He strode impatiently across the room to look out her window. "There will be knowledgeable technicians to disassemble the warheads aboard the C-17. It's good that we'll be there to meet them." He was tapping the edge of a manila folder against his palm as he looked down the street that ran along the canal. Her eyes focused on the document. Where in the world did he ever get anything labeled "Of Special Importance"? Did he know it was a state crime to even have such a folder? The pig must have set him up! He knew Pete didn't read Cyrillic.

Stunned at Vostrov's continued treachery, she stood up, reaching for the file, her new book sliding from her lap onto the floor. "Peter, you can't have that!"

Peter thrust the folder behind his back. "Vostrov gave it to me."

"I just bet he did! He is an asshole!"

"He was helping."

"Peter, he is a thug! He helped his own uncle into the Gulag." She reached around his waist with both arms for the folder. "Just let me have it. We need to burn it now, before anyone comes – quickly!"

He put his hand on her chest, "I asked for a favor. I…"

Expecting a favor from the pig was beyond stupid. She thought Peter was smarter than that…

"…who had betrayed you. He gave me this." Peter was looking everywhere in the room except at her, which was difficult, since his hand was now in the middle of her chest pushing her away as she continued to impatiently reach for the folder. He spoke even faster now: "I don't know if this is a setup, or what Vostrov was trying to accomplish." Now he was speaking to the door behind her head. "I already asked the Ambassador to courier a copy back to the Secretary of Defense."

He took a deep breath, his gaze shifted to a window over her other shoulder. "If this file is true, the traitor should be arrested shortly after the Secretary receives the diplomatic pouch."

She gave up struggling with him, took a step back and folded her arms. It was either that or reach for her knife. "Peter, give me the damn thing!"

He reluctantly handled over the folder and walked away to stand at another window. He still didn't look at her. She inspected the manila cover, opened it, and gave an involuntary gasp. A candid photo was neatly glued in the top left corner of the first page. It had apparently been surreptitiously taken on a busy sidewalk. It was an old photo, but the individual had not changed much. She placed the dossier on the table and dropped back into her chair.

She read through the first three pages before her eyes began to blur and she had to look up for a second while they cleared. Pete was still staring out his window. "Did anyone translate this for you, Peter?"

"No."

She let her breath slowly ease out and then took another even deeper one. "Then I shall do so."

Her finger moved down the first paragraph until her lips involuntarily tightened and she paused to summarize. "It says he was recruited by a fellow bisexual while he was at Yale. He received $2,000 a month for the first five years. After he obtained his initial political appointment, his stipend was increased to $5,000 a month.

"There follows a list of the Russians he identified as disloyal, along with when they were executed or to which concentration camp in the Gulag they were assigned." She turned a page. "In most cases, they were dispatched the usual way." She tugged her left ear. "A bullet in the back of their brains." She had thought herself long removed from this, but it was not as if this were the first such profile she had read. She steeled herself and continued her quick summary for Peter as if the pages were only an excerpt from a touring guide. Her finger paused and then again began moving down the page, "A few individuals, mostly non-Russians, including me, are listed as unconfirmed."

She turned a page and her finger moved faster, "It records every time he met his handler or made a drop, what he provided and the dates on which he was paid. It lists where he lived, where he drank, who he tried to recruit, his daily routine, where he partied, who he slept with, as well as his partner's sexual preferences." Her finger hesitated as she read silently for a moment, and then continued to paraphrase aloud, her voice shaking for a few words before steadying, "It identifies those individuals he suspected might be susceptible to bribery..." She turned the page and looked up at Peter. "There are pages missing."

He turned away from the window and moved toward her, but she warded him away by extending her left hand. Her right arm was wrapped tight around her stomach.

"Vostrov tore out some pages out before he handed me the file."

She nodded and slowly flipped through several pages of tight script. "Over the 15 years, he had two handlers. Each wrote yearly evaluations of him. Both believed him to be loyal to Russia, very reliable, knowledgeable and worthy of continued cultivation. After the United States attacked Iraq, he requested his salary be increased to $10,000 a month. Because of FSS fiscal pressures, he was informed that he would only receive a 10 percent increase."

She read the last page carefully: "In his last evaluation, he is noted as being concerned about his safety, and also voiced the opinion that now was the time for Russia to re-establish control over the border countries, especially rich ones like Kazakhstan. He offered several suggestions on particular events that could be manipulated to serve as triggers to initiate new policies."

Asya turned the last few pages and let the folder close. She pushed the file away from her. It slid across the desk and fell on her Hermitage book. The file lay open on its back, the photograph staring up at both of them.

"Peter, I slept with him."

He silently nodded, his eyes focused completely on her.

"I made love to the man who arranged for my mother to be killed." Her right hand reached under her skirt and drew her jeweled knife from its sheath. She stood and raised it toward the window. The sun rays glinted off the blade. She knew her voice was rising. She tried to keep it from becoming shrill. "That man owes me *kun*."

"Anastasia, Vostrov could be running a game."

"No," she closed her eyes and slowly shook her head as tears welled in the corners of her eyes. "There are things in that file we did in private, Peter. I will bury this knife in his throat."

Pete stepped toward her and took her in his arms, but she kept the knife between them, tip up. She looked up into his eyes. He had to understand. "I will take his blood, Peter. No matter what else, I must avenge my mother."

"Asya, I don't want you to live with his blood on your hands. I want you with me. I don't want us to begin our lives by watching blood gush from his throat. We need to put him in jail."

She held both his gaze and the knife steady. "Peter, she was my mother. This is my land, my culture. If you seek to love me, then..."

Before she could finish, Peter had grabbed her right hand, rotating their arms together. He took her knife from her unresisting fingers and deliberately made two cuts parallel to the faded scars already present in their arms, "Take my blood, Asya." He pressed his arm against hers so their blood joined before it continued down his arm. "Take my blood for *kun*."

She pulled away so her breasts no longer touched his chest. "I cannot, Peter. It is not enough."

Between them, unnoticed, their joined blood dripped on Winsor's smiling face.

CHAPTER FORTY-THREE

Asya was so exhausted, Pete was surprised she made it to the plane. As soon as they boarded, she buckled her seatbelt, pulled a blanket to her chin, curled up in her seat and closed her eyes. She didn't stir through takeoff or for the landing in Moscow. Pete couldn't tell if she overheard him thanking the Ambassador and his wife for their support as well as the use of the Embassy plane.

As soon as the airplane reached altitude out of Moscow, Pete used the secure telephone to check in with the Secretary of Defense, updating him on events and thanking him for positioning the cruiser. He then had a short conversation with Bob Farrell at the CIA and a much longer one with the Duty Officer at the Transportation Command at Scott

Air Force Base. By the time he hung up, he had a good grasp of the capabilities of the C-17 in route.

Since Anastasia's eyes remained closed, Pete went up to the cockpit to get to know the pilots. In the left seat of the turbo prop was Lieutenant Commander Suzanne Metcalf – "Suze is fine, Captain." She was lean, blond, attractive, and in her late thirties, Pete guessed. Her co-pilot was the slightly younger Lieutenant Marco Rattone – "Ratt for short, Captain." His Mediterranean coloring would have declared his Italian heritage even if his name had not. He was probably an inch shorter than Suze. He had black hair and alert, sharp eyes, and wore a large gold Naval Academy ring on the third finger of his left hand.

The plane was on autopilot but both aviators' eyes constantly scanned the horizon as Suze and Pete talked. "I'm jet-qualified, Captain, but if I can't fly off carriers, I'll probably opt out of the Navy. I might as well be piloting one of those big sky buses around for an airline. It will be more money, more time at home and it can't be any more boring than flying VIPs around. No offense, sir." She took a quick sideways glance to gauge his reaction as she diplomatically changing the subject. "By the way, I noticed you weren't using the headset in the cabin. If you put it on and press the throat-mic switch, you can speak directly to me without leaving your seat and you will hear more easily above the engine noise."

Pete shifted the discussion to the business of the day and how events might play out. It was another half-hour before he closed the cabin door and returned to the silent Asya. Her eyes were now open, but she was staring out her window, apparently focused on the gray cirrostratus clouds that blanketed the horizon. She did not turn to look at him.

Pete dutifully donned one of the available headsets and checked communications with the pilots before losing himself in his own thoughts. A hunger for vengeance seemed to be consuming Asya. Was there any room for him?

Suze's voice rang in his ear, "Captain, we are almost at the airfield. Do you want to make a reconnoitering pass over the cave you were talking about? I can fly down practically any canyon if you can point it out."

Pete looked out the window. They were about 5,000 feet above the ground. The narrow road that ran past the airfield was clearly visible. He keyed his mic. "Good idea. Use the airfield as a checkpoint. Then follow the road north a few klicks looking for a turn off to the left. I'll ask Asya to help us identify the right one." He looked over, but in response, Asya only closed her eyes.

"Suze, the canyon goes about 10 miles back into the mountain range before it stops. Just pick one that seems likely. It won't take but a few moments to determine if we're wrong and then we can check another. I'm sure we will recognize our cave from the abrupt way the canyon ends."

As they passed the airport, Suze descended another thousand feet. From the lower altitude it was even more obvious that the mountains in this area routinely received tens of meters of snowfall.

Pete keyed his throat mic again. "Suze, just up ahead. Aren't those pretty deep ruts? Someone got stuck there. I'm sure those mark the turnoff to our road!"

A minute later, they passed the destroyed guard shack. Suze had pulled the aircraft up another 2,000 feet to keep them above the canyon walls.

"Hey! Sir! I count four trucks and a jeep. Where did they come from?" She had put the plane into a lazy flat circle to the right for better visibility. Her surprised intercom report mirrored his own uneasiness.

She keyed her mic again. "I thought you said the Americans were bringing their own equipment. I didn't see anything when we flew over that airport. It looked like there was still snow on the runway. I certainly wouldn't have missed seeing a C-17!"

He was doing his own evaluation of the situation on the ground, "A platoon from the Air Assault Brigade was assigned to provide site security. It must be them."

As they completed their first full 360, a truck – one warhead strapped to its bed – rolled out of the cave door. Suddenly, several of the soldiers in the vicinity of the truck raised their rifles. Small bursts of rifle smoke indicated firing.

"Commander, get us up!

"Lieutenant, contact the President of Kazakh's airplane. I need to talk to him!"

Suze had already two-blocked both engine throttles and Pete and Asya were thrust back in their seats. As the plane rose, Pete spoke sharply to Asya, "Buckle your seatbelt tight and put on a headset! You need to get your head in the game. Now!'

When the aircraft climbed to an altitude of 12,000 feet, well out of small-arms range, Suze winged over to circle back toward the canyon. Ratt achieved contact with Rafi mid-turn and patched him through to Pete's headset.

Pete angrily asked, "Mr President, did you tell anyone to start disassembling the warheads?"

"Absolutely not! My orders are to keep everyone out of the cave. The door is to be barricaded and locked."

"Then you have a problem. There are men in the cave, people are shooting at us, and someone is stealing your missiles!" The plane was again passing over the canyon. A second flatbed truck was exiting the cave with another warhead strapped to it. The smaller vehicle was gone.

"Sir, the jeep is almost out of the canyon!"

Suze had also been counting vehicles. Now that she had alerted him, he saw a cloud of snow tunneling down the canyon road.

Pete returned his attention to communicating to Rafi. "How long until you can get enough soldiers here to really secure this place?"

"You're breaking up, Pete, I don't understand."

Asya broke in over Pete with a burst of Kazakh, and The President's voice immediately answered. She turned to Pete, her pupils in the process of rapidly shrinking to their normal size. "He says he will get troops on the way to the cave and some jets over the area as quickly as possible. Rishael is contacting the 38th Airborne right now. Rafi will also call Vostrov."

Another burst of Kazakh assailed their ears and Asya held up her hand as she listened. "Rishael just got through to the 38th. They now report they have been unable for the last several hours to raise the detachment responsible for guarding the cave!"

Over Asya's shoulder, Pete could see Suze shake her head. They both knew what that report meant. The 38th should have known the detachment was history when the first call wasn't returned. Only inexperienced commanders expected chicken shit to magically turn to chicken salad.

Asya was staring at the cabin floor, using both hands to press her headset earpieces tight against her head. She turned to shout to Pete above the noise of the airplane: "The Airborne Commander says they are scrambling jets and assembling soldiers. They will have four jets here in an hour and, if it doesn't snow again, three squads of troops will be on the ground in another six hours."

Pete frowned as he thought. There would be no telling where those vehicles they had seen in the canyon would be by then. The jeep was already racing past the airport, a wide cone of snow in his wake, and two trucks still near the cave entrance were busy hurriedly turning around.

The vehicle they had seen pulling out of the cave had already passed the old guard shack. Each warhead that exited the canyon could make eight to 10 nuclear bombs. Who knew where in the world they might show up?

He keyed his throat mic: "Suze, we need to stop some trucks."

"I know, sir. But this is a VIP plane. Ratt and I only have pistols."

"You don't carry anything else?"

"We also have a special survival kit if we go down in a bandit area. It's in the cami roll behind your seats. But it only includes two rifles, a couple of 9mm clips and a half-dozen grenades…" Her voice rose a bit in excitement, "If they are getting away with nuclear weapons, we could set this crate down at the entrance and use the rifles. Maybe if we get a lucky hit on the first truck's tires it will block the others."

Pete heard Ratt mutter 'suicide,'" but was distracted when Asya placed her hand on his arm and motioned for him to remove his headset. As she leaned up to speak directly in his ear, he could see color was returning to her cheeks. "Didn't Rishael or Saken say they had trouble keeping the canyon open in winter?"

Right! Pete looked at her for a second and nodded, before redonning his headset to speak to the pilots. "Do either of you ski?"

"Of course," Suze replied, "I was born and grew up in Denver."

"Think you can identify where an avalanche might be brewing?"

Five minutes later, Suze had brought the plane down to 500 feet above the north canyon wall and throttled back to just above stall speed. Pete had succeeded in breaking out one of the airplane's plastic windows after emptying nearly a full rifle clip through it. When Suze announced she was flat and level, Pete and Asya began lobbing out all the grenades, one after another. Suze immediately began a climb, wheeling the plane 30 degrees up and to the left so they all could watch.

Below, the snow plumed twice, then nothing. The third time, the snow suddenly dimpled for 100 yards. A small white puff rose straight up like a geyser from the center of the dimple and the entire mountain side slowly began to move, as if a huge sand dune were sliding before the wind, except, once started, the white flow slipped ever faster, quickly beginning to pick up rocks and tree trunks along with the snow. By the time Suze completed a half-circle and returned, several hundred meters of the canyon was filled high with snow and debris. As they watched, all the trucks halted behind this barrier.

Pete wrapped Asya in his arms, "Brilliant idea!"

She looked up at him. A smile was beginning to play around her lips, when Suze's voice interrupted in his ear, "What about the jeep?"

Damn! He had forgotten about the one vehicle that gotten out of the canyon. "Let's find it. We can tail it until someone arrives who has more than a popgun."

At 12,000 feet, there was still just enough oxygen to breathe, but one could see nearly a hundred miles. After five minutes, Ratt spotted their target, now headed due west, snow billowing out in a distinct vapor trail. As they closed the distance, they saw the jeep abruptly slow once as wind shear blew drifting snow across the road in front of it. Evidently, at the speed he was going, the jeep driver was having occasional trouble seeing.

"Captain," Suze's voice was concerned, "we have a problem. I am going to need to put this plane down someplace to refuel before those jets get here. Looks like the jeep may reach that forested area up ahead in 15 to 20 minutes. Following it will be iffy after then." She paused, "Do either of my VIPs have any more great ideas like the avalanche thing?"

Pete looked over at Asya and she shook her head. He thought for a moment before keying the mic: "I do, but I don't know where I could possibly find the exceptional pilot I would need to carry it out."

The plane's wings wagged and Suze's voice boomed in his ears. "You are one lucky Captain today, sir." His ears clicked as she changed radio frequencies. In a second she was back: "By the way, the jets are in the air."

They would be too late.

"Commander, look down ahead of us about 025 where there is a thin line of trees, and then a few yards further on where the road appears to buckle. See it? Are you really good enough to land on a carrier?"

Suze's answer was to abruptly nose the airplane over so that Asya and Pete fell forward against their seatbelt webbing.

A minute later, the Ambassador's plane skimmed across the road, engines at full throttle, landing gear and flaps down, just in front of the jeep. The airplane's right wing passed within a few feet of one end of a stone bridge that arched over a frozen stream. As Suze banked the plane sharply to the left and back toward the road, Asya reported the jeep was skidding sideways as it entered the thick snow plume their propellers had thrown up.

The Commander began taxiing the plane squarely down the road toward the snow cloud, the aircraft's wings snapping against the flexible aluminum side-road snow markers like playing cards on a bicycle wheel. She nosed into the cloud before Pete closed his hand on her shoulder and she finally set the brakes. Less than 20 feet in front of them, the vehicle they had been chasing was nosed up at a slight angle against the left abutment of the bridge, steam pouring from under the hood.

"Stay with the plane, Commander. If these guys start shooting, get the hell out of here." Pete swung the door open, pushed the folding staircase out, and leapt from the plane. His right foot skidded on an icy patch, his knee buckled and he pitched face-first into the four-foot snow bank alongside the road. As he used his good arm to struggle to his knees, Asya passed him, running toward the jeep.

"Asya," Pete yelled, "Help me!"

She didn't pause. He saw a gun in her right hand and the glint off the blade in her left. Damn it! They both suspected who was in that jeep. Pete got to his feet and began limping as fast as he could, dragging his protesting right leg.

Ahead of him, he saw her reach the driver's side of the jeep. She hesitated, raised her pistol and lowered it. He was within 10 feet. "Asya, don't."

She fired once, and then again.

He saw the blade of her knife gleam in the sunlight as it slid through the air like a scythe. Blood arced in the air around her and Peter stumbled the last three feet. He fell forward, using his upper body to pin Asya against the vehicle.

The bodies of two swarthy men were belted into the front. The corpse in the passenger seat was leaning back against his door, his rifle in his lap, his eyes clouding, a last pulse of blood still oozing from the two bullet wounds in his chest. The man in the driver's seat hung forward in his seat belt, head tilting downward and left at an unnatural angle, his right hand still closed on a Glock in his lap.

Asya's voice was emotionless. "They were just coming around when I got here. The one you thought I was shooting is in the back seat. I hope he's dead, but I don't think so."

Pete pushed himself to his feet, opened the jeep's back door and pulled the unseatbelted body from the floor. Blood was still welling from a gash above the unconscious man's right ear. Pete pulled him out and pushed him face down in the snow. He was not about to ask Asya to help immobilize their prisoner. He suspected it was difficult for her to continue standing by the hood.

Winsor moaned once, but did not move, and after Pete had located and removed both a pisto and a knife, he began trying to unbuckle Winsor's belt.

A feminine voice came from behind him, "Captain, could you use another hand and some duct tape?"

"I could." Pete struggled to his feet and let her tape Winsor's arms behind him. "Suze, I thought you were going to stay with the plane?"

"Ratt is in the pilot's seat. I am not about to lose one of my VIPs during one of my boring flights."

"You may need to work on following orders, but I like your attitude."

"Commander, go back and have Ratt feather the props and idle the engines. Then he can help you put this bundle in one of the seats and secure him. I want you to fly us back to the air strip. Asya and I will get a ride home on the C-17."

"Peter." He turned around. Anastasia had moved away from the jeep's hood and was standing immediately behind him. Her pupils were dilated again, the gray shadows beneath her eyes even larger than before. She extended her knife and gun to him. "Take these. I want to go with them. I want to return home to Astana."

"Asya, please." Peter heard his own pleading clearly in his voice.

"I am going home to my uncle."

"Uncle?"

"Rafi, Peter." She said the words slowly, as if she were in a deep sleep. "How did you ever think I got out of Russia alive? President Parzarev is my mother's only brother."

Pete waved as the Ambassador's plane wagged its wings leaving the airfield. As he watched, its silhouette rose above the rapidly incoming smudge and black dots that, a minute later, separated into silhouettes – a lumbering C-17 along with two Kazakh escorts.

CHAPTER FORTY-FOUR

Pete and Rafi were sitting across from each other on the couches in front of the fire. At the beginning of their conversation, the fire had been crackling quite briskly. Now the only noise was the occasional quiet murmur as a log broke further open. Outside, a drenching cold rain was soaking the city of Astana.

Pete was staring down at his hands. "She won't see me."

Rafi sighed. "I'm helpless, Pete. My guards are more loyal to Asya than they are to me. She was a legend when she was only a beautiful Olympic champion." He shrugged. "Now that it's rumored she personally killed Chechen terrorists who were trying to steal our riches" – Rafi held his hands out, palms up in mock despair – "they take her every wish as an iron-clad order."

Pete looked into the flames. He had already spent 72 hours in Astana. The plutonium had been removed from the warheads with 15 hours to spare. He had requested the C-17 make a slight detour on its way home to America. It had dropped him off at the Kazakh capitol.

After three days, he knew only that the hotel had no concept of how to properly make poached eggs and that the shortest path to Rafi's private residence involved crossing through the backyard of a woman with a second cousin in Duluth. His experience at the hotel during breakfasts was the same as at Rafi's residency: he had been disappointed every time. The heavily armed guards at the President's house were unfailingly polite, but Pete was simply not permitted to enter.

Rafi got up from the couch and picked up a dark blue diplomatic pouch from his desk. "I have something for you. The Secretary of Defense sent you a personal cable. Given the circumstances, your Ambassador entrusted me to ensure you received it."

Rafi's secretary entered with coffee, placing the service on the low table between the two couches and wordlessly poured two cups. Pete nodded his thanks.

After she left the room, Rafi handed Pete the courier pouch, placed his personal letter opener on the coffee table and sat down across from him, cradling a delicate coffee cup.

Pete unzipped the pouch and a sealed envelope slid out. "Captain

O'Brien's eyes only" was neatly typed as an address. Pete slipped the letter opener under the flap and cut the end open. He spread the yellow sheet flat on the table, bending over it to read the decryption machine faint printing.

Pete,

Thank you for your phone call. The C-17 contents arrived safely at Oak Ridge and everything is proceeding as planned. The President had a very good conversation with Vostrov, and appropriate arrangements are being made.

The President is very pleased, as am I.

I have some not-so-good news with respect to the passenger you shipped us. There are several considerations, some having to do with our friends in the Congress. An agreement has been struck, of which we believe the subject is as yet unaware. He is to be wrung dry by Bob and his friends at the Farm for six months, and then permitted to return to private life.

The file proved invaluable in several peripheral discussions. I personally excised some non-essential information relative to your assistant.

The President wanted to speak personally to you and I have asked him to wait as your office (Maureen) informs me you deserve time to resolve some personal issues. You have my number if I may be of assistance.

Cordially yours,

Bill Johnson

Secretary of Defense
United States of America

Pete, please destroy this note.

Pete reread the message once. He then placed it on top of the leather pouch and, using the tip of the letter opener, sliced out the paragraph about Winsor's file and put it in his billfold. Pete balled up the rest of the yellow sheet, tossing it into the fire. The paper ball hit a log and fell near the brick hearth, apparently escaping destruction. As Pete reached for a poker, it began to darken on one edge. In a few seconds, the brown became black. Ultimately, a small wick of flame appeared.

After a long silence, Pete finally spoke. "I can't leave without her, sir."

"I understand that is your hope." Rafi selected two brown cubes of sugar from the bowl on the tray and slowly stirred them into his coffee.

There was nothing for Pete to say. He was out of ideas.

"Pete, are you familiar with the St Nicholas Cathedral here in Astana?"

"No, sir."

"It is quite a famous church locally. Quite beautiful. It is the tallest building in Astana, constructed without using any nails. I believe it is the most stunning Orthodox Cathedral in Kazakhstan.

"When the Russians were here, they closed it, but I had it refurbished and reopened as soon as we achieved independence. The Cathedral is quite near our home. Often, when I face a difficult problem, I walk there, light a candle and think. I find it peaceful. Many an answer has come to me while I was standing in the *sabor*." Rafi paused, sipped some of his coffee and glanced at his watch. "You might consider doing the same."

Peter stood and held out his hand, "Thank you for your time today, Mr President."

"Would you like the address of the cathedral?"

"Sure." Pete was only being polite and both of them knew it.

Rafi shook his head. "You would probably only get lost. I am leaving the office early today. Why don't I drop you off there?" Pete considered objecting, but it would have been churlish, for Rafi had his hand in the small of his back, an umbrella over his head, and was guiding him out the office and down the front steps to a waiting car.

The cathedral was squarely in the middle of a park. It was a surprisingly deserted place, given the beauty of the cobblestone paths and the long tree branches swaying in the wind. It appeared the perfect spot for lovers, but it was a cold, overcast day. Maybe Kazakh lovers weren't the hardy types. The sun was hidden by dark, heavy clouds, although the rain was already beginning to stop. Above the graceful sub-arches, six steeples reached skyward, their ornate round peaks gilded with gold leaf. Each of the high windows held clear glass, rather than the stained glass of Pete's Protestant background.

When he had climbed the eight wide stairs to the heavy door, he looked back. Rafi's car still sat, motor idling, now 50 feet away. It looked as if the President had no intention of moving until Pete entered the cathedral.

Actually, going inside wasn't going to hurt anything. It was a remarkably unique church and Rafi was right, Pete would have left Astana without seeing it if Rafi hadn't forced his hand. If nothing else, it was aptly named – Nicholas was the patron saint of sailors.

As he swung the tall door open, he heard Rafi's car begin to finally rumble across the cobblestones. Pete turned and lifted his hand in farewell, but Rafi's head was buried in his paperwork.

Inside, it was almost eerily quiet. The entire church was deserted. The hollow flickers from guttering candles were the only sounds to be heard. A lone wick illuminated the altar screen. A few more wavered in icon coves. A large chandelier, hung in the exact center of the cathedral, burned brightly, but no light penetrated the gray shadows along the walls. It was unlike any church Pete had seen. There were no pews, just a few scattered simple chairs along the sides. He pushed the tall wooden door firmly shut.

As his eyes adapted, he realized he was not alone. There was a single penitent inside. A slight man, his head covered by a hood, stood in an alcove around to his left, praying to himself. Three burning white tapers behind him cast long smudges against the icon and the wall in front of him.

Pete closed his eyes and eased his shoulders back against an ancient beam. He let the silence, the age and the simplicity of the structure seep into his bones. Time passed. He may even have dozed. He had certainly lost track of time. Something had changed. His headache was nearly gone and the penitent was praying louder. What the hell didn't Asya understand about the two of them?

The chanting voice of the penitent was growing even louder. It was seriously damn annoying. He could feel his headache returning. Didn't the guy realize this was a church?

Maybe he should follow Rafi's advice and light himself a candle. Pete moved toward the nearest brass candleholder, reaching in his pocket for a donation.

CHAPTER FORTY-FIVE

The little hairs on the back of Asya's neck had begun prickling the second Pete pushed open the Cathedral door. It was in St Petersburg that she had first realized she felt different when she was near him. She wondered if he felt the same? Had he even taken the time to notice? If he ever stopped hitting people for five minutes, he might be more aware of things.

She had lost her concentration as soon as he physically closed the door. Her uncle should be thrown into her aunt's pig pen!

She restarted her prayer and searched again for her mother. She knew what she wanted her to say. She had been her mother's only child and her mother had been her best friend. They had engaged in make-believe conversations all their lives. Asya hadn't stopped the practice just because her mother had died.

"So, a very handsome man. He looks strong."

"Not ugly, but also not very sensitive. Not the type of man you take to the ballet."

"You live now in the United States. You go to baseball, not ballet. Besides, you were always sensitive enough for three people."

"Mother!"

"Anastasia. You know it is true. You need someone who loves you and can put up with you, not someone to coddle you."

"He will never understand me."

"Child, even I never fully understood you. My brother says he loves you. That is more than enough. Bring him over here so I can better see him."

Asya stood still for a moment.

"Don't roll your eyes. You think I can't see? Bring him over here so I don't have to cause you to do something that will embarrass you. Show me some of that stuff those nasty Russians taught you in spy school. You were always better at that than me."

Asya thought about stamping her foot, but instead, began praying again, this time a little louder. She thought the anguish in her voice was a nice touch. Behind her, Peter started to move. He was now about 20 feet from the candleholder.

She sensed he was uncomfortable approaching closer. He glanced at the closest icon to her and began edging away. He probably assumed she was praying for the soul of a child. Damn it! Mothers, even dead ones, were such pains. She was going to have to bring out the big guns. She was going to have to commit.

She switched mid-phrase from Kazakh to English "…hear me, Mother, in the English you taught me!"

He was still backing away. Over the past two days, she had made her peace with her Kazakh family. She was finally ready. Of course, Uncle was not about to let her announce her decision on her own timetable – oh no… She added a few tears.

"Mother, I have betrayed you. I betrayed you for my own love. I owed you *kun*, Mother, I owed you *kun*. I left your death unavenged. I wanted love for myself."

She sensed a mental nudge. "I think you were about to go over the top, but he appears to love you more for yourself than for your sense of timing and drama. He has begun walking your way and I am just going to watch the rest. I love you, Miss Sensitive."

She heard Pete light a candle and then felt him place his hands lightly on her shoulders.

She stifled her tears. He looked up at the icon in front of them and spoke, "Please also forgive me, Mother. I begged your child not to avenge you. I love her so much. I do not want her broken. I want to live with her for the rest of our days."

His words echoed in the empty church and slowly died away into the grain of the wood.

Pete continued, bending to pour his words into her hair. "I know I can only truly live if she is with me. I would die, Mother, for her happiness." He paused, dropping his voice even further, his lips moving in her hair, his whisper barely discernible. "Please forgive your daughter, so she may forgive me."

Asya's head nearly rocked from her mother's nudge. "I thought you said you were the sensitive one."

"He may be showing signs of improvement."

Pete nuzzled her ear, "What, sweetheart?"

She leaned back into him, reaching her hands back to his arms, and, as he touched her hands, she cupped her fingers into his. She shook her scarf-covered head loose from her hood, leaned back against his chest and shifted her hips back into him.

"I said the visibility is improving, dear Peter. Look up."

High above, the sun had broken through the clouds. The light, diffused by the dusty air, drifted down upon them, gently illuminating the icon of the mother and child.

Later, holding hands, they walked through the bare trees toward Rafi's house. "I will need a few more weeks, Peter. I want to visit with Rafi and Rishael, as well as with Rishael's family. I want to be able to remember them, if I can never return to Kazakhstan. I know you need to return to Washington. I will join you."

A FINAL NOTE

A novel is a story that lives only in the imagination of the teller and readers, and that is surely true here. However, the roots of this tale grew from real world events and include the extraordinary service to America provided by Dr Thul Vanle, very late one snowy evening, when she introduced me to President Nazarbayev. Her service to America deserves historic recognition. The world should also note the exceptional judgment during this period exercised by Kazakhstan President Nursultan Nazarbayev, American Secretary of Defense Bill Perry and President Bill Clinton. Acting together, these three significantly reduced the danger of a nuclear Armageddon.

A THANK YOU

Intent to Deceive inserts facts among fantasies, mixes missteps with memories and plays emotions against real events. I have taken too long to tell this tale and I fear I have forgotten several of the individuals who should rightfully be acknowledged.

I know I particularly appreciated Steve Spruill, who provided the great title as well as his personal encouragement and Marlene Adelstein was invaluable as a book doctor. Jane Hubbell Lund did yeoman work personally looking for appropriate apartment buildings in downtown Indianapolis. Daniella King critically reviewed the uneven parallel bar scene and Bill McDaniel told me how Asya could most effectively wield her brass letter opener. Of course this story would never have been written if Rich Haver had not pulled out of the long lane of incoming traffic when I flagged down his car at the entrance to the CIA headquarters in Langley, Virginia early one dark winter morning to let me ask if he had anyone who could dust and check the set of crystal salt and pepper shakers I had lifted during my breakfast with the purported President of Kazakhstan.

I also welcomed the help of:
Fred Rainbow
Ginger Oliver
Jay Davis
Leslie Zimring
Michael Zimring
Mike Hough

Nancy Merrick
Nancy Spruill
Sunjin Choi
Tim Oliver
Vago Muradian

CPSIA information can be obtained
at www.ICGtesting.com
Printed in the USA
BVHW03s1950280318
511787BV00027B/52/P

9 780999 471807